For the first time in Marc's long life, he cursed logic.

Being with Cece had taken him to a new place, a wild place, a place he felt free.

He wanted the same for her, but as she pulled further away, he knew that he'd lost her, knew she was slipping back into the werewolf she thought she should be rather than the woman she was.

He couldn't let that happen. He wouldn't.

He pulled her from the booth and down the short hallway. Then he spun her around and kissed her again...and reveled in their differences. She was pack; he was a loner. She was soft and warm; he was hard and cold.

They had nothing in common, but he wanted her more than he had wanted anyone or anything in his undead life.

Books by Lori Devoti

Harlequin Nocturne

*Unbound #18
*Guardian's Keep #32
*Wild Hunt #41
Holiday with a Vampire II #54
"The Vampire Who Stole Christmas"
*Dark Crusade #62
*The Hellhound King #82
Zombie Moon #91
The Witch Thief #136
Moon Rising #176

*Unbound

LORI DEVOTI

grew up in southern Missouri and attended college at the University of Missouri-Columbia, where she earned a bachelor of journalism. However, she made it clear to anyone who asked that she was not a writer; she worked for the dark side—advertising. Now, twenty years later, she's proud to declare herself a writer and visits her dark side by writing paranormals for the Harlequin Nocturne line.

Lori lives in Wisconsin with her husband, daughter, son, an extremely patient shepherd mix and the world's pushiest Siberian husky. To learn more about what Lori is working on now, visit her website at www.loridevoti.com.

MOON
RISING

—

LORI DEVOTI

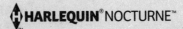
HARLEQUIN® NOCTURNE™

Recycling programs
for this product may
not exist in your area.

ISBN-13: 978-0-373-88588-6

MOON RISING

Copyright © 2014 by Lori Devoti

Printed in U.S.A.

www.Harlequin.com

Dear Reader,

Thanks so much for reading *Moon Rising*.

I had the opportunity to research this book one very hot summer in Cave City, Kentucky. Cave City is home to Mammoth Cave National Park and numerous other smaller caves. It was great fun exploring with my family and thinking of challenges werewolves and vampires might face in such a setting. Other attractions, like horseback riding and visiting Dinosaur World, were just as fun, especially for my kids, but didn't make it into the book. Maybe in the next one...

To learn when that next one might be coming out, or to find information on some of my other books, stop by my website. While you are there, be sure to sign up for my newsletter. I have monthly contests, and right now, all new subscribers get a coupon code for a free vampire novella.

Thanks again and keep reading!

Lori Devoti

To my werewolf-and myth-loving children.

Chapter 1

The human lived in squalor.

Not exactly what Marc Delacroix had been expecting from a man who claimed to have found a fortune in hidden treasure.

He flicked his tongue over one fang and plucked a rotting banana peel off the table beside him. Holding the thing with two fingers, he frowned. If the man had found the vampires' treasure, he was hiding it well.

Or perhaps he was spending it now.

The blog article had appeared on the internet only this morning. Still, by now the man could be in another city. Or he could be hiding in the cellar. It was the only part of the house Marc had yet to investigate.

He dropped the banana peel onto the floor.

Behind him a door creaked.

Instantly alert, he slid into the shadows. Ideally, he

didn't want to encounter the man. Of course, ideally, the man would have been fast asleep with his stolen goods sitting conveniently by the door.

But few things worked out ideally.

With a grimace, he made sure his appearance was cloaked, that he would blend into the background should the treasure hunter look in his direction, and waited.

Two people entered the room. The first, despite an athletic build, was most definitely female, the second male. Both moved slowly with the stealth of an animal stalking prey.

Marc slowed his heart almost to a standstill and stood completely still. Then he inhaled.

The telltale scent of woods and wild greeted him.

Werewolves.

If he hadn't been afraid of discovery, he would have cursed. Wolves weren't known for their technological prowess, and Marc certainly hadn't expected them to be monitoring RSS feeds. He had hoped the vampires had a jump on them.

He had hoped they would miss the significance of the man's supposed "find" entirely, but obviously, they hadn't.

"How long do we have?" the male asked.

The female pulled out a flashlight and switched it on. "How drunk was he?"

"Four beers and three shots."

"The bar was packed. I doubt anyone has even spotted him yet, much less done the Good Samaritan thing and called him a cab—if they even have cabs in Cave Vista."

The male grunted.

"To be safe, we need to be out in thirty. I'll do the other rooms. You check here." She motioned with her flashlight for him to search the area where Marc stood hidden.

He stayed calm and still, waited for her to leave, and then focused his energies on the male she'd left behind. The wolf passed him twice, taking a step toward him each time, but then paused and turned.

After ten minutes and two more close calls, the female returned.

"You find anything?"

The male wolf frowned. His jaw jutted to one side. Marc could see that he was struggling with what had happened while he was alone in the room.

The thrall Marc had cast had worked on the werewolf, but not entirely. Marc filed the information away for future reference.

He hadn't dealt with werewolves for sixty years, not since the war. And stealth hadn't been an issue then; speed and strength had. His job at the time hadn't been spying on wolves. It had been killing them.

A much simpler task.

The female stepped around the male. She was tall for a woman, close to six feet with dark hair that reached the middle of her back. Despite her simple clothing and lack of makeup she was striking. An interesting choice of emissary if the pack wanted their arrival in Cave Vista to go unnoticed.

Standing in the middle of the room, she spun slowly on one foot, assessing the space. When her attention turned to the area Marc occupied, he doubled his efforts at deflection.

A line formed between her eyes. They were hazel,

with shadows that shifted as she moved. At one moment they appeared green, the next gray. As she stood still, focusing on where he hid, they settled on gray.

Thinking it fit her indecision, he smiled.

The break in his strict stillness cost him. She blinked and took a step forward.

"CeCe." The male who accompanied her grabbed her by the elbow. He pointed toward the cellar door.

With another frown, she followed him, but as he opened the door, she hesitated.

The scent of damp earth flowed out of the underground space. Marc resisted the urge to inhale deeply and pull the smell into his lungs.

"I'll wait here." The female, CeCe, took a step backward.

"Are you sure?" The male paused with one foot through the doorway.

Her hand tight on the flashlight, she nodded.

The male disappeared down the stairs.

Marc waited, content to let the wolves find his treasure and bring it up to him. Even more content to spend the moments in the meantime taking in the female werewolf's form.

As he had first noted, she was athletic. In her shorts the muscles in her legs were easily visible. She was a runner, but more than that. A swimmer or a skier, he guessed. She had that kind of all over toned body, with some bulk in the shoulders and thighs.

As if feeling his focus, she spun. Her gaze was on him, so intense he couldn't trust that she didn't see him. He ran his tongue over the back of his teeth and wondered how she would taste.

Feminine and wolflike. Sweet and wild. Like berry

wine, he guessed. He inhaled, testing her scent. She smelled of forests and fresh-turned earth, but with something else, something he hadn't expected…a spice. Vampires smelled of spice. He hadn't realized werewolves did, too.

Without shifting her gaze, she crouched and plucked something off the floor. Then, in one fluid movement, she pulled back her arm and flung the object toward him.

The banana peel Marc had dropped earlier smashed into his favorite black shirt. His jaw tensed.

Lights shone through the front window. She spun again, this time toward the cellar. She threw the door open. "Russell. Company," she called.

In front of the house gravel crunched under the tires of a sedan pulling into the driveway.

For a moment, Marc didn't think her companion would reply, but just as he thought whoever occupied the vehicle would arrive inside before the wolves could exit, toenails sounded on wooden steps and a giant black-and-tan dog, a Rottweiler, shot out of the cellar.

CeCe cursed and widened her stance. Her hands in front of her in a protective manner, she stared the beast down.

"Russell?" she called, but low.

The dog lowered its head and growled.

The male wolf appeared in the doorway. His shirt was torn and there was blood on his arm. "He was locked in a room—"

CeCe waved his response off. "No time. Get out. I'll keep him busy."

To Marc's surprise, the male didn't argue. He

moved to the dog's left and, sticking to the walls as much as possible, worked his way out of the room. In a second a door banged shut.

"Vampire?" The female werewolf didn't move her attention from the dog, whose low growl had changed to snarls. A tiny ridge of hair now stood along the creature's backbone.

"Vampire? Do you hear me?" the female repeated. "This dog doesn't like me being here because I'm a wolf and in his territory…but a vampire?" She shook her head. "He'll like that even less."

Still staring at the dog, she lifted her lip and made a low barking noise. The dog's snarls shifted, still there, still warning, but less intense. Her hand reached to the side and closed over some object Marc couldn't see.

Before Marc could formulate a plan, an object flew through the air toward him.

He dove to the side, completely ruining his efforts at blending.

One hundred and forty pounds of dog crashed through the crowded room. Busy rolling out of the animal's trajectory, he didn't see the werewolf leave, but he heard her muttering something as she did.

The dog would slow him down, but it wouldn't stop him. He hoped she was smart enough to realize that.

He rolled over and faced the animal. Every tooth in its mouth appeared to be visible. Drool flowed from its gums. It lunged forward, jaws snapping. Marc dove and grabbed it by the hind legs, then he spun his weight to the side, sending the creature sliding and skittering across the floor. Furniture and beer bottles crashed.

The animal roared to a stand, but back on his own

feet, Marc was ready. He leaped onto a nearby table and jumped from one solid surface to another, the dog snapping at his heels.

Only a few feet ahead of the animal, Marc grabbed hold of the door's frame and swung out of the room. Safe in the hall, he slammed the door shut behind him.

The dog's body thudded into solid wood. A human's heart would have been pounding. Marc's barely changed its beat. He smoothed his hands over his shirt, frowning at the tears and stains.

Down the hall another door smashed against a wall, the front door to the house being flung open by the sedan's occupants. Some Good Samaritan, Marc guessed, who had found the human treasure hunter after he had succumbed to the wolves' liquor.

The dog slavering on the other side of the door, completely immune to any thrall Marc tried to cast, ruined any chance he had of blending back into the shadows…killed any hope he had of waiting for the man to pass out so he could continue his search.

The werewolves had assured that his time here was wasted…except, perhaps it wasn't. He had seen the wolves, knew who and what they were. They, however, had not seen him; at least he didn't believe the female had had a chance to spot him before sprinting out the door.

So, for now, the advantage was his and he had every intention of using it.

As the drunken homeowner stumbled into the hall, Marc retreated again, but this time with a goal in mind…a sweet, wild, athletic goal that he couldn't wait to taste.

* * *

CeCe Parks paced outside Russell's motel room. She'd knocked twice and he hadn't answered. Finally, as she balled her fist to pound again, the door flew open.

She pushed past the younger wolf and into his room. He hovered near the entrance for a minute, then pulled the door closed but left it unlatched.

She continued her pacing, wearing a path in the already worn and stained carpet. Russell seemed equally tense. His gaze darted around the room, traveling to the bathroom and back to her, only to shift again when she tried to meet his eyes.

Finally, losing patience, she came to a stop in front of him. "A vampire was there, watching."

His head snapped up. "A vampire? Are you sure?" His fingers tapped against his canvas shorts. He ran the back of his hand over his forehead, swiping away sweat.

The temperature in Cave Vista, Kentucky, had topped one hundred and five degrees today. Even now, with the sun down, it couldn't be much under ninety-five.

"Yes. I—the dog sensed him." All she had seen of the vampire was a blur of dark movement. "After you went into the cellar, I felt something strange, but I couldn't see anyone." It annoyed her that she had doubted her own senses when the dog had been so confident in its. But that came with having a human half, having a more logical brain that at times interfered with the senses of her wolf.

"What did he want?"

She frowned. "The treasure, I'm sure. I need to call Karl."

"No." Russell placed a hand on her forearm. "Not yet."

She pulled her lips into her mouth. She understood Russell's reluctance. They had been given a simple job—take back what was theirs—and they had failed.

Russell shifted so he stood sideways to her. "You know they don't accept me."

"You won't be blamed." She said the words with confidence because she knew they were true, knew who would be blamed—her. This trip had been a chance for her too. A chance to prove that she was worthy of being a good mate for Karl, the alpha, that she had more than her genetics to offer the pack.

"Maybe not." He shoved his hands into the front pockets of his shorts. He looked young and vulnerable and CeCe wanted to console him, but werewolves didn't console…they toughened. Another wolf might have ridiculed him for his lack of confidence. She couldn't do that, but she couldn't play nurse to his feelings, either.

She swallowed the soft words that had formed and turned away.

"Karl will want to know the vampires are here."

"Vampires? Or vampire? There is a difference." Russell still sounded sullen, but at least his fight was back.

She walked to the window and looked out. It was still dark. The vampire could be out there right now, watching.

"Does it matter?" she asked.

"Yes. If it's only one, he's probably just an opportunist. He saw the blog and came looking for easy money."

CeCe closed the curtains back over the window. "Coincidence that we're here too? That it's the pack treasure the man found?" She couldn't buy that, and she didn't think Karl would either.

"Maybe not, maybe he had a vendetta."

"Hates werewolves?" It wasn't impossible. Despite the fact that the war between them had been over for sixty years, there was still no love between vampires and werewolves. Her father had taught her of their dangers, shown her how one had tortured and killed her mother.

Russell interrupted her dark reverie. "The point is, if it is just one vampire there's no reason to call Karl. It will make us look like we're afraid to make a decision on our own. Like we need his guidance on every little problem."

What Russell said made sense. One vampire CeCe could handle on her own; she had been trained. Plus, she needed to prove to the pack she could solve problems, be of value; calling Karl and getting his advice would undermine that. They would only hear that she had failed and needed the alpha to bail her out.

"It was only one," she said, confirming the idea in her mind. Vampires didn't work together like werewolves. They didn't have packs to depend on. They were antisocial, even with their own kind, like cats. It made sense that one would be here alone.

"So, we fix this ourselves?" Russell asked. He leaned forward. CeCe could almost feel him pulling the agreement out of her.

"Yes."

At the younger werewolf's relieved smile, CeCe smiled too. They could do this. They could find the treasure and if necessary, fight off the vampire to get it.

If she couldn't, she didn't deserve the position at Karl's side.

An hour after leaving the human fortune hunter's house, Marc was back. This time armed with steak and sedatives.

Dogs might be sensitive to preternatural beings, like vampires, but they were also loyal and loyalty meant predictability.

They also liked steak.

He pulled a sirloin from his pocket and shoved four sedatives that he'd stolen from a local vet's office inside. Then he shoved open the man's bedroom window. As expected, the dog was pacing the floor, nose in the air. When he saw Marc, he snarled.

Before his reaction could build to full attack, Marc flung the steak into the room. Then he waited.

Fifteen minutes later he was back inside. He pulled the bedroom door shut, leaving the animal and man inside, and went to finish his search from earlier.

The male werewolf had come up from the cellar with empty hands. If he had found anything, it hadn't been much, size-wise anyway. There had to be more.

With that in mind, Marc scoured the underground level.

The area was small and smelled like such spaces in older houses did, a unique mix of cleaning supplies and fresh earth, even though the walls and floors were concrete.

He searched the main room first and found nothing, but he had expected that. If he had found a treasure, he wouldn't leave it lying out on top of the dryer like the latest load of laundry.

He'd hide it, but where?

Where would a human think others wouldn't want to go?

His gaze lit on a small space behind the furnace. The area was shoved full of discarded furniture, old framed prints, and other yard sale fodder. As he moved closer, he realized that someone, the werewolf he guessed, had been there before him. Two framed prints had been set to the side and a chair had been pulled out also.

Marc crouched and peered into the open space where the objects had been. Unable to see anything that would qualify as treasure, he reached into the hole and groped around for anything of interest. His hand hit a cold metal loop. He pulled it out.

Handcuffs, but not any handcuffs. These were made of silver.

Marc rolled onto his heels.

Silver was for werewolves, stopping them, controlling them, killing them. Cuffs like this had been used before, in the war.

What would a human be doing with them? After another moment of reflection, Marc shoved the cuffs into his back pocket and searched the space again. Nothing but cobwebs.

If there had been treasure here, the werewolf or someone else had taken it.

Satisfied that he had closed this loop, he left.

Outside he stared at the house. If the treasure wasn't

here, where was it? Or had the whole tale been a lie? Perhaps the drunken human inside had created the story. For what? Free drinks and slaps on the backs?

Glancing around the weedy yard, Marc could have swallowed that idea. Except for one thing...the handcuffs.

The human had gotten them somewhere. And Marc didn't think it was his local fetish shop, unless that fetish shop had a specialty in werewolf domination.

And there was the even bigger coincidence. The werewolves.

Whatever was going on in Cave Vista was a lot more complicated than what Marc had been led to believe.

Time to get some answers.

Chapter 2

The next night, CeCe stood outside the bar, waiting for Russell. The human, Mike Porter, who'd found the treasure, had been inside for an hour. She'd phoned Russell and left a message on his phone, but he had yet to arrive.

An hour was too long. Porter could be passed out by now, and CeCe needed him coherent if not sober.

Unwilling to wait any longer, she stalked into the dingy bar. The theme was 1970s chic. Unfortunately, based on the torn upholstery and dirt-encrusted walls, CeCe guessed the decor was original. The dirt probably was too.

A bartender stood behind a red upholstered bar. He was wiping it down, but when CeCe entered, he stopped.

In fact, everyone in the place stopped what they were doing.

Trying to ignore their stares, she let her gaze wander over the tables. She spotted her target at the far end of the bar.

"You need directions?" the bartender asked as she walked by.

"No, but a drink would be good." After ordering a beer, she slid onto the stool next to the treasure finder.

"Told you," the bartender murmured as he placed a beer bottle down in front of her.

It took her a second to realize he was talking to Porter.

"What did he tell you?" she asked, trying for a tell-me-everything smile.

"That the gold diggers would be after me," the man rebutted, plopping his beer bottle down and staring at her under the brim of his feed hat. "You a gold digger?"

"Uh." CeCe blinked.

"Does she look like a gold digger?" A man dressed in slacks and a long-sleeved shirt stepped behind them.

Porter turned to look at him over his shoulder.

"I believe gold diggers spend a bit more time on their…appearances," the newcomer added.

CeCe sat up straighter at the insult. She was clean and her hair brushed. But Porter seemed to like the other man's answer. He raised one bushy brow, guffawed and took a sip from his bottle. "I'm not much on fancy clothes and lipstick myself. That's how I lost my first wife…damn lipstick telling tales on me."

He stared at CeCe with new interest.

Not sure how to get the conversation back on track

and to get rid of the unwelcome newcomer, she asked, "Are you married now?" She knew he wasn't. His home had zero signs of a female touch.

"Not at the moment." He leaned closer. CeCe could smell beer and peanuts on his breath.

She closed her eyes for a second and reminded herself of why she was here. She had, as far as she could see, two choices in getting him to talk: intimidation or making friends. In her opinion the second would be both easier and a lot less complicated. Werewolves might be half animal, but they tried to obey human laws, at least when it came to things like battery and murder.

A hand landed on her thigh. Her eyes flew open. *Porter's hand.* In deference to the heat, she'd worn shorts tonight. Now she regretted the decision.

The newcomer was staring at her with amusement in his eyes.

Porter, however, seemed to have forgotten his existence. CeCe had wanted his attention and now she had it. Gritting her teeth, she tried to ignore the feel of the human's sweaty fingers touching her bare skin.

He leaned closer and for one horrifying moment CeCe thought he was going to kiss her. She stood up. As soon as her legs straightened, she realized her mistake.

Porter frowned and pulled back. His face closed off.

"Never mind her. There's plenty more out there, right, Mike?" The newcomer slapped Porter on the back and took her spot at the bar. She was left standing behind them, unsure what to do next.

"Let me buy you a beer to help you forget."

Within seconds a new round sat in front of the

two men. The man grabbed her half-empty beer and handed it to her. "You might want to move on now." His gaze was intense and knowing.

She realized then who...or what...he was. The vampire. She hadn't noticed his scent before this. The stench of beer and cigarettes all but blocked out the peppery scent she now realized came from the male.

He smiled. His teeth were smooth and white and even. No fangs.

She frowned.

When she didn't move, the man stood and motioned Porter to stand too. Together they walked past her to an empty booth.

The human's steps were even, but jerky, as if he was being operated by some outside force.

Suspicions renewed, she followed them.

"I thought you had things to do." The vampire tugged at his sleeves, pulling them lower over his wrists.

Her eyes narrowed, and she slid into the booth next to him. "Not at the moment."

The three sat in silence, CeCe and the vampire sitting side by side, each aware of the other, each daring the other to make a move first. It was obvious to CeCe that the vampire was casting some kind of spell on Porter. She suspected that he'd somehow gotten the man to make the advance on her, thinking that would drive her away. But if he thought a sweaty hand on her thigh would be enough to send her running, he was wrong. She had endured a hell of a lot worse, and to keep the vampire from learning the location of the treasure, she would do so again.

She took a sip of her beer and waited.

The vampire did the same.

She'd never been this close to a vampire before. In fact, she'd never met a vampire before. He wasn't at all what she'd expected. There was nothing thin or anemic about him. In fact, he radiated strength and power. He was, she hated to admit, magnetic. Her body seemed to lean toward him. Her energy seemed to focus on him. She could barely keep her mind on the task at hand, listening to the mindless prattle of the human Porter.

She adjusted her weight, pulled her leg up under her body and dug her fingernails into her ankle. The pain helped her focus, helped her ignore whatever magical magnetism the vampire was throwing her direction.

But still her body tingled.

Completely unaware of the energy zinging between them, Porter happily sipped his beer and told them everything he knew about fishing, hunting and exploring the area's many caves in search of Native American relics. The one topic he didn't mention, however, was the treasure.

Again, CeCe suspected the vampire was involved in the too-obvious omission from the human's story repertoire.

Finally, frustrated and fed up with her own body's reactions to the vampire beside her, CeCe could take it no longer. She turned to face him. "I know what you are," she said.

"What is he?" Porter asked. She shoved a beer across the table toward him.

"It belongs to us."

The vampire arched one brow.

"What?" Porter started.

Barely suppressing the growl that formed in her throat, CeCe pinned him with a glare.

The human took a quick sip of his beer and looked elsewhere.

"You need to leave," she murmured. She tried to keep her expression bland. Her face ached with the effort.

The vampire picked up his beer and took a sip. "Mike, would you like to take a walk? Get a bit of fresh air?"

Porter, busy draining his sixth beer, froze. His hand slowly lowered. His eyes blinked. "Yes, I think I would."

"Good." The vampire smiled and turned to CeCe. "If you don't mind." He raised his brows, indicating that she needed to get out of the booth and his way.

Her first instinct was to refuse, but Porter was already moving. Blocking the vampire would do nothing but allow the human to get away.

Fisting her hands, she stood.

"Mike, do you need to use the facilities?" The vampire's face and stance were casual, but CeCe could feel power pouring out of him. Her body tingled again. She itched to move closer to him, to be part of whatever enticing spell he was creating.

She gritted her teeth and called on her wolf. The animal crept forward, suspicious. It sniffed and growled. CeCe clung to the creature, used it to tear through whatever net the vampire was casting around her.

The shroud of magic lifted, but the spell of the vampire didn't totally go away. In fact the power around him seemed more evident, as if he'd been using magic in some way to hide his true strength.

A shiver of awareness danced up CeCe's spine, tightened her core and made her breasts tingle. And her wolf, traitorous bitch, just stood by watching.

"Yes, the john."

Then before CeCe could stop him, the human had shuffled into a bathroom, one clearly marked "men." With a smile, the vampire slid into the room after him.

She muttered a curse and tried the knob. It was locked. She pulled back, prepared to shove her shoulder against the thin wood and force her way in.

"You looking for the women's?" The bartender stepped out from behind the bar. A line of curious faces turned to watch her. The bartender stepped closer. "You got business to conduct, you need to take it elsewhere."

Business. She frowned.

The bartender titled his head toward the door Mike and the vampire had disappeared behind. "Mike's a good customer, but there's plenty of people who don't like us serving alcohol, much less…" He gave her a knowing look.

With a start, CeCe realized what he meant. A prostitute. He thought she was a prostitute.

"I am not—" Her instinctive defense was cut off by another patron pushing past her on his way to the bathroom.

He pounded on the door.

"C'mon," he complained. He pounded again. "Who's in there?" he asked.

The bartender stepped past her and pressed his ear to the door. "Mike, she's not coming in. Might as well get your ass out of there."

Ignoring the stares of the other bar patrons, CeCe crossed her arms over her chest and waited.

"He's not answering." The bartender looked at her as if she might have some explanation…and she did, but no one in this room would want to hear it.

Past caring if her actions seemed odd, she pushed the two men out of her way and slammed her shoulder into the door. The hinges creaked.

"What the hell? I got a key." The bartender grabbed her by the arm. She shook him off and slammed into the door again.

It flew open. Porter lay sprawled faceup on the floor. His eyes were open and glossy. CeCe's wolf twitched. Dead, it said.

CeCe leaped over Porter and into the room. The space was tiny, a one-seater with nowhere for the vampire to hide. But then he didn't need to. Mosquitoes and hot, muggy air flowed through an open window.

With a curse, she grabbed the sill and tried to force her body through the opening.

The bartender grabbed her by the waistband of her shorts. "Not so quick. The sheriff will be wanting to talk to you."

He jerked her back inside.

CeCe sat at a sticky table inside the bar waiting for the EMTs and law enforcement to finish whatever they were doing with Porter and release her. She'd been sitting here for thirty minutes, plenty of time for the vampire to have disappeared completely.

She edged her chair out and glanced at the door. The bartender, seeing her movement, walked over. "Don't be getting any ideas."

Wishing she had the vampire's power to control humans or the freedom to show her own skills, she pushed her chair back with one foot and crossed one leg over the other. "Just getting comfortable."

"Good."

Choosing to ignore the ignorant human, she pulled her cell from her pocket and checked for missed calls. Zero.

"You expecting a call?" A man dressed in the brown uniform of the sheriff's department walked up. A strip of plastic pinned to his shirt declared his name as Al Davis and his rank as deputy. He pulled out a chair and straddled it.

He pulled a notepad from his pocket. "Barker says you were with Mike tonight."

"I was standing in the hall with—" she glanced at the bartender "—Barker the whole time Mr. Porter was in the bathroom."

"Yeah, Barker said that, too."

"So I didn't kill him," she prompted, placing both feet on the floor.

The deputy's pencil paused. "Kill him? Anybody say something about killing him?"

She stiffened. "He isn't dead?"

"Oh, he's dead as last Thanksgiving's turkey dinner, but nobody killed him. At least, we didn't see it that way." He tapped his pencil against the pad.

"There was no…blood?"

Wariness crept into the deputy's eyes. "Where did you say you were from?"

No blood. Had the vampire killed him or not?

"So, it was what? A heart attack?"

"Might be best if I ask the questions for now. Address?"

Seeing she would get nothing else from the deputy, she gave him her name and the address the pack used when humans got too nosy. After another ten minutes, he released her.

Outside, a crowd had gathered. For three in the morning, it was impressive. All the bar goers must have called their closest thirty or so friends to share what had happened, but for once, CeCe embraced the throng of humans.

Humans gossiped and she needed information.

It took her less than half an hour to learn that yes, they did think Mike Porter had died of a heart attack. She also learned that he'd been cavorting with some big-city hooker trying to pass herself off as a tourist who'd come down trying to get a piece of the treasure he'd stupidly told the world about finding.

Grateful that none of the people she spoke to seemed to tie the hooker in question to her, she dug a bit more, asking if anyone had seen the man Porter had been with before tonight. To her annoyance, no one seemed to have seen the vampire at all.

It was as if he was mist, had flowed in and left, completely unnoticed by anyone except her.

Which made her wonder what else he could do. Could he have killed Porter, then done something that convinced this group of humans that the death was natural?

How big of a threat was this vampire? And before he killed Porter, what had he learned? Had he already found and stolen the treasure?

"Damn it, Russell. Why did I let you talk me out of calling Karl?" she muttered to herself.

Now she was stuck. Her only lead on the treasure, Porter, was dead; Russell was AWOL; and somewhere in Cave Vista was a vampire who knew *she knew* he'd killed a human.

Killing humans was strictly forbidden. It was one of the three laws of peace laid out in the treaty that ended the vampire-werewolf war.

No killing of humans by either group.

No killing of werewolves by vampires.

No killing of vampires by werewolves.

Both groups were free to kill their own kind whenever and however they wanted, at least as far as the peace treaty was concerned. Werewolves had their own laws governed by the pack alphas. And alphas had the right to dispense with any wolf who broke one of those laws in any way they saw fit.

CeCe had no idea how or if vampires had any regulation on such things, but based on what she knew of them, she sincerely doubted it.

But bottom line, this vampire had broken one of the three laws and he knew CeCe was a witness. Would he break the second law to cover breaking the first?

Of course he would.

Chapter 3

Across the street from the bar, Marc sat cross-legged on the roof of a T-shirt shop.

Something had happened inside, something interesting enough to pull the residents of the small town out of their homes at…he slid a watch from his pocket…2:30 a.m.

He considered dropping onto the ground and mingling with the crowd, seeing what he could learn, but he'd gone to great lengths to ensure that none of the humans he'd encountered earlier would remember him. Seeing him again so soon might spoil his efforts.

A gurney appeared loaded down with a short, round-bellied form. The sheet was pulled up completely, covering the body's face.

EMTs didn't roll people around with their faces covered, not if they were alive.

It could have been any short, stocky occupant of the bar tonight, met with some ill fate, but Marc knew immediately it wasn't. He knew immediately his only real lead was dead.

And he knew who was responsible…the female werewolf.

She must have come into the bathroom after he left through the window, found Porter passed out on the floor and killed him.

Why kill him? Had she learned where the treasure was and wanted to ensure that Porter told no one else? Or was she just crazed from being outsmarted by Marc? Had her frustration sent her berserk?

He'd heard of wolves losing all control when their canine halves were ignited. There was no reason to think her female form would make her resistant to the weakness.

He waited, expecting to see her hauled out in handcuffs or dragged out dead in her wolf form.

Another half an hour passed before she appeared. The crowd outside was determined; only a few had given up and gone home, and more, including local media, had shown up to replace them. The werewolf strolled among them seemingly free. People talked to her without fear.

So if she was responsible for Porter's death, she'd managed to clean herself up afterward and cover her crimes.

He waited for her to leave the crowd and wander farther down the street, where he assumed she had left her car. Running along the rooftops above her, he followed. When she turned to go into a parking lot, he dropped down onto the concrete in front of her.

To her credit, she didn't jump. She stood perfectly still and watched him.

He inhaled, checking for the scent of fresh blood. Just her normal werewolf scent of forest and things wild, plus the strange spice he had yet to explain, came back to him. His nostrils flared and his body hardened, but he pushed the annoying response aside, pretended it didn't exist.

"What happened?"

She ran her tongue over her teeth. "You tell me." Her fingers moved for no reason, like a cat's tail twitching. He thought of the handcuffs he'd found in Porter's basement, wished he had them with him to keep her from shifting.

"I can't. I wasn't there."

"Weren't you?" Her jaw slipped to the side, determination warred with anger in her eyes. "You broke one of the laws. Do you intend to break another now? It might not be as easy as you think."

"Laws? Me?" He laughed. She was going on the offense, a smart tactic to throw your accusers off, if they were easily thrown off.

Marc wasn't.

Within one exhale of her breath, he had moved forward, so he was in front of her, his shirt brushing hers. "What happened to the human? He was alive when I left. Stupid drunk, but alive."

It was why Marc had left. Porter had passed out on the bathroom floor before he'd had a chance to question him. He'd tried waking him up, but the human had been out cold.

This time she laughed. "You expect me to believe

that? Why did you kill him? Did he tell you where the treasure is?"

"Treasure?" He crossed his arms over his chest and leaned back.

She shook her head. "Turn it over and perhaps I won't report you to the pack." Her eyelid twitched.

He angled a brow. "Quick to sell out what's right for reward, aren't you?"

Her jaw tightened. "I'm quick to do my job."

"And your job involved treasure. Interesting." He pretended to process the information, even though he'd had no doubt as to why she and her wolf friend were here. "Where is your friend? Why wasn't he with you tonight?"

"I don't owe you answers."

"No, you don't, but then I don't owe you anything either." He turned his back on her to walk away. Dawn was approaching. He had appearances to keep up. If she thought he had to stay hidden in the light, he could follow her and be at a complete advantage.

"I won't let it sit. The laws of peace exist for a reason. I don't know how you did it, how you covered up what you did, but killing humans is asking for discovery. It's dangerous to us all," she called after him.

He stopped and turned. "And, lest you forget, *wrong*. Taking a life, human, werewolf or vampire, is just wrong…isn't it, little wolf? Or does the pack believe differently?"

"Of course—"

He raised one hand. "Not to give you the wrong idea. I have done all three and will do them again—if I think it is necessary. I've walked this earth for over two hundred years, long enough to know that nothing can be taken at face value. If you want to survive, the only law that really matters is the one that keeps you alive." Without another word, he leaped onto a Dumpster and from there the roof.

Then he sprinted away to a spot where he could watch her, follow her and wait for her to screw up.

Werewolves always did.

Chapter 3

The next morning, CeCe pounded on Russell's motel room door. When no answer came, she went to the office and claimed to have lost her key. The woman behind the counter, busy watching some talk show, didn't bat an eye as she handed one over.

So much for security.

Key in hand, CeCe let herself into Russell's room. The bed was made and the bathroom tidy. It appeared no one had been in or out of the place since the maid had visited the day before.

Uneasy, she walked around the room looking for any sign of what might have happened to Russell, but everything seemed in place. His suitcase was on the floor beside the bed and his razor was in the shower.

She had checked her messages ten times since last night—no calls to her cell or to her room.

Where had he gone?

Her mind went back to the bar…the dead human… and the vampire.

Her hand drifted to her phone. She needed to call Karl. He needed to know what was happening.

Her finger hovering over the keys, she hesitated. Russell had asked her not to call. He'd told her it would be admitting defeat, confirm both his and her positions as failures in the mind of the pack.

But that was before everything had gone south, before Porter had turned up dead and Russell gone missing.

She had to call Karl now. It was her duty.

She dropped her gaze to the floor. Dirty footprints from some occupant or another were clearly visible on the tan carpet.

If only Russell had left such a clear trail… She paused.

But then, of course he had, at least to a wolf.

Annoyed that she hadn't thought of tracking him earlier, CeCe roamed the room. Russell's scent was everywhere. She went to the door and stepped outside.

The heat was working against her. The best conditions for air scent tracking were cool, cloudy days with a light wind, but despite the oppressive heat, she managed to find two main trails—one leading toward downtown and one going the opposite direction. She could think of no reason Russell would have headed out of town, toward the woods.

She had a lead.

Karl could wait.

Leaning against a car bumper across the street from the werewolves' motel, Marc folded the morning paper and set it aside. There had been no news of Porter's death in it, but based on a conversation he'd had with a woman who had strolled by, the death had been natural causes.

No mysterious puncture wounds, no gruesome crime scene.

No reason for the female werewolf to accuse him except for her obvious prejudice against his kind.

As he pulled his wide-brimmed hat lower and adjusted his sunglasses, the female wolf stepped out of what he assumed was her companion's motel room. He'd seen her leave another room earlier, then return to this one with a key.

Wearing pants and a loose-fitting top, she looked almost as out of place as Marc in Kentucky's heat. He had chosen a long-sleeved shirt and pants to protect him from the sun, but wondered at the werewolf's choice of clothing. The one-hundred-plus temperatures had no effect on a vampire, but the werewolf's shirt already clung to her back, perspiration spots showing through. By noon she would be sweltering. The only concession to the heat she seemed to have made was a ponytail that swished as she walked.

Her stride was strong and determined. Perhaps a bit too determined for the slow pace of Cave Vista, Kentucky. More than one person turned their attention on her as she walked by.

When the werewolf entered the woods, he let out a relieved breath. The stress on his system of functioning in the full light of day was draining him. He would need to rest or feed soon.

The shadow of the trees would offer some relief.

The female moved along the path quickly. The

roots, holes and half-rotten logs that broke up the path didn't slow her even slightly.

Concern that here in the quiet of the woods she would hear him caused him to slow his steps more. He was forced to let her disappear from sight, to follow on faith that she would stick with the path and that eventually he would find her and whatever she was seeking.

As he turned a bend, a new smell froze him in place.

The unmistakable scent of dead and rotting flesh hung suspended in the thick, muggy air.

Marc gagged and spat. Vampires didn't feed on the dead.

Where was the werewolf going? What had she done?

His instinct was to rush forward, but there was no reason. Whoever, whatever, he smelled was past saving.

The smell hit CeCe like a baseball bat to the gut. Rot, decay…decomposition.

Her pace slowed as she walked closer. She prayed that the stench came from some animal, that her nose telling her it was wolf was wrong, but as she stood over the body, stared at the too-familiar canvas shorts and blue T-shirt, she was faced with a nightmare.

Russell was dead.

She closed her eyes and fisted her hands. Why was he in these woods? Why hadn't he come to her? Damn the young wolf for trying to prove his worth to a pack that didn't accept him.

She'd accepted him. Why hadn't that been enough?

Because she was nothing to him, not mother, not

lover, barely friend. He'd needed more, a stronger connection, one he would only find through respect hard earned.

Anger came next…at the vampire. He had to have done this. She had yet to turn over Russell's body, but that truth burned through her mind. This wasn't natural causes. Wolves didn't drop dead from heart attacks, especially ones as young as Russell. And a human couldn't overpower a wolf, not without a gun with a silver bullet inside.

That left one option—the vampire.

Anger welled up and threatened to spill out, to blind her to everything except hunting down the vampire and tearing into him, seeking revenge…but the laws of peace forbade that. The laws of peace bound her to following channels, telling her alpha, letting him inform the vampires…waiting to hear if punishment had been meted out.

She gritted her teeth and forced back the wolf inside her. The animal growled and snapped, scratched at her mind for release, but CeCe held strong. Finally, her wolf took a step back and whined, let sorrow replace the anger, let CeCe feel it too. She lifted her head and howled.

Emotions spent, she stared down at Russell. Her eyes were damp and her throat was hoarse, but the worst wasn't over. She had to search his body for any proof that tied the vampire to his death and she had to get him out of these woods and back to the pack— alone. She couldn't leave him here for wild animals to feed off him.

Her mind focused and her wolf back under her control, she knelt.

She hadn't seen or heard from Russell in more than twenty-four hours. Based on the condition of his room, she suspected he hadn't been in it since that time either. Which meant he very likely had come here then and been killed soon after. The state of decomposition seemed to support this guess, further along than she might have suspected in a day, but the heat and humidity of the area would have sped the rate.

So, a day. She stored the information and moved on.

The next key piece of information was the most obvious. He had been killed in his human form. Contrary to what some monster movies showed, when werewolves died, they stayed in their current form. So Russell had been human when he was killed.

The easy part over, she knelt and placed a hand on his arm. She had to roll him over. It took both hands, and a pause to push aside the reality of what she was doing, but with minimal physical effort, she pulled him onto his side and finally his back.

Russell's round human eyes stared back at her. Human. She blinked and tried not to see the lack of expression, the glossy look of death—just concentrated on the shape.

The eyes changed first, but Russell's hadn't. Which meant he hadn't even tried to shift. Another small piece of data, but a piece that might prove important. After filing it away too, she shifted her gaze from Russell's face to his chest.

This time what she saw wasn't as easy to file away, wasn't as easy to accept.

The flat end of a stake protruded from his chest.

A breath hissed from between her closed teeth.

The werewolf had been staked through the heart, like a vampire.

She reached to touch the weapon, then paused and leaned forward instead, sniffing the leather, searching for some unique smell that would identify the last hand that had been wrapped around the handle, but there was no smell—none, not even of the leather itself.

She sat back on her heels and frowned.

There should have been some scent, even if only Russell's.

However, there wasn't, and puzzling though this fact was, spending time on it now would get her nowhere. She pushed the question aside and concentrated instead on what she needed to do next.

Russell's murder changed everything. This was not a simple retrieval mission any longer. This was personal, and criminal.

She no longer had the choice of not calling the pack. She had to let Karl know what had happened. Saving face, hiding her failure, was nothing when compared with the loss of Russell.

The tiny screen of her phone glowed as she punched in the numbers, but the sign of life was deceptive. Instead of a ring, a high pitched squeal sounded.

No reception. The region was hilly and sparsely populated. She'd had a signal in town, but even there it had been choppy.

She snapped the phone shut and shoved it back into her pocket.

She was on her own, at least for now.

Her gaze returned to the stake.

She hadn't come prepared to take away a murder weapon, or a body, but she couldn't leave Russell behind. Couldn't risk his being found by humans before the pack arrived. She would have to drag him somewhere, hide him until she could get back into town and cell coverage, and call Karl.

As she was glancing around, looking for a likely hiding place, the woods went silent. She froze, stood so quietly she could hear her own heartbeat, solid, steady, reassuring. Nothing else moved, not even a frog or bird. The woods were noisy places, birds and insects searching for mates and defending territory.

There was only one thing that could make the creatures still to the point they had. A predator was in the woods, and not one the tiny creatures that called the forest home recognized. They might see her presence as unwelcome and watch her with guarded interest, but wolves were natural encroachers.

Whoever, whatever, was approaching now wasn't. Her mind went one place—the vampire come back to cover his tracks, to take Russell or at least the weapon that had killed him. But it couldn't be…not in the day.

Perhaps he had an accomplice. Some human he had brainwashed into doing his bidding.

The quiet intensified. She could feel it.

With no time to do anything else, she pulled off her shirt and wrapped it around her hand. She'd worn the voluminous shirt to protect her skin from sun allergies, but here in the woods, that wouldn't be an issue—besides, she had no other choice.

Wearing just her jog bra, she jerked the stake from her pack mate's chest. It was heavy and obviously made of metal. With Russell's blood covering what wasn't covered by leather, she couldn't at the moment know what type, but she assumed iron. It was a common choice for stakes.

She moved through the woods with care, hid the weapon beneath a rotting log and then returned to spy on whoever, whatever, had followed her.

She crouched behind a bush, then waited and watched.

The vampire, dressed in long pants and a long-sleeved shirt and wearing a wide-brimmed hat and sunglasses, shoved aside a patch of brambles and stepped into view.

Despite the one-hundred-plus temperature, a chill moved over CeCe's body. A vampire in the day.

It broke every truth her father had taught her about the creatures. Rattled her faith that anything she knew and believed was true.

Shocked, she didn't move; the vampire, however, seemed focused. He walked in a direct path toward Russell.

Her suspicions fell into place, like coins dropping into a jar.

He had killed Porter and Russell. The only question left was, had he come here to cover his crime, or had he followed CeCe with plans to kill her too?

Before he had drawn a second breath, he knew exactly which tree the female crouched behind.

Deciding to let her believe for the moment that he was ignorant of her presence, he turned his attention to the dead werewolf.

The male lay faceup and alone in a flattened area of brambles. Marc recognized him instantly—the wolf who had been with the female, who had raced up the stairs ahead of the dog.

Keeping a portion of his attention on the tree where he knew the female hid, he moved toward the body. There was no sound from her quarter, no hint of life.

But she was there. Of that, Marc had zero doubt.

Still, as long as she stayed hidden and made no move to attack, he might as well take advantage of the time and study the dead wolf.

He hadn't had time or reason to analyze the male werewolf too much earlier, but he was young. Not puppy young, but even considering the extended lives of weres and their deceptively slow aging, this wolf was too young to have had any real life experience.

In other words, an easy target. For the female? Had the other wolf challenged her claim to the treasure? It went against everything he'd heard of werewolves and their blind pack loyalty, but the evidence that someone had wanted the wolf dead was irrefutable.

Marc moved to the side, so he was facing the hidden female, and crouched next to the body. The pose had dual purpose. It both assisted in his examination of the body and gave the female the false impression he was off guard, inviting her to make some move.

Alert for any movement, he lowered his gaze to the werewolf's body. Lost in his investigation, for that moment he all but forgot the female and his plan to lure her out of hiding.

A gaping rectangular hole marred the wolf's chest. His shirt, stiff with blood, stood away from the wound like a ragged crown.

The young wolf had been staked in the heart...like a vampire. Cold shock rolled over Marc. He did nothing for a moment, giving his brain time to process what this meant, but the time offered no answers.

Stakes were for vampires, to pin them to their beds while they slept, keep them from rising again. They weren't for werewolves.

Werewolves were shot or torn apart or like all hunted supernatural beings...burned.

No, that wasn't true. He had heard stories from the war that wolves had been staked, but he had never witnessed the act and had never really believed them. Why use a weapon that requires such up-close inter-action when a gun will do?

He brushed his finger over the wound. Whatever had happened or not happened before, this wolf had definitely been staked. The opening, while not large, hadn't closed in on itself. Which meant the weapon hadn't been removed when the werewolf was alive; it had been removed after his death, quite a while after his death.

From behind her bush, the female moved.

Instantly alert, Marc sprang forward. Attack or be attacked. The motto had kept him alive for two hundred years.

He landed in the brush, two feet from the female, close enough he could see the glimmer of gold in her amber eyes and smell the wildness of the wolf inside her.

Her hands tensing into claws, she stepped back. She'd removed her shirt for some reason. Her skin glistened with sweat.

He stored the thought away and assessed the threat. In her human form he could take her; as a wolf he wasn't as sure.

Knowing he had only a few moments before she realized this too and shifted, he glided forward.

She leaped to the side. He paused. The grace and ease of her movement wasn't lost on him, but it also served as a reminder of the animal inside her.

Now six feet away, she stared at him, within easy reach if she had been human and not capable of leaping impossible lengths.

Her eyes slanted in her face, the first sign that she was close to changing. It was the first time he'd seen her in the day. Her skin was pale like a vampire's; it made her hair seem darker, glossier.

"So, you killed Porter and Russell too. Which first?" She threw the words out like tiny exploding bombs.

Sensing that aggression would only push her closer to the animal she was so close to becoming, Marc stilled. Like her, his true nature clamored to get out. His fangs descended and his senses sharpened.

He could see her pulse throbbing at her throat, hear her heart pounding and smell the sweet heavy aroma of her blood as it coursed through her veins. He pressed his tongue against the sharp tip of one canine and concentrated on the small but shooting pain.

"Stop with your frivolous accusations. You know

I didn't kill him. You saw me arrive." He flexed his hands and lowered his shoulders.

The female took a step forward, her dark hair bristling like a wolf's ruff raising. "You obviously killed him earlier and came back. Why? To hide your sin or to stop me from telling my alpha, stop him from declaring the laws of peace broken?"

The idea that she would falsely accuse him, reignite the aggression that simmered under the surface of all vampire-werewolf interactions, and possibly restart the war, angered him. No treasure was worth bringing back the decades of death and destruction.

He moved forward to meet her and this time he showed his fangs. "One dead wolf, killed by a stake through the heart. The weapon of choice for vampire hunters."

"And a human. Or is Porter too far below a vampire's notice to count? Have you already forgotten him?"

"Why would I have killed Porter? What would be my reward? And I spoke to someone. The death was natural causes, most likely a heart attack."

She laughed. "I saw how you confused him, confused everyone in that bar. They didn't even remember you were there. How much harder would it be to convince them a body drained of blood was a simple victim of a heart attack?"

He made no attempt to hide his humor. "If only it was that easy." When she didn't seem to share his levity, he continued, "The people didn't remember me because I kept them from seeing me while I was there—they had no chance to acquire a memory of me. But to hide fang marks, or blood loss…I would have had to be present when the body was found, and even then, later, when someone new viewed the body at the morgue or hospital, they'd see the truth."

Her body stiff, she grunted. She didn't want to hear that he was innocent and her bias would keep her from seeing the truth, whatever it was.

"Let's say I did perform this miracle. What would my motive have been?"

She jumped on the answer. "Treasure. You took him into that bathroom, spelled him into telling you where it was and then you killed him to keep him from telling anyone else."

"Then why am I still here?" Her logic was idiotic. This conversation was idiotic and frustrating.

She hesitated.

"If I had the treasure, why would I stay here? Why would I bother following you into these woods?"

"To keep me from telling the pack what you have done."

He leaned back onto his heels. "The pack. You think vampires fear the pack? You think vampires would trust the pack, believe them over one of their own?" He didn't add one of the Fringe, the vampire regulatory body he'd joined one hundred years earlier. The Fringe was a secret shared only among the vampires, created to keep the group in line. Keep them from killing one another off or letting one rogue vamp endanger them all by doing exactly what she accused him of doing—killing humans.

If he had killed Porter, he wouldn't be worried about the werewolves. He would be worried about the Fringe.

"I didn't kill Porter and I didn't kill your friend. Look at how he died—a stake through the heart. We both know that isn't how a vampire would kill a were-wolf." He held her gaze, kept his own doubts brought on by the remembered tales from the war off his face.

Something flickered in her eyes.

Doubt.

The emotion was real. He realized then that she had truly suspected him, which meant *she* was inno-cent. Porter could easily be just what the humans had said, a heart attack, but this… He let his gaze flicker to the dead wolf.…

If the female hadn't killed this wolf, who had? Per-haps another wolf? Perhaps hiding in the woods now… watching them?

He tensed. His eyes on the female, he listened for any other sign of life in the trees. He would have sworn they were alone, but he'd been through too many bat-tles to trust even his own instincts.

The forest was silent. He inhaled, searching again for other life, but all he could smell was the heady sweetness of her blood. It overwhelmed every other sense he had, even that of the dead wolf.

Her expression shifted again. Logic warred with a belief…bias against vampires…that she couldn't shake.

"I don't believe that. Russell didn't kill himself."

Then a vampire must have done it. Her prejudice was so complete, it was beginning to bore Marc.

"Doesn't the pack have cable? Watch crime shows? The most likely killer is always the person closest to the victim. Who would that be?"

Her jaw tightened. "The pack is a family."

He laughed again. "And families never kill each other."

She stared back at him, ire clear in her gaze. But

then he was questioning everything she held dear. He pitied her, almost. If her beliefs were that blind, she deserved to have the chains of lies that kept them in place snapped in two.

"Who was closest to your pack mate? Who had reason to kill him?"

She squared her shoulders and turned to look at the woods. "No one."

Marc wanted to laugh again, but he suppressed it. "Think again, because someone did."

"During the war—"

He cut her off. "The war is over. The vampires ended it." The Fringe had ended it. They had gathered up the weapons used and threatened any vampire who didn't let things lie.

She shook her head. "Vampires started the war and werewolves ended it." She glanced toward her fallen pack mate. "Perhaps someone…some vampire…is trying to do the same thing again. Perhaps that's who has reason to kill Russell."

He laughed. "Is that the fairy tale they tell pups before they snuffle into their blankies for the night?" He tilted his head to meet her gaze. "How old were you when the war ended? What could you possibly know of it?" Werewolves were long-lived, but if this female had seen over seventy new years, he'd be surprised. The war had ended only a decade after that.

"I…" She closed her mouth, her lips pressing into a thin line. Then just as quickly she opened them again. "I know not to trust a vampire's lies."

"Because wolves don't twist the truth, won't say or do whatever it takes to protect the pack?"

"That at least you are right about, vampire. We protect the pack." Her hands formed fists at her sides. She lifted her upper lip, flashing a snarl. "Tell me what you know. If you didn't kill Russell and Porter, who else is here with you? Who are you protecting?"

His lips twisted into a sardonic smile. "Protect? Who would a vampire protect? We have no pack, no loyalty, no love…isn't that what you believe?"

"I—" Her words broke off. She turned on the ball of her foot. "Damn. Humans." She shoved past him, grabbed the dead werewolf by the wrists and began tugging him across the uneven rocky ground.

Annoyed the female had heard or sensed the entrance of humans into the trees before he had, Marc pressed his tongue against his fang and watched her.

Jerking the body through the trees, she seemed to have forgotten Marc. Brush snapped and the spice of some wild herb she had trampled filled the air. Being dismissed so thoroughly annoyed him anew.

Moments earlier she had accused him of not one, but two murders. Now she acted as if he were no bigger threat than one of the trees that stood between her and whatever destination she was headed toward.

He crossed his arms over his chest and arched one brow. As she tugged and then pulled the body backward, she left a flattened line of grass and scratched earth in her path. Even a human wouldn't miss the trail she was creating, not without some aid.

She could…should have…shifted, left him standing here with the body.

Of course, that would have meant leaving her pack mate for the humans to find, and as he had just pointed out, werewolves would do anything to protect the pack, even dead pack.

"How far?" he asked.

She paused. Hair clung to her face; the heat and humidity of the woods wore on her, unlike him, causing her clothing to cling to her athletic but feminine form and sweat to bead on her brow. "You mean a vampire can't—"

The sound of branches snapping cut off her response. The human was close, too close.

Marc waited, interested in what she would do.

She would have to shift now, or she'd be caught with her dead pack member's body. No matter who was wandering through the trees toward them, explaining that would be difficult. The police would be called and she'd be stuck answering questions, which, after being seen at the bar with Porter so near to his death, wouldn't be good.

She must have realized this too.

With a curse, she grabbed up branches and tossed them over the dead wolf's body.

The human was close now. Marc could finally smell him, a male who smoked and drank excessive amounts of coffee. His blood would taste of both. Marc wriggled his nose with annoyance. The human's scent edged into the female werewolf's, would soon stomp out the wild beauty of hers.

Unaware of his thoughts, she picked up another branch and tossed it onto the pile. She seemed lost in her work and unaware exactly how close the human had gotten.

In fact, he was here.

A man, fifty-plus in years and excess weight, shoved back a bramble. He was standing sideways; he hadn't seen Marc, the female werewolf or the dead

Russell yet. And he wouldn't see Marc, not if Marc didn't want him to.

The vampire prepared to slip out of the man's awareness, to let him focus instead on the two wolves.

He glanced at the female.

She stood with her hands at her sides and her body taut. She'd waited too long; she couldn't shift, not without the human witnessing her transformation.

Without thinking, Marc moved and jerked her toward him, until her chest, damp with sweat, pressed against his. She looked up; her eyes flashed with surprise.

"Play along." Then he dropped his mouth onto hers. Her lips were soft for a second; then she realized what was happening. Her body stiffened, her lips hardened and she tried to break free.

His hands on her upper arms, he pulled her body closer and pressed his lips tighter against hers, until their teeth touched.

"Relax," he murmured. "Give the human something to see and he won't see anything else."

Before she could comply or fight more, the human turned and froze. "What's…?" He slapped his hand against his thigh as if calling a dog.

Marc ignored the annoying noise. It wasn't hard to do. It was, in fact, much more difficult to remember that what the human was seeing was staged, would under any other circumstance have never happened, could never happen again.

The female tasted wild and sweet, like honey stolen fresh from a hive. Her blood pounded through her veins. Her skin was warm and slick with perspiration. Marc wanted to slip his lips from hers, trail them down her face and onto her neck…sample and explore everything she had to offer.

His fangs hung heavy in his mouth. He pulled his lips from hers and grazed her skin with one tip, enough to give him one tiny taste.

The female jerked and the human cleared his throat.

"You two…is everything all right here?" The man took a giant heavy-footed step forward.

"Fine. We're fine." The back of her wrist pressed against her lips, the female slipped from Marc's embrace. Her voice was husky, but at least she had a voice. With a desire he hadn't felt in a century swirling through him, Marc was unsure of his ability to place words into sentences.

"You sure?" The man shot a glare Marc's direction. He turned to the side, giving the human his profile. His fangs were extended. He needed a moment to harness the desire and hunger pounding through him.

The female hesitated, but only for a moment. "I'm sure."

The man didn't reply. Instead he bounced his gaze over the area surrounding them. Remembering the purpose of his act with the werewolf, Marc focused on the middle-aged human, forced his attention back to the female werewolf and Marc.

"Got a call of a smell. Something rotting. Either of you smell something like that?" His attention settled on the female werewolf. He frowned.

Marc stepped forward to sling his arm around her shoulder. She stiffened, but didn't pull away.

"I'm afraid we haven't been aware of a lot," Marc replied.

"Huh." The man snorted; then reached into his front

pocket and pulled out a pad. "You look familiar, miss. Were you at the bar last night?"

It was then Marc noticed that the drab outfit the man sported was actually a uniform. Marc lowered his gaze, checking for a gun. The man was unarmed and not, Marc guessed, with the local or state police. More likely in this area, a sheriff's office.

The officer's pen tapped against the edge of the notepad.

Marc shifted his gaze to the female. "You should answer him," he whispered. Stalling would only make the man question more.

She twisted as if to step away. Marc pressed the tips of his fingers into her bare skin. "I wouldn't do that. Sudden moves might shake our friend from his trance." It wasn't true. Even days from a feed and decent rest, Marc's powers were stronger than that, but he enjoyed having the female so close, all the more because he knew having her body pressed against his made her uncomfortable.

"You say something?" The man's brows lowered and his pen wavered.

Marc relaxed his fingers, let them brush over the female's upper arm, up and down. Her skin was soft and damp with a combination of humidity and sweat.

If Marc bit her, she would taste sweet and salty. A heady thought.

"You—" the human began.

"I was. I gave a report." The wolf twisted in place, made it obvious she was ready for the conversation to be over.

"That's right. I thought I remembered you. My deputy talked to you. You want to remind me of your name?" He wrote something on his pad.

Marc smiled, enjoying the female's discomfort. He could have made it easier on her, poured more of his powers into making the sheriff go on his way, but she'd give Marc no reason to help her. That he'd done as much as he had deserved recognition and thanks. Neither of which he guessed would be coming his way.

"CeCe. CeCe Parks."

The female's response startled Marc out of his thoughts. He hadn't expected her to answer, at least not that easily.

"And you?" The man stopped his scribbling to look back at Marc.

"Is this necessary, officer? Have we done something wrong? Trespassed perhaps?" Marc had no reason to keep his name from the human, but he knew that the female werewolf, CeCe, was waiting to hear it. Knew not knowing his name, when he now knew hers, was pricking at her, like a burr caught in her fur.

The man rolled back on his heels and then forward again. "Probably, but I doubt anybody cares. Just need the information for the report's all." He grinned, a friendly act to gain Marc's trust that the vampire did not believe. "Gotta keep the pencil pushers happy."

Marc paused another second, just to tweak the female more, then pulled in a breath as if the information had been forced from him. "Marc Delacroix, but I'd really rather this little—" he waved his free hand to indicate the woods around them "—incident not be reported. You see..." He dropped his arm from CeCe's shoulder. "She's married, not happily, but still..."

The officer grunted, but kept writing. CeCe, however, glared.

"Got ID?"

With a smile at the werewolf, Marc handed the man two business cards, one from his dry cleaner's, the other from his favorite hunting grounds, a bar in D.C.

The officer nodded and scribbled some more. The werewolf's eyes widened, but wisely, she kept her mouth firmly closed and her feet firmly planted in one place.

After a few moments, the man returned the business cards, gave the pair a warning to find a new spot for "whatever" and left.

"You spelled him."

Marc tucked the business cards back into his pocket. "It is called thrall, and only a little. Besides…" He pinned her with a look. "You should be thanking me. I didn't have to include you or your pack mate into my 'spell.' I could have simply stood by and watched as the human cuffed you and dragged you in for questioning."

She snorted. "Werewolves have their own way of escaping human detection."

He tilted his head. "Shifting, then running? Effective, if you don't have a 175-pound body to drag behind you. Or are you saying you would have left him behind?" He walked to the body and kicked off the branches she'd thrown over the dead werewolf.

She didn't answer and he didn't expect her to. They both knew he'd saved her from, at the very least, a few hours of uncomfortable questioning.

Her wild scent crept back into his consciousness.

She had moved to stand beside him. Annoyingly silent on her feet, he hadn't even noticed.

"If you're so powerful, why play the game at all? Why not just cast your spell wider, make him think he saw nothing but trees?"

"Thrall," he corrected.

Her brows inched upward.

Marc shrugged. "What would have been the fun in that?"

As he reached for the dead were's arm, he felt her glower.

And for the first time in decades, a true smile curved his lips.

Chapter 5

C eCe clamped her jaws together, refusing to growl. The vampire knew he was annoying her. He was toying with her on purpose, playing with her as a cat would a mouse.

But she was no mouse; she was a wolf. She needed to act like one. Do what her pack and alpha would do in her place.

She stepped between him and Russell, knocking against the vampire and cutting off his access to the wolf. "Don't touch him."

The vampire raised a brow, but didn't move from his crouch. "Have you smelled him? Seen if he smells of wolf?"

"He is a wolf."

"Another wolf, one that might have killed him."

Despite the fact it hadn't worked earlier, she pulled

her cell from her pocket. "I've already told you, that is impossible. I have my facts. The pack will decide what to do with them."

In one fluid motion, the vampire stood and knocked her hand aside. The phone flew from her fingers, landing deep in the brush.

She snarled.

"What next, vampire? You think you can toss me aside as easily?" She let the wolf inside her raise its head and sniff the wind, let the vampire see the animal that was so eager to escape. Her frustration with the vampire, his quick confusing words, had agitated the beast.

A shift would come easy, swift.

"What makes you think I want to toss you aside?"

The question was simple, polite even, but brought with it memories of being pressed against the undead vampire. His body had been cool against her too-hot flesh. She should have been repulsed, but instead she had been tempted to stay with her body flush against his.

Her body still tingled with awareness.

Attraction, to a vampire. It was unheard of…sick and disloyal. No wolf would think of a vampire that way.

Still, a tremble ran through her. She tried to hide the unwelcome reaction, forced her mind, her body, everything inside her to remain still…strong.

Back under control, she looked at him.

The vampire, damn him, smiled.

He knew.

Then before she could react, snap at him, curse or

do something else she would regret, the smile disappeared and his face went earnest.

"What side are you on, CeCe? The pack against all else? Against right? Against truth? How far does your loyalty go? Would you give up lives, your soul to give the pack what it wants?"

The use of her name startled her almost as much as his questions confused her. "Calling the pack won't stop the truth—it will hurry its discovery. If you truly had nothing to do with Russell's or Porter's death, you have nothing to fear." Even a wolf with as much reason as she had to despise the vampires wouldn't hang…or stake…an innocent one.

A look of knowledge she didn't like filled the vampire's eyes. He stared at her as if he knew things she didn't, had experienced things that she hadn't.

Which of course he had; he was a vampire. There was no way of knowing how old he was, what times he had lived through. But even if he was a thousand years old, he wouldn't understand werewolves or the pack. Only a wolf could truly do that.

She turned to retrieve her phone. His fingers on her arm stopped her. Her heart thumped in her chest. He touched her too easily, and damn everything, she didn't mind.

She jerked her arm more violently than necessary to break free and spun. Her hands balled into fists and her lip rose.

He held out both hands. "Let me look at the body. I can tell you things no werewolf could."

She wanted to argue the point, but couldn't. How he had manipulated the people outside the bar and now the sheriff spoke for itself. Vampires had powers werewolves didn't, and he might notice something she couldn't.

If she could trust anything he said.

Still, she was curious what he might say, what wild explanations for the stake wound he might create.

"Fine." She stepped back. "But I'm watching."

He didn't acknowledge her threat, just lowered his body back to a crouch and began a cool, controlled examination of Russell's body.

"He was stabbed, once." Marc's voice was professional and detached, like a doctor's. "The wound didn't close as you would expect." He glanced at her. She could feel his suspicion, but didn't acknowledge it. She kept her gaze as dispassionate as his.

After a moment, he continued.

"No signs of struggle." He tilted the werewolf's head to the right and then the left, examining his neck. "No bites."

"The neck isn't the only place a vampire will bite," CeCe commented, instantly suspicious that he was trying to mislead her.

He looked up; no emotion showed on his face. "No, but unless the relationship is intimate, it is widely preferred."

His gaze stayed on her a little too long.

Intimate. It was as if he'd whispered the word into her ear. She could feel his breath against her neck, could feel the tingles again, creeping up her body, but, she told herself, the sensation was only in her mind, the vampire causing it somehow to bring her discomfort.

CeCe ran her palm up her neck. Realizing what she was doing, she jerked her hand away.

The vampire was still crouched on the ground next to Russell, five feet away. He didn't seem to notice her unease. His gaze back on the dead werewolf, he picked up one of Russell's wrists then the other, rotating Russell's arm back and forth as he did, obviously looking for any marks.

"Clean," he announced.

"So, no bite. That doesn't mean a vampire wasn't involved," she added, shifting her feet.

"No." Marc rolled Russell's body onto its stomach and lifted its shirt.

Unsure what he might do next, if the vampire would try something Karl would question later, CeCe edged closer.

Marc released an impatient sigh. "I am looking for signs of struggle. There are none. If I attacked you, would you fight back?"

"Of course—" She cut off her own reply. "But you could have put him under—" she struggled for the word "—thrall."

Surprise and then indecision crossed his face. After a moment, he sighed. "You saw me at the bar. You even sensed me at Porter's house when you had no reason to suspect I was there. Thrall doesn't work as well on other preternatural beings. If it did, the war would have lasted only a matter of months. The vampires would have picked the werewolves off one by one."

What he said made sense, but he had reason to lie. "I didn't see you at Porter's, though." She hated admitting it.

"Because I didn't move. One flicker of my eyelash and you would have sensed me—you did sense me. And once the dog revealed I was there, there was no hiding from you again. So, as much as I would like to be all-powerful, let me assure you this wasn't a product of thrall."

She blinked. She believed him.

"But perhaps you think this werewolf would have stood still, let a vampire, let anyone he didn't know, walk up and shove a blade through his heart—"

"Stake," she corrected.

Silence greeted her. Marc's eyes turned appraising.

"The wound was caused by a stake," she added.

"And you know this how? Are you an expert in stake wounds?" He tilted his head and for a moment she thought an accusation would follow, but he simply continued, "I see a wound, and while I'll admit my first reaction was stake, it could be from something else, a knife or a dagger." He looked back at the Russell's chest. "I do know it was something sharp and that there are no bits of wood or debris in the wound… but…" He turned his attention back to her. She could feel his gaze, weighing, assessing. "I can't tell you one hundred percent for certain it was from a stake."

"It's too big." She gestured over Russell. "Too far across. I arrived before you. I had longer to look."

"You removed his shirt and put it back on?"

She crossed her arms over her chest. "Look—more carefully this time. Tell me I'm wrong." If he did, she'd know he was lying, she'd know she had more reason to suspect him of being involved.

His lips thinned, but Marc did as she said; he raised Russell's shirt higher so the wound where the stake had been lodged was fully visible. He ran his finger around the opening; then without asking for permission, he prodded the gap in the flesh.

"Don't." She dropped to a kneel, her hand reaching to pull Marc's away. Allowing a vampire to look at Russell was one thing, allowing him to get Russell's blood on his hands was too much. The pack would object; Karl would object.

A growl sounded in her head; hairs rose on the back of her neck. The pack, even unaware of exactly what was happening, sensed her distress, and was reacting two hundred miles away. She wondered why it had taken them so long, why they hadn't felt her need for support when she was being held by the humans at the bar, or when she had found Russell.

Did the vampire affect her that thoroughly? Cut through her control that completely?

She removed her hand without touching Marc and pulled in one deep, calming breath. Agitating the pack while they were so far away would do nothing to help her now.

The vampire slowly removed his hands from Russell's body and held them palm out. Blood streaked his right index finger. She stared at the stain. Werewolf blood on a vampire's hands. To the pack it would be cause for war.

But this blood wasn't fresh, wasn't a mark of guilt, she told herself.

Still, she knew how Karl would react, and seeing Russell's blood on Marc's skin made her uneasy, feel guilty, as if she was hiding something.

Miles away the pack sensed that too. They milled around sniffing, wondering; she could feel them as clearly as if they stood inches away.

Suddenly desperate to quiet the increasingly agitated wolves, she grabbed Marc's hand and wiped his finger across her pants. The vampire didn't question her strange move. He just sat and watched. When the blood that had stained his hand was instead streaked across the leg of her pants, she closed her eyes and breathed again.

The wolves snuffled…then slowly they quieted.

She opened her eyes and found herself staring directly into the vampire's.

"You're important," he said.

She widened her eyes. "Isn't everyone?"

He flipped his hand so he gripped her wrist. "No, the pack heard you. Whatever you were thinking or feeling…they heard you."

She jerked her arm free. "Wives' tale. Wolves are individuals, not bees or humans. There is no hive mind."

"Don't lie to me. It's a waste of time and only tells me I can't trust you. Sure, wolves are individuals, if they choose to be, but the closer you are to the pack, the more important you are in their survival, the more keyed in they are to your hurts, wants, desires…."

The damned whisper again. Her skin tingled.

She squared her shoulders. "The pack senses things. It's part of what keeps us strong." And they watched her. She didn't know why, but they had since her father had first delivered her to them.

Marc jerked his head back toward the dead were. "It didn't help him."

CeCe swallowed. He was right. If anyone in the pack had sensed Russell was in trouble, it hadn't been in time to help the young wolf. She hadn't sensed he was in trouble. She had failed him.

"My guess? He wasn't important, not like you."

Her gaze snapped back to the vampire. The truth was complicated and none of the vampire's business.

She stood. "You can leave." She knew she should hold him, keep him here to answer to Karl, but suddenly she wanted him to leave and take the strange way he made her feel, made her question things, with him.

Also standing, he cocked a brow. "I've always been aware of my ability to leave. Should I thank you for verbalizing it?"

She ground her teeth together. "I can take it from here. I'll call the pack."

He laughed. "Didn't we cover that earlier?"

"The pack has to be told."

He waved a hand. "Of course, as does the…do the vampires. A werewolf was killed, possibly a human, and according to you, by me." He grabbed the cuff of his shirt and tugged it lower, over his wrist. "The vampires will definitely want to hear of this, but—" he scratched at a spot that covered the stitching on his sleeve "—there's no reason to tell them now. Why not wait? Neither the human nor this werewolf is getting any deader."

She growled at the callous remark.

His eyes flickered, but he didn't apologize. Instead, he stepped closer. There were lines around his eyes she hadn't noticed earlier. They made him look tired, more human and less monster. They also for some reason, for just for a moment, made her forget that she couldn't trust him.

"If you didn't kill Porter or this werewolf—"

"Russell. His name was Russell." Suddenly it was important he acknowledge that, that they both acknowledge Russell as a person, not a body, a thing to be coldly examined and discussed.

He paused, then nodded. "Russell. And I didn't kill them either, then someone else did. Chances are, another werewolf—" At her growl, he added, "Or vampire. If you call your pack here, there will be too many bodies, too many voices. The truth will get lost. Is that what you want? The pack will arrive. The vampires will arrive and where will we be?"

"In the middle of a war." A war. Started by one simple, easy assignment—steal back some treasure, from a human, a drunken human too stupid to keep news of his discovery to himself. It shouldn't have ended like this, and maybe it wouldn't have if she'd called Karl when they first discovered that the treasure wasn't at Porter's house. At that point everything was still okay; Porter and Russell were still alive.

And despite the fact that she didn't want to start a war any more than the vampire claimed he did, she couldn't dig the hole any deeper. She had to call Karl and the pack.

However, the vampire didn't need to know that.

She turned back. "Agreed."

"You won't tell the pack, or any other werewolf?"

"I said I agree. How about you?" Her voice held steady. She was lying to a vampire. That hardly counted.

"This is our secret. To assure it, we hide the body together."

A breath she hadn't realized she'd been holding escaped her lips. She'd been afraid he would insist on taking Russell with him. She would need to know where the werewolf was so she could bring Karl back to him.

Marc's next comment, however, sliced through her relief.

"And we work together."

"Together?"

"Together. You don't trust me and to be honest, I don't trust you. The only way to be sure the other isn't behind this, or working with whoever is, is to work together. Share information."

Share the treasure—or steal it from her when she found it. She realized now that was his plan, keep her from calling in the pack so he would only have to deal with her.

He didn't see her as a threat.

Some piece of her wanted to prove him wrong.

She dropped her gaze to the ground, but Karl would never agree to her working with a vampire, not even as a spy.

The sound of Marc's laugh brought her head back up. "Are you honestly trying to make me believe you were going to let me walk away from here? Not follow me? Not try to listen in on every conversation I have? Isn't it better we just share the information as we get it? We do both want the same thing, right? To find out who killed the human and your pack mate?"

"And the treasure. Don't deny you want that too." She couldn't let it lie, couldn't let him believe she was that stupid.

He slipped forward, fast and silent as the wind, so his chest was inches from hers and his breath stirred her hair. She didn't step back; she didn't let herself.

"Perhaps. It is why we both came here, but some

things are more important than treasure. Don't you agree?" He looked down at her. She couldn't look up, couldn't meet his gaze. Her body tingled. She wanted to believe it was with the excitement of lying to him, playing him, but she couldn't lie to herself, not that thoroughly.

"If you don't agree, I'll have no choice. I won't be able to let you out of my sight. Not until I know without a doubt that you or one of your pack didn't set all this up to frame me."

She stared at a button on his shirt. It was shell, expensive, and nothing like anything a werewolf would put on his body.

But he was right. She wouldn't let him walk away. She couldn't. And what good would following him do, when he knew she was watching him? Better to pretend to work together, to pretend to share. If she could get his trust, he would tell her more. Then she could sneak away and call Karl, tell him everything.

With the pack here, she'd be stronger, better able to resist whatever magic the vampire cast around her. Able to see it as false. And once she delivered him to Karl, the pack would accept her too, see her loyalty.

Russell would still be dead, but after she found the treasure, she'd have everything she came here to get…a mate, a place, a family. Russell would have appreciated that. It's what he had wanted too.

Chapter 6

Marc knew CeCe didn't trust him; he also suspected that the first chance she got, she would contact the pack unless he could think of a way to stop her, and unfortunately, he had gone without sleep for four days. As he aged, he could tolerate more and more time in the day, but he had pushed himself too far already. Before the sun set, he would be out, lost in the cursed vampire death, and the werewolf would be free to do whatever she chose.

He slipped his hands under the dead werewolf's shoulders. Then, while he waited for CeCe to grab hold of the wolf's feet, he glanced at the sky.

The sun was high and hot. He could feel it draining his resources. He didn't know how much longer he could last. He needed a plan.

"Where are we headed?" she asked from six feet away...the length of the dead wolf's body.

Marc could easily have handled the other male's weight on his own, but CeCe was easier to keep an eye on when she was busy carrying her half of the burden.

"Somewhere no one will find him."

"You're familiar with the area?"

The question was innocent, or appeared to be, but Marc knew better.

"No. I'm a vampire." He paused and sniffed the night air. "And the town's name says it all."

"A cave? We're looking for a cave?" CeCe adjusted her grip on the werewolf's feet and glanced around the dark woods.

"You don't like caves?" Marc guessed. Caves were cool, dark and closed in. The perfect place for vampires hiding from both daylight and would-be slayers.

She shrugged, but Marc could feel her unease.

"Caves are underground, cold, with no light. Who could like that? Besides bats and—"

"Vampires," Marc murmured, and sniffed again. The scent of the underground was closer. He jerked his head to the right. "A few more feet. Watch your step."

He moved another ten feet, then motioned for CeCe to lower her half of the dead werewolf to the ground. She followed his instructions, then stood back, her hands grabbing her upper arms. "I feel a breeze. It's cold," she said.

Marc walked a few more feet, then knelt. The scent of the underground was strong. Two feet in front of him was an opening in the ground. He could tell by the chill and scent of the air he'd found what he'd been searching for, a cave.

Without speaking, he returned to where CeCe stood, slung the dead werewolf's body over his shoulder, and walked back to the opening. Then he dropped the body. The dead wolf fell through the partially obscured opening and into the cave.

He waited for the body to hit.

"What—" CeCe leaped forward. Marc slung out his arm, stopping her from falling through the opening too. Her weight pressed against his arm. He shoved her backward, causing her to fall onto the ground.

She sprang to her feet, her hair bristling and her eyes glowing. "You threw him into a hole. How deep is it? How will I—?"

"Get the pack to him?" As Marc had suspected, despite what she had said, she had every intention of calling the pack into their investigation. She was making it nearly impossible for him to trust her. Unknowingly, she was sealing her own coffin with her actions.

Not wanting to reveal his thoughts, he shook his head. "Surely wolves aren't that afraid of the dark."

Ignoring him, she moved forward. Inches from the opening, she stopped and fell to her knees.

Before the werewolf Russell's body had fallen through, vines had covered the cave's opening. Now the entrance was glaringly obvious.

Obvious enough that he knew that any hiker who wandered this direction would find it. Ignoring the female werewolf, who seemed intent on tumbling into the cave after her dead pack mate, he began gathering vines and fallen limbs.

As he approached, CeCe looked up. "What are you doing?"

Marc dropped his load and began positioning branches and vines across the entrance. "The idea was to hide the body. As I told you before, I'm a vampire, not a magician. Once I leave, any ability I have to keep people from seeing something leaves with me. Your friend's weight broke through what covering there was. I am simply replacing it."

He dropped a limb onto the hole in front of her, then stared, telling her without words to move. After a few tense moments, she did. He knelt in her place and fluffed the greenery they had crushed while milling around the opening.

Satisfied the cave was as hidden as it could be, he turned to face her.

"He's gone now," she murmured. Worry was clear on her face.

"Not gone, hidden. There is a difference."

"I felt inside and dropped a rock. The hole is deep. We…"

"Once we learn who is behind this, who killed him, you can retrieve the body. The floor of the cave isn't that deep, maybe thirty feet. Surely even a wolf in human form and outfitted with ropes can rappel that far."

He dropped the remaining vines that he had gathered and strode into the woods. Her obsession with the pack was frustrating. Such blind loyalty is what made the war possible. Vampires had trusted vampires; werewolves had trusted werewolves. And neither had allowed themselves to see any truth or fairness in the other. If anyone had been thinking for themselves, analyzing all the information, the war could have been settled with a simple meeting between the two groups.

But no one had, not even Marc.

And that was the fact he had to face. Sixty years ago, he had made a bad choice, trusted when he should have questioned. He wouldn't do that again, and he wouldn't let the female werewolf do it either.

Truth was all that mattered, was the only thing in the end that could save any of them from the mistakes they had made before.

And Marc was willing to do anything, risk anything to make sure that this time, the truth was what everyone saw.

As the vampire strode away, CeCe stared at the hole he had covered. She poked the largest of the branches he had dropped over the opening with her foot and considered her options.

Thirty feet. Wolves leaped, but they didn't climb, and thirty feet was well past even Karl's vertical leaping ability.

She or another wolf might survive jumping into the cave, but they wouldn't be getting back out, not without the climbing gear Marc had mentioned.

Which meant Russell's body was lost to her, at least for a while.

She had also, thanks to the vampire, lost her phone. She could find it easy enough, but not now. Retrieving it would have to wait until later today, after she lost the vampire and placed her call to Karl using the phone in her hotel room.

And that, despite what she had told the vampire, was her first move: return to her room and call her pack. Begin to make right the wrong she had done.

Ready to put on her cooperative face and follow the vampire, she turned.

But Marc had returned and now stood only inches away, a dark expression on his face.

"You can't do it. It's too much for me to expect that you can." He sighed after he spoke, as if accepting something of great personal upset.

Prickles of unease wove up her spine. She took a step back, only to be reminded by the crackle of breaking wood that the cave entrance lay less than a foot behind her.

Marc blew air out of his mouth. He looked tired. She realized then the reason for his hat and sunglasses. Not the same as her reasons for choosing skin-covering clothing, not sun allergies.

The sun was wearing on him, draining him.

Calling the pack would be no problem at all, not with Marc weakened like this. Perhaps he would even pass out. Perhaps that part of vampire lore was true.

And if Karl and the pack traveled fast enough, they could be in Cave Vista before nightfall tonight, before Marc awoke. All CeCe would have to do is follow the vampire and see where he slept. Then taking Marc, questioning him and finding the treasure would be no problem at all.

Triumph shot through her.

Marc grabbed her by the arm.

"I would like to trust you, but that would just be stupid of me, wouldn't it?"

She jerked backward. Her foot plunged through the vines and she sank to her thigh through the cave entrance's makeshift covering.

She realized then what he planned to do with her. How he would stop her from getting to the pack. "No." She wouldn't be dropped into that hole.

She couldn't be.

* * *

Marc's fingers dug into CeCe's arm as her body slipped and threatened to fall into the cave where her dead pack mate now lay.

He could feel her fear and see her panic.

Her eyes slanted and her pupils turned to slits. She was shifting. She yelled again. This one turned to a bark.

Minutes, seconds, he had no idea how much time he had.

His gaze dropped to the ground, where her leg had already descended into the cave's entrance.

The quickest, simplest solution to his problem was obvious.

He loosened his hold and lifted his foot to break more of the covering he had just added.

"No." Panic shone from her eyes.

Thirty feet. She was a werewolf; she'd be fine. He knew this, but still…fear emanated from her.

He stared into her wild, now golden eyes, seconds counting down, neither of them moving. Her fingers wrapped around his forearm, grasping, asking without words for him to help her, not to let her fall.

He cursed, then jerked and pulled her free.

She lay on the ground, breath heaving from her chest, her hair and eyes feral.

He cursed again, knew his weakness was a mistake, that he should rectify it while he still could, shove her into that hole, but he couldn't.

Wild and beautiful, trapping her would have killed some part of her, stolen something he feared could never be replaced.

Instead, he reached into his back pocket and pulled

out the handcuffs he'd found at Porter's. He'd brought
them with him today and was glad of it. With the wire
of pure silver hidden beneath their hard steel exterior,
they would stop her from shifting.

Not looking at the female wolf, he slapped one
around her wrist and the other around his.

Now, if she wanted to get to her pack, she would
have to drag his soon-to-be-lifeless body along with
her.

CeCe shuddered. So close. She'd been so close to
falling into the dark pit. She still was at risk. The vampire was still near, could with one good kick shove
her back toward the hole and watch as she clawed to
keep from falling.

Images flashed through her mind. She closed her
eyes, but they kept coming. Damp earth under her
nails, rocks gouging into her palms, nothing to hold
on to, nothing to keep her from falling…no one to save
her…no one who cared.

Something snapped and cold metal wrapped around
her wrist. Her skin itched.

Her eyes flew open. She jerked her arm, only to
have it jerked back. Confused, she spun to a sit.

Marc sat two feet away. A steel bracelet shone from
his wrist. CeCe blinked and moved. Marc moved too,
or his arm did. Stupidly, she stared at her own wrist.
Silver metal glinted and winked in the increasingly
strong rays of the sun.

"Are you all right?" he asked.

She pulled her hand toward her chest. Marc's arm
moved closer.

"You…chained us together," she muttered. "Like dogs."

"We need to go." He stood and held out his hand as if he expected her to take it.

She shook her head. "You were going to throw me into the pit."

He shrugged. "Should have, but I didn't."

If he expected her thanks, he expected too much.

"I'm not going with you." He might think he had her trapped, but he'd forgotten what she was. Her hand might not fit through the cuff, but her paw most certainly would.

She smiled and called to her wolf. The creature edged forward. Then ears folding backward and legs stiffening, it stopped.

CeCe frowned and called again. This time her wolf didn't move, not at all.

Instead, pain wrapped around her like a snake squeezing her from inside. She gasped and rolled onto her stomach, and, desperate, called again.

A new wave of pain rolled over her. Her wolf yelped and pulled back. CeCe's legs curled up toward her core.

"Stop. The cuffs aren't mundane." The vampire knelt beside her and yelled into her ear.

Not mundane. For a moment, the words made no sense, then as the latest wave of pain faded, the meaning became clear. "Silver. You used silver on me." She spit out the words.

She knew she couldn't trust him. What did he have planned for her now?

He grabbed her by the shoulder. "As if you give me any choice. We made a deal, but you meant to break it. Do you deny that? Do you expect me to believe that when I fell asleep, while I was helpless, you didn't plan to call your pack? Break our pact?"

A pact with a vampire had no meaning. Only the pack mattered. Only her duty mattered. It was a truth that her father had pounded into her from the time her mother was killed by one of the undead beings.

She lifted her lip to snarl, then called for her wolf again. She was strong. She'd been trained. She'd gone through worse. She could beat this.

Agony like a boot in the snout knocked her back down.

Somewhere nearby the vampire cursed, then he lifted her into his arms and slung her as he had slung Russell over his shoulder and strode through the woods.

She bounced against his shoulder, hard. The world moved up and down with each step. She clawed at his back, cursed him to death and beyond, but he kept moving and her wolf refused to come out, refused to save her.

Through the woods and away from the cave, he walked. Whatever he had planned for her, it wasn't the pit.

Exhausted, she thanked God for that. Then she passed out.

Chapter 7

CeCe awoke in the dark. Cave-dark.

The vampire.

The hole.

Her heart rate surged; a cold sweat broke out on her body. Unsure where she was, what position she had landed in after being tossed into the cave, she lay still.

Near her a hum sounded. She sucked in a breath and struggled to identify the noise. Steady, loud and man-made…a machine. What the hell? Then the noise clicked off and recognition hit…an air-conditioning unit.

Relief swept over her like a reassuring breeze.

She wasn't in the cave…wasn't even in the woods. She was instead in a room, windowless or with black-out coverings on the windows, but a room.

Her pulse settled and as her panic subsided, her other senses kicked in.

Wherever she was, it was cool, but the air was stale as if sometime in the past someone had smoked here. Like an old motel room.

She moved; beneath her springs creaked. A mattress. Her guess was right; she was on a bed. She dragged her hands over the surface, double-checking. Cheap quilted polyester brushed against her palms and a weight—the cuffs—dragged at her wrist.

She rolled onto her side toward her restrained wrist and felt for the metal bracelet.

It was still there. She followed the chain with her fingers and felt the cold skin of the vampire.

She held his wrist for a second, unsure if he was awake, asleep or dead.

He didn't move and her fingers, now pressed against the underside of his wrist, felt no pulse.

She jerked back her hand. Then, curious, she reached out again. His skin was still soft and pliant, cold to the touch but without the dead, unresponsive feel of a corpse. She rolled closer, so the front of her body touched the side of his. He lay on his back, his hands at his sides.

She ran her fingers up his torso and over his chest. He still wore a shirt, the cotton stiff and formal feeling, but through the material she could feel his body. He was muscled, as were wolves, but he was bulkier than a wolf.

The cut of his clothing had hidden that from her when she was depending on sight rather than touch, but as her fingers traced over raised pectoral muscles, there was no denying this vampire was in shape.

An image of him without his shirt flitted into her mind. She lifted her hand. Guilt lanced through her. She curled her fingers into her palm and moved to roll onto her back.

The handcuff he had snapped around her wrist got caught on the quilt, pulled at her, reminded her that she wasn't lying here in a place unknown of her own choice. She'd been trapped, and if she wanted to escape, she needed to find the key—now—while the vampire was still out.

Slowly, her fingers unfolded and she let the pads of her fingers graze over his chest again. Her palm touched the space where his pectorals met...the area over his heart. Suddenly, she had to know, had to listen for herself to see...was he truly dead, did he die and rise each night as her father said, or had he, like some animals, slipped into a short if deep hibernation?

With her free hand, she unbuttoned the vampire's shirt and pushed the material aside. Then she pressed her ear to his heart.

At first there was nothing, no sound, no sensation. Then as her skin warmed his, as she felt herself relax against him, she heard it...the faint and slow but steady thump of his heart.

She froze, contemplating what this meant.

Her father was wrong. Vampires weren't dead. They weren't even that different from many wild creatures. Yes, they slept, hibernated at least to some degree during the day, but in the animal world that was far from unnatural.

Her father was wrong…. She had never considered the possibility before.

She thought of Marc, of his offer, his reasons why she shouldn't call Karl.

But then she thought of Karl.

So what if her father had one tiny fact wrong? It didn't change that a vampire had killed her mother, and it didn't mean that what this vampire asked of her was right. She shook her head.

Vampires weren't truly dead. Interesting, but not significant. Not a fact that changed anything she believed or had to do.

She pulled back and continued her search. Ten minutes later she had searched every logical place on the vampire's body where he might have stashed the key. His pockets were empty, there wasn't so much as a grain of sand in his socks, and he wore no chain around his neck. The key wasn't on him.

She rolled onto her back and stared into the darkness. She was alone in a space she couldn't see, shackled to one hundred eighty pounds of, for the moment, dead weight.

Dead weight that had taken every precaution to eliminate all light. She thought back to his long pants and long sleeves.

Her father and the legends weren't totally wrong. Vampires might not be dead, but sunlight did harm them…weaken them.

It's what every cut-rate monster flick taught. Find a vampire where he sleeps, destroy him with a stake through the heart or drag him into the light. If just being in the light, while his skin was fully covered, had weakened him, what would being exposed to the sun, without his layers of clothing, do?

The room, no matter how big, had to have a door, and beyond that door there had to be sunlight.

If she wanted to escape, all she had to do was find it.

If the exposure did kill him, it would be breaking a law, but the law had already been broken and she would be justified.

He'd taken her prisoner and killed Russell.

He'd convinced her for a time that he hadn't killed her pack mate, but trapping her like this showed how stupid she had been to believe him.

Karl would approve of her decision. The pack would approve. They wouldn't turn her over to the vampires; they would celebrate her victory. They would, perhaps, even accept her.

She rolled over to face Marc, and then sat up with every intention of shoving him off the bed. Leaning over him, she paused. Her hand lowered and her fingers brushed over his bare chest where she had pressed her ear earlier.

His pulse might be too light to feel, but he had a heartbeat. Her father had been wrong.

The hairs on the back of her neck rose. A growl escaped her throat. Her hand shaking, she touched the vampire again.

Alive…

Another growl…her wolf, its loyalty to the pack, objecting to her thoughts.

She grabbed the chain that connected her wrist to the vampire's. He'd done this. He'd trapped her and dragged her into the dark. Another vampire, like him, had killed her mother. She couldn't trust him, couldn't let this opportunity pass.

She growled, but the noise was faint…false, just an attempt to push her body to move.

A wolf, a real wolf, wouldn't hesitate. A real wolf would attack its enemy. No regrets. No weakness.

She ground her teeth together and wrapped her free arm around the vampire, surging forward before she lost her resolve.

As one they fell off the bed. She hit the floor first, landing on her back. The vampire landed on top of her.

She placed her palm on his chest and levered her leg under his, to shove him aside so she could get under his arm and drag his weight as she searched for an exit. Again they tumbled as one, coming to a stop with CeCe on top…her ear pressed against his chest.

And there it was again…the steady soft beat of his heart.

Defeated. She closed her eyes.

She couldn't do it. She would have sworn a thousand times over that she could, but she couldn't.

She just couldn't.

Hours had passed since CeCe had faced her failure. She had moved, but only slightly. She had simply rolled off Marc's body and onto the hard floor. Some kind of indoor/outdoor carpeting was all that lay beneath her and concrete.

Her body was stiff and her back ached. She'd lost track of time, but hadn't drifted into sleep.

The room was still dark. Pitch dark, and the air conditioner had come back on, then shut off again, leaving the space silent.

She had nothing to do, nothing to occupy herself except memories. Memories she wished she didn't have.

They rolled over her, pulled at her. She closed her eyes as if that would shut them out.

Learn. Train. Be strong. Be ready.

She gritted her teeth, but a growl escaped.

Frustrated, she rolled toward the vampire and straddled him. She had to get out of this room.

One way or another, it was time for Marc to wake up.

Fingers twisted into the front of Marc's shirt. His body was jerked upward then dropped onto a hard, flat surface. His back and then his head hit too. A weight straddled his waist and curses flowed over him.

"Damn you for being alive. Damn you for not being what you're supposed to be."

Another jerk upward. This time, fully awake, Marc kept his body from dropping again. He surged to his feet, taking whatever clung to him up too.

"Damn you—" The words stopped, cut off with an umph as Marc plowed forward into a wall.

With his assailant trapped between his body and the cinder block walls of the room he'd rented, he snarled, revealing his fangs.

"You're awake." The words startled him.

He'd expected fear and alarm, instead he got exasperated relief.

"Put me down and unhook these damned things."

Adrenaline poured through his body as he struggled to focus. Finally, his mind cleared and the feminine face of the werewolf, CeCe, came into clear view.

The need to bite, to savage, didn't, however, recede as quickly. The need for blood pounded through him and CeCe's scent called to him, stronger even than it

had in the woods. He pressed two fingers to the bridge
of his nose and tried to leash the monster he was at
risk of becoming.

His head ached and his body shook. As his fangs
sank into his own lip, he tasted blood. It wasn't
enough; he needed more. Needed to taste the sweet
blood of the wolf pressed tight against him.

But he couldn't, not now, maybe never.

He gritted his teeth until his jaw ached and concentrated on things outside of this room, duties and
responsibilities, his job for the Fringe.

Finally, he was able to breathe.

"What time is it?" he asked.

Based on the pounding in the back of his head he
guessed he had not had the full eight hours he needed
after four days without rest.

But then, of course, the pounding could also have
been from having his head bashed into the floor. He
grimaced and moved backward. As he did, CeCe slid
lower, reminding him of the intimate position of their
bodies.

Suddenly, the ache in his head was gone. He leaned
toward the female wolf, inhaling her scent. Thoughts
of biting her returned, savaging, too, but in an entirely
different manner. "Do all wolves smell like this?" he
murmured.

"Like what?" Her voice was harsh, almost hoarse.

"Wild, like a creature that roams the night, but
with…spice." He could think of no greater compli-
ment, but at his reply, she shrank back.

"Wolves are nocturnal," she replied. "Werewolves
aren't."

He realized then that her face was strained and pale.

"You don't like the night." It was a comment as much as a question. The idea was foreign to him. "But I met you in the night—"

She frowned. "The night is fine. It's this unnatural—" She cut off her own response, pressing her lips together.

The dark. She was afraid of the dark. It explained her response to the cave.

He had never met an adult who was afraid of the dark and certainly wouldn't have expected the phobia from a werewolf. He glanced at CeCe, but her face was turned to the side, and she avoided his gaze.

He stepped away from the wall, cradling her in his arms. She didn't fight him, telling him more than he wanted to know. Her hair brushed against his check and her scent called to him. More than anything, he wanted to lower her onto the bed and investigate her scent, her body, her.

Based on how he felt, there was, he guessed, still an hour or more of day left. Without his full rest or feeding, he wasn't ready to go out in the sunlight again yet. Which meant, they had plenty of time with nothing to do. However, tempting as the idea of lowering her onto the bed and joining her there was, her current cooperation wasn't real, was instead a product of her discomfort. A discomfort he was responsible for creating.

Slowly, he let her body slide from his, forced his arms to loosen as her weight made contact with the mattress. Then he found her hand and pulled her to her feet.

"I'm sorry," he murmured. With her fingers tucked into his, he led her across the room. Within seconds, the yellow glow of cheap lighting glared overhead.

Pain shot through his ill-prepared eyes, but beside him CeCe released a breath.

It was his turn to look away, to hide how he knew his eyes would appear until they had time to adjust.

"A light switch," she murmured. "A stinking light switch."

He didn't understand her disgust, but with his eyes and head throbbing, he also was in no state to analyze much. He walked back to the bed. With no choice but to follow him, CeCe trailed behind.

"No phone at least," she commented, gesturing without purpose around the room.

"I removed it." He pointed to the door, which he had padlocked from the inside before losing consciousness. The lights he had never turned on, but he'd known they were there. He realized now that she hadn't, or hadn't thought to look for them.

Her fear, then, was strong. He was in the habit of storing such information to use later if needed, but for some reason his only reaction to this tidbit was regret.

"What's that?" Her finger traced over his arm, over the quarter inch of his tattoo that had become exposed when his sleeve edged upward. It was a casual gesture that emphasized how she'd changed from the wolf he had met in the woods. She seemed tired…resolved… as if the fight had left her. At least for now. He didn't trust that it would stay away long.

He pulled back. "A tattoo. Product of a misspent youth."

"It's raised." Her voice was curious, but not suspicious. He wished his eyes would adjust and allow him to see her expression.

"Vampires react differently to tattooing. I'm surprised werewolves don't too."

She didn't reply. He took that as a sign that she'd accepted his answer. Hoping that was the case, he knelt and felt for the spot where he had hidden the key to the cuffs. With the key hidden in his palm, he sat back onto the bed and closed his eyes, waiting for them to adjust.

He could feel anxiety flowing from her. She paced, or tried to. The cuffs kept her from moving more than a foot from his side.

Finally, she turned and growled. "You have to take these off of me sometime." She lifted her hand, pulling his arm up also.

He let her.

The ache had subsided in his head, and his eyes no longer burned. With a sigh, he opened them. The pain didn't return.

The werewolf stood beside him, one hand on her hip, one hand held out toward him as if she were considering striking him.

"I intend to." He opened his fist and showed her the key.

Her growl growing louder, she reached for the key.

He snapped his fingers closed and moved his arm to the left, making it impossible for her to reach the key, not without throwing herself on top of him.

Which he wouldn't mind, not even a little. He waited again, half hoping she would do what the stiff line of her body told him she was considering—throw herself on him and attempt to wrestle the key from his grasp.

When she didn't, he sat the key on the bed beside

him and stared up at her. "Someone killed your friend.
We should figure out who."

She crossed her arms over her chest, or tried to.
The cuff around her left wrist kept her from complet-
ing the motion.

"I want to trust you. With the two of us working
together, we can cover more ground, each talk to people the other can't. If we work together we can find
out the truth, not just what the vampires or the werewolves want to be true."

Her gaze had shifted, from him to a spot on the
wall.

"Can I trust you? Do you want to know the truth?"
he asked.

She licked her lips and her nostrils flared, but her
expression was guarded. He had no way of knowing
what she was thinking.

"Vampires aren't dead," she said.

Her observation surprised him. He wasn't sure if it
was a comment or a question.

"We never claimed to be," he replied. He kept his
tone light, but not without effort. Even after two hundred years in this state suspended between life and
death, it was a topic he avoided—that, as far as he
knew, all vampires avoided. He grabbed the key and
twisted his body so his feet rested on the floor. "The
term is, I believe, undead."

She nodded, but didn't seem to be listening to what
he was saying. Her mind was elsewhere.

"But the light. That part is true, at least partially."

"That it destroys my kind? You saw me in the day.
You know better."

"But it weakens you, doesn't it?"

The key digging into his palm, he stood. "Why? Are you planning to off some vampires? Be warned, you wouldn't be the first to think trapping us in the day would be an easy venture. But you'd be wrong. We're used to being despised, hunted, destroyed. There are entire families bred and raised to kill our kind. And why? Because we remind them of what they could become, of their own weaknesses."

He stopped himself from saying more, plucked at his fang with his tongue instead. He'd said too much, given away too much.

But she only tilted her head to the side, making it appear she was actually considering his words.

"Werewolves too. We don't have slayers, but we have hunters. Hunting wolves, blaming wolves for being wolves. If they realized some of those wolves had started as humans it wouldn't matter. It might even make the hunt more fun."

A shadow crossed her face and for a moment they only stood together sharing what few other creatures could…the haunting feeling of being hunted by what had once been your own kind.

"I didn't move you."

Startled, he tilted his head toward her.

"While you were…out…I didn't look for the door or a window."

His gaze darted to the floor beneath them.

She waved off the challenge. "Okay, I thought about it. How couldn't I have?" She raised her hand and shook her arm so the cuffs bounced up and down. "You trapped me and carried me here, but I didn't drag you to the door. I didn't try to open it. I didn't try to destroy you."

"And you could have," he murmured. He had pad-locked the door, but with only a steel lock. Werewolves were preternatural creatures. He hadn't known for sure that she wouldn't be able to break through the door, at least enough to allow light into the room. Which, she was right, would have weakened him more. And then she could have broken a piece off the wooden head-board, fashioned her own stake and been done with him completely.

Staring at her now, he realized how stupid of a risk he had taken. Except it hadn't been, because she hadn't even looked for the door and somehow he'd known that she wouldn't.

"The pack wouldn't approve of you harboring a killer," he added.

She tensed and immediately he regretted reminding her that she had accused him of killing her pack mate.

She started to turn, but key in hand, he stopped her. He slipped it into the lock and let the cuffs fall onto the ground.

For a moment, she rubbed her wrist and said noth-ing.

He picked up the cuffs and slipped them into his back pocket.

He held up the key. She didn't reach for it, but he extended his hand anyway. Suspicion clear on her face, she took the tiny tool and shoved it into the front pocket of her pants.

"Partners?" he asked.

Her hand inside her pocket with the key, she met his gaze. "In answer to your question, no, the pack wouldn't approve." She turned and walked to the door. She grabbed the padlock in one hand and twisted. The metal bent and broke. Then she dropped the useless lock onto the floor, turned her back to the door and slid to a crouch. "How long until dusk?" she asked.

"Under an hour," he replied.

She nodded. "Good, and tomorrow you're on your own."

He walked across the room and sat beside her. "Fair enough." His idea that they could work together, stop new trouble from building between the vampires and the wolves, had been naive. He'd need a new plan, one he could implement on his own. He would play along with whatever act she put out and pretend he thought they were working together, if she acted as if they were. But he wouldn't believe her. He couldn't.

A good inch of space between them, they sat together in silence, waiting. His hand dropped to the broken lock. He tossed it up and down in his hand, wondering if she could have done the same wearing the silver-laced cuffs, wishing he really could trust her, and wondering why he'd given her the key at all.

He was smarter than that. Smarter than a lot of things he'd done, risked, since meeting this female.

It was just as well that he'd realized his suggestion they work together was foolish. She just might have been his final mistake.

Chapter 8

At dusk, Marc had stood and opened the door for CeCe. She'd said she needed to get her phone from the woods and call the pack, report in so they wouldn't send others to check on her.

He didn't believe her that she wouldn't tell them of Russell's death and that a vampire might be involved, but he couldn't keep her chained to his side forever, and the alternative, killing her to hide a murder he didn't commit, was ludicrous. He would just do his best to cover his own bases and prepare the Fringe for the stories that were about to come. And then he'd go back to his purpose for being here—finding the treasure.

"Two hours…at the diner." It would be plenty of time for her to betray him.

"Vampires eat?" she asked, one foot outside the door, one foot still on his side of the threshold.

Surprised by her question, he answered, "Vampires do whatever it takes to survive." A sad, bald truth.

"To blend, you mean."

Her answer annoyed him. He didn't like that to survive he had to pretend to be something he wasn't. He started to push the door shut, but she placed a hand on his chest, halting his forward movement. His gaze lowered. Her fingers spread out, but just for a moment. Then she snatched her hand back.

"You'll be by yourself?" she muttered, her gaze dropping to her now-curled fingers.

"Of course. There are no other vampires here." None that he knew of.

His tattoo throbbed, reminding him of the call he needed to make. His check-in was overdue. Still, he took a moment to ask, "And you? Will you be alone? No other wolves?"

She stared at the dark street. A wind had formed since they had left the woods. A paper cup rattled through the parking lot that lay to the north of his temporary home. The light for the motel was out. The innkeeper had most likely left early. The odds that the concrete-cube rooms had sold out were slim.

CeCe looked back. Some strange emotion floated behind her eyes—sorrow or resolve. Marc couldn't place it.

"I'll be alone." Then she walked into the wind. It lifted her hair and tore at her clothes, and she tilted her face to meet it.

She looked strong and confident. Marc would never

have pegged her for being afraid of something as mundane as the dark.

Within minutes she'd turned a corner and was gone. Reluctantly, he closed the door.

Alone again. It was a vampire's lot.

His tattoo tingled. He placed his hand over it, applying pressure to lessen the throb. Then he walked to the bed and pulled a laptop from under the mattress where he had hidden it.

After plugging the computer into an outlet and establishing an internet connection, he made his call.

"Marc. It's past time for you to check in. Have you found the treasure?"

Marc recognized the face on the screen immediately. Rudolph Van Bom, one of the oldest and most revered of vampires. But Van Bom wasn't an active part of the Fringe, not any longer. He shouldn't have answered the call.

"Rudolph. This is a surprise." Marc didn't like surprises.

"These are surprising times," the older vampire countered. He was dressed in long-sleeved workout gear, the type that was advertised as wicking away sweat, not that a vampire needed the feature. The room was dark and shallow with no decorations to give Marc a clue as to where the vampire was while taking the call.

"True." Marc paused. He'd called to report on what had happened, prepare the Fringe for whatever rage the werewolves leveled at them. He'd hoped to talk with Andre Moreau, who was known as a diplomat, at least as far as vampires went, but seeing Van Bom caused him to reconsider. Van Bom was old and powerful, but he was also harsh and quick to judge.

"You are back with the Fringe," he stated.

"Did I leave? Have things changed? I thought the only escape from the Fringe was a trip into the sun or an embrace with a stake. At least that was the pledge those of us who founded it made." Van Bom plucked some kind of red ball from his desk and squeezed it. The toy disappeared in the vampire's grip, only to expand again as he opened his fingers.

"No, that hasn't changed, but you have been—"

"Absent? Not from my own choice; it seemed I was unneeded." There was no malice in the words, but something about them pricked at Marc. He had assumed the vampire, as old as he was, had no interest in the drudgery that came with being a member of the Fringe, hunting their own, executing orders and vampires.

"Your connections and knowledge are impressive," Marc replied. "The Fringe is lucky to have you." The words were placating, but also true.

The older vamp made a dismissive noise and sat the ball on his desk in front of him. "Even among vampires there is little that can replace age and experience. It is our only source of real power."

"Very true." Marc glanced at the door where CeCe had left earlier. Van Bom might well have insight into why the werewolf Russell had been staked, and the vampire had been active during the war. He might know if the stories of werewolves being staked then were true. If they were, there might be some tie to the wolf here.

Marc stared back at the computer, weighing his words.

Van Bom's eyes glimmered. He leaned forward, his elbows on his desk. "Did you find the treasure? Tell."

It was an order, but Marc was under no compulsion to comply. However, he'd already decided to use the older vampire as much as he risked, but he would start slow, with something else that had been nagging at him.

"I need some information." Marc paused. "On weapons."

The older vampire raised a brow. "Weapons? What type of weapon? Have you found something?" The vampire's voice rose and he edged closer to his computer screen.

"Only this." Marc held up the handcuffs he'd used on CeCe.

Van Bom's eyes shuttered. "Cuffs? Not that unusual."

"There is silver in them." Marc dropped them onto the bed.

"Silver, like from the war?" Van Bom twisted his lips to the side.

"Yes."

"There's more. Tell me."

Marc hesitated, but he had gone this far. He had no choice but to finish the tale. "A werewolf has turned up dead."

"A werewolf? How?"

His gaze steady, Marc answered, "He was staked."

"Staked?" Van Bom pushed himself back then leaned forward again. There was no missing the excitement in his eyes. "Did you find him? Did you find the weapon?"

"No. The stake was missing, but the werewolf wasn't here alone. He was with a female. She blames me for the death."

"You?"

"Yes."

"Did you kill him?"

"No, of course not."

Van Bom shrugged. "Worse things have happened. Why are you telling me this?"

Annoyed that the other vampire seemed to think Marc was wasting his time, Marc growled. "She will tell her pack, claim I broke one of the three laws, maybe two."

"Two?"

"A human is dead too, but the police have termed it natural causes, a heart attack."

"So no crime there." Van Bom seemed to accept that it would all be that simple, no problem because he didn't wish it to be. "You need to get back to your job. Find the treasure. Do you think this female may have it? Could she have killed the other wolf?"

"No, but she is…" Marc clenched his jaw, strangely unwilling to share details about CeCe with Van Bom.

"She is what?"

"Different."

"Different? How?" Again Van Bom leaned closer.

"Her smell…do wolves smell of spice like a vampire?"

A smile curved Van Bom's lips, but it was fleeting. "Not that I've heard. Perhaps it is just her perfume."

Perhaps, but Marc didn't think so. He was old

enough to distinguish between a natural scent and one applied from a bottle.

"What else?"

"Nothing, except…" He thought of her long sleeves in one-hundred-plus heat and how she had reacted when he had Russell's blood on his hand. He knew the pack had reacted too; knew that connection meant something. "Nothing," he confirmed.

"You're sure?"

It was obvious Van Bom didn't believe him, but Marc wasn't concerned with the fact. Van Bom would take what information Marc chose to give him.

After a moment, Van Bom grunted and reached for his mouse. "Then do what you were sent there to do. Find the treasure."

Before he could cut the connection, Marc replied. "There's more I need to ask."

Van Bom paused, his hand hovering.

"During the war, there was talk of werewolves being staked. Is it true?"

Van Bom seemed uninterested. "There are better weapons to use on a werewolf. Silver."

Marc knew, of course, that weapons targeted at werewolves always contained silver, but he hadn't considered whether the stake that had killed Russell would have. "Have you ever heard of a silver stake?"

Van Bom's brows lowered. His impatience with the questions was clear on his face. He waved one bony hand. "Wives' tale. I don't know who created it."

Marc waited. He hadn't mentioned any specific stake or story.

After an annoyed pause, Van Bom continued. "During the war there was talk of a weapon, a stake. The werewolves claimed it was created by a female who was bitten as a teen. She was in love with a vampire, but the wolf stole her. Changed her. After that, of course, the vampire would have nothing to do with her."

Of course not. The other vampires wouldn't have allowed it.

"She hated both groups." Van Bom tapped his fingers against the desktop. He looked back at Marc. "And, according to the werewolves, she created a weapon that could be used to kill both werewolves and vampires."

"A silver stake," Marc filled in.

Van Bom lifted his chin in agreement.

"But the stake was nothing special."

"So, it was real?"

"Real, but mundane. There was no magic in it."

Marc hadn't mentioned magic. He glanced at the older vampire, wondering at the statement, but the extra embellishment wasn't important. What mattered was a silver stake did exist or had.

A silver stake through the heart would most certainly kill any werewolf, and if the stake was werewolf-created and owned, Marc could hardly be blamed for Russell's death.

"Where is it now?" he asked.

"When the war ended, it was stored away with other relics the vampires and werewolves thought might be…misused."

"Like these?" Marc held up the cuffs.

Van Bom's eyes flashed. "Yes, cuffs, silver bullets, stakes. Things both sides used to kill the other. Hiding it all away was part of the treaty." The ball reappeared in Van Bom's hand. He squeezed it.

"Where?"

Van Bom's lips twisted. "I don't know. No one does."

"Someone must. Who hid it?"

"A vampire."

"Then he—"

Van Bom cut him off. "He never came back. He took the weapons and never returned. We all assumed he'd hide them and come back, that the weapons would be ours."

So, the vampires had wanted the weapons for themselves, had felt they had some importance. "But the stake wasn't special?" Marc prompted.

Van Bom lifted one shoulder in a dismissive manner. "I told you, the wolves believed it was. It was made by one of their own, of silver. And they are a superstitious lot. We acted as if we were as afraid of it as they were."

"To get them to throw it in with the other relics. Then if things went wrong, the vampires would have control of the one weapon the werewolves truly feared."

Van Bom smiled. "Now you understand." He placed one long finger against his chin. "But why the interest in the stake?"

"I told you, the werewolf here was killed with a stake."

"But a stake through the heart…surely that would kill a werewolf, silver or not."

It was a good point and one Marc had considered. Could a mundane stake through the heart have killed the wolf? If so, Marc could easily be blamed. As a member of the Fringe, he was always armed, and stakes were part of that weaponry. But if the answer was no, then someone had either found the legendary stake that Van Bom described or made one of his own.

"Perhaps you should go home."

Marc's head jerked toward the screen. "Leave? Why?"

"You said this female werewolf blamed you for her pack mate's death. If her pack arrives, there will be trouble. There's no reason for you to be involved in that. If you leave, what will they do? We aren't that easy to find."

It was true. The vampires weren't like the wolves. They had no central location. Even the Fringe had no set meeting place. They operated independently with very few ties to any one place. When you lived for eternity it became a necessity—if you didn't want the locals hunting you with pitchforks and torches.

But Marc had called for ideas and information, not the suggestion that he run.

He wasn't going anywhere, not until he found the treasure and proved his innocence. He told Van Bom as much.

"If the werewolves take you, we can't be responsible for saving you."

Marc had never depended on someone else to save him, but he had thought his century with the Fringe would be worth something.

Van Bom stared back at him, cold and dispassionate.

Apparently, Marc had been wrong.

Without even a nod, Marc broke the connection.

He didn't need the Fringe's protection. He didn't need anyone. He'd been alone too long for that.

Chapter 9

CeCe had gone to the woods first. Not to Russell's body—she had accepted that the werewolf's remains were beyond her, at least for now. She went to find her cell phone and retrieve the stake.

She had returned to the woods with a battery-powered lantern. Even with it strapped across her chest, bandolier-style, it took close to an hour for her to find her cell. She punched a button to see if the phone powered on, then shoved it into her pocket.

She was running short of time with less than an hour left before she had to meet Marc. She didn't want to be late; she didn't want him to change his mind and run. She needed him to be here when Karl arrived.

Her phone secure, she went to retrieve the stake. It was where she had left it, undisturbed. Again using her shirt as a glove, she dropped the stake into an oversize plastic bag and carefully rolled the weapon inside. Then she placed the newly protected stake into her backpack and covered it with three pounds of fresh mushrooms she'd purchased at a roadside stand. If the sheriff returned, she'd claim she was hunting the fungus, and had a particularly profitable day.

With the pack hitched onto one shoulder, she began the trek back to Cave Vista.

In her hotel room, CeCe dumped the mushrooms on her bed and unwrapped the stake. Not wanting to touch the metal or disturb whatever evidence might possibly have survived, she studied the weapon through the plastic.

It was, she estimated, fourteen or so inches long and tapered at one end. The handle was wrapped in leather and the butt was flat, to make it easier to pound the stake into a body with a mallet. CeCe had seen stakes before, but they had all been wood, usually aspen. A few had been iron. This, however, she could now see was silver-toned.

A sick feeling crept over her. She hadn't touched any part of the stake except the leather-wrapped handle, and that with her hand covered. Slowly, she slid the stake out of the bag. At the very top, right where the leather ended, there was a spot of bare metal.

She touched her finger against it. A charge like walking into an electric fence zapped through her. With a curse, she jerked back.

Her knees weak, she collapsed onto the bed. The stake lay beside her…the bare spot of metal shining like a warning.

Silver. The thing was laced with silver, and something else. Silver weakened a werewolf, shut off his strength, ability to shift and heal quickly, but it didn't deliver a punch like this stake.

Her hand moved toward it; strangely, she wanted to pick it up again.

She curled her fingers into her palm and pulled her hand back.

What the hell was the thing? She stared at the weapon for another moment as if it might shift itself or fling itself at her. Finally feeling somewhat recovered from the shock of touching the thing, she considered what this discovery might mean.

A stake made of silver.

Was it meant for a vampire or a werewolf? Her father had never told her that silver affected vampires as it did wolves, but there were obviously holes in his knowledge.

Maybe there were more clues on the weapon itself.

Wary, but determined, she wrapped the plastic back over the metal and carried the weapon to the bedside table. Under the lamp that sat there, she studied the stake further.

There were faint designs on three of the four sides. She smoothed the plastic tight against the metal and studied the first set of thin lines—the lightning bolt symbol of the wolves.

The symbol had been used by the packs for centuries. However, after the Nazis stole the image to symbolize their own movement, the bolt had fallen out of favor. Seeing it on the mysterious stake somehow wasn't surprising. And knowing she had pulled it from a werewolf's chest, she had no doubt that in this instance the meaning involved the werewolves.

She bit her lip. There was something strange about the mark here, however. The Z was broken and not just by the line that traditionally ran through it. No, the Z, which should have been drawn in one smooth stroke, was actually in two pieces, as if someone had chopped the bolt in half.

The pack broken? A wolf separated? As her mind sorted through various possibilities for this new version, she flipped the stake past the blank side to the next symbol. This one she didn't know.

It was similar to something she had seen before. What appeared to be a snake was biting its own tail. However instead of the usual circle, symbolizing something that came in cycles, it was twisted into the figure eight. She turned the stake so it ran perpendicular to her body...infinity. An eight on its side was infinity.

Vampires didn't age, didn't die unless some outside force took their life. The infinity sign seemed a likely symbol for them.

She paused, recalling Marc's tattoo. She hadn't seen much of it, but what she had seen was curved like the bottom half of a circle and covered with scales. The coincidence was too great. Marc's tattoo and the symbol on the stake had to be the same and they had to mean vampire or something involving vampires.

It also, quite possibly, tied Marc to the stake. The realization should have thrilled her. She had suspected the vampire from the beginning, but for some reason she was unnerved, disturbed.

Not ready to admit success or failure, she rotated the stake under the light a bit more. Like the werewolf lightning bolt, the vampire infinity symbol was broken. A hairline of space ran through the center of the design.

So, not infinity after all. Not any longer.

What did that mean?

She turned the stake again. The third symbol seemed to be a combination of the first two—a bolt running through the eight, and with no break in the original designs.

This was perhaps the most puzzling design of all. Frowning, she flipped the stake around again, taking a moment to study each side once more.

She glanced at the clock. There were twenty minutes remaining until she was to meet Marc. Luckily, Cave Vista was small. It was less than a five-minute walk to the diner. Leaving her a decent amount of time to make the call to Karl, and after studying the stake, she felt even more beholden to do so.

She pulled her cell from her pocket.

Her thumb grazed over the numbers, but she didn't immediately start dialing.

She was about to admit that she had failed completely and in the process had allowed one of the pack to be lost. She had not been directly responsible for Russell, but she still felt as if he had been in her care.

Karl answered the phone himself. If that hadn't warned her that he was tense and waiting for her call, his tone would have.

"What happened? Last night the pack sensed something. Then no word for almost twenty-four hours." The anger in his voice caused her wolf to whimper. She had to force the noise not to escape from her lips. She lowered her body onto the bed to keep her knees from collapsing.

Karl was the alpha. She couldn't stop the urge to crumple in the face of his annoyance, but rolling onto her back on the hard floor with him two hundred miles away would help nothing.

"I was…busy," she murmured. She hadn't considered how she would explain why a day had gone by without her calling, a day where she had lost the treasure, lost Russell and been trapped by a vampire.

"Busy how? Did you find something?"

CeCe stared at the stake. The broken infinity sign faced her.

"I did. Find something that is."

"The treasure?"

"No, the treasure is still missing, and the human who found it is dead." This she guessed the alpha would already know; he would have been monitoring all news coming out of Cave Vista. Surely, by now a death notice had been posted somewhere online.

"Dead?"

So, it hadn't, or the alpha wasn't being as vigilant as he normally was.

"How?"

"The sheriff here says natural causes."

"He says?"

She glanced back at the stake. "It just seems…coincidental, him finding the treasure and all."

"When did he die?"

She told Karl about being at the bar, about Marc and Porter going into the bathroom and Porter not coming back out.

"So the vampire killed him."

"I told you, the authorities said natural causes."

Karl grunted, letting her know he had little faith in human detective skills.

"There's more," she said. "Russell is dead."

There was a pause.

"Dead?" he repeated. "The vampire."

"No. At least, I don't know that." She hurried through the tale of going to the woods and finding Russell.

There was silence on the other end of the line.

"He had a stake in his heart," she finished.

"The vampire. It had to be."

CeCe'd had the same thought, but hearing the alpha's words from Karl, she felt the need to defend Marc, to give him the benefit of some doubt. "He was killed while he was human. He didn't even try to shift."

"And that means what?" There was warning in the words, but CeCe pushed on.

"Russell was young, but he wasn't stupid. He wouldn't have stood still and let a vampire shove a stake through his heart."

"Meaning what?"

What did she mean? How did she think that stake got into Russell's chest?

"I don't know. I just don't think we should blame the vampire without investigating some more. We'd be accusing him of breaking one of the laws. It could restart the war."

"Worse things could happen."

Karl's response shocked her. Worse than war? What could be worse than war?

"Why is the vampire there? He must be looking for the treasure."

"He is…at least I assume he is." She couldn't admit she had spent as much time with Marc as she had. It wouldn't help his case with the alpha, and it would damage hers.

"Then he has every reason to kill the human and Russell."

Karl was too calm, too…almost relieved that the human and Russell were dead and that Marc was around to tie to their deaths.

"I don't think he did it." It was as close to standing up to the alpha as she dared.

"You don't think he did it?" Silence.

She could feel Karl's anger vibrating through their connection. She understood the emotion; she should want the vampire to be guilty. She closed her eyes, but didn't take her declaration back.

"Then who do you think did? Or are you admitting to the crimes yourself?"

Before she could answer, he continued, "Vampires are not our friends. They never have been. During the war, they carried guns loaded with silver bullets and wore silver caps on their fangs. They filled us with holes and drank our blood. But you think this vampire didn't do it. Why, CeCe? Why?"

She had no reason, not one that Karl would understand. Not one she understood herself.

"So, we're clear. The vampire killed Russell."

Like that, Karl had decided Marc's fate. A sick feeling filled CeCe's stomach.

"But if we assume—" she began.

"Assume?" His voice was sharp and filled with warning. It wasn't her place to question him. She knew that. Marc had said she was important, but he was wrong. She was nothing to the pack, not until Karl accepted her, made her position as destined mate official.

"What about the stake?" he asked, making it clear the decision of guilt was over.

"I have it." She wanted to feel good then, proud that she had done one thing right, but she couldn't.

"That's good. Everyone knows stakes are for vampires."

"Except…" She hesitated.

"Except what?" The edge had returned to his voice, warning, reminding her of her role.

"Slayers. Slayers use stakes."

"Have you seen any slayers?"

"No."

"But you have seen a vampire, near both the human and Russell."

"Yes." She was an automaton now, answering his questions as she was supposed to, cutting off any real emotion she might have felt.

"Good, then we have a plan."

A plan? She hadn't realized they had been looking for one.

"Is there anything else?"

Wanting to feel better about what was happening, CeCe picked up the stake. "It has a symbol on it, three actually."

"The stake?"

"Yes…one is the werewolf lightning bolt, the second…I think it means vampire, and the third is a combination of the first two."

She could hear Karl adjusting in his seat, hear the wheels on his chair moving over the floor. Except Karl didn't own a wheeled chair. She frowned, her focus briefly diverted.

"None of that matters. The stake itself doesn't matter," Karl declared.

"But the single symbols are broken, and what does the combined one mean?"

"I said, it doesn't matter."

Any feelings of pride she'd had at recovering the weapon disappeared. She dropped it on the bed.

"Where's the body?"

Drained, she collapsed onto the mattress next to the stake. She assumed he meant Russell, but she was too tired to clarify.

"Safe. Out of reach of humans."

"Humans? Were humans there too?"

"Yes, a sheriff, but he didn't suspect anything and he didn't see Russell."

"What do you mean? How didn't he see him?"

She told him how Marc had used his powers to hide the body from the sheriff, realized as she was telling the story that it added to Karl's version of things… that of course Marc would have hidden the body. The killer would always hide the body.

"The entrance to the cave is actually a hole, a straight drop down. Someone might find it, but they wouldn't be coming back up to tell anyone about it. Russell's body is safe for now," she murmured.

"Not if the vampire knows where he is. We will have to move him and capture the vampire. Until we get there, you'll have to watch him."

All life seemed to have left CeCe, all fight. She murmured some kind of agreement.

"Find the vampire. Make sure he doesn't take Russell or find the treasure. And keep your cell on."

Then he hung up. No goodbye. No words of concern for her and what she had been through.

But then she and Karl had never had that kind of relationship. It was silly to expect it now.

She glanced at the clock. She had maybe three hours before whatever team Karl chose arrived, and she was five minutes late for her meeting with Marc. If he left without her, she would be spending those three hours tracking him.

She would have the stake, but Karl apparently had no interest in it.

Her attention moved to the plastic-wrapped weapon. She couldn't take it with her. After glancing around the room, she settled on the mattress. Cliché, but the best she had on short notice. She tore the material with her teeth, then shoved the stake inside. With the mattress and bed coverings back in place, she was ready for her date with a vampire.

A vampire whom members of her pack were on their way to kill, or at least frame with a crime.

Chapter 10

Marc waited in the shadows outside CeCe's hotel room. He'd seen her enter the room almost an hour earlier, a pack on her back. When the light clicked off and she stepped out into the night, she was ten minutes late for their meeting.

Her heels hit the concrete first as she speed-walked to the diner. He hesitated, his gaze lingering on her hotel room's door. She'd carried the backpack for a reason and he didn't think it was to keep her lipstick fresh. Treasure or stake? He'd like to find both.

However, if he investigated now, he wouldn't be able to beat her to the restaurant, or appear to have beaten her.

Deciding for now that keeping CeCe's guard low was most important, he cut through an alley, his feet moving over the ground so quickly he almost took flight. Within minutes, he had arrived at the diner and climbed through the restaurant's bathroom window. After taking a moment to wash and get the scent of soap on his hands, to further convince the werewolf he had indeed arrived before her, he opened the door and strolled into the dining room.

CeCe stood near the jukebox, scanning the room.

He lifted his chin and gestured to a booth in the back.

She hadn't changed or bathed since he'd last seen her and tiny bits of dead leaves clung to her clothes. Bits too small for a human to see. Either the werewolf assumed the same was true for a vampire or she had been too rushed to check her appearance.

The woods then. She could have simply gone to retrieve her phone, but she wouldn't have needed a backpack for that. Rolling the possibilities around, he stood to one side and let her choose the side of the booth she preferred.

She slid into the seat that kept her back to the wall and offered a full view of the dining room and main entrance.

Always a smart choice, but it made Marc wonder if she was expecting someone. No, it *told* him she was expecting someone.

"Did you make good use of your time?" he asked, picking up the photocopied menu that had been tucked between the salt and pepper shakers.

"It's only been two hours. I'm afraid I wasn't able to solve the world's problems in that time." Her jaw was tense and when he reached for a second menu to hand to her, she jumped.

"Coffee?" he asked.

"No, thanks. I don't drink caffeine."

"I meant, have you had any? You're on edge. What happened?" In her current state of mind, being direct seemed his best method of getting information.

She stared at him for a second as if surprised at his question. Then she sucked in a breath and dropped her gaze to the table. "Nothing."

"You called your pack."

She looked up. "You knew I was going to."

"And what did you tell them?"

She picked up a menu. "That Russell is dead. That he had a stake through his heart."

"Did you mention me?"

Her jaw tightened. He could see that she didn't want to answer, but finally she did. "Yes."

Her honesty surprised him. He lifted his head. "You told them about me. Did you tell them you suspected me?"

She met his gaze then. "No, I told them I thought you were innocent."

"Really?" He tilted his head, not sure he believed her. "Then I guess I'm in the clear. We can each go back to what we were doing here and you can look for the real killer." Casual, believing. He moved his gaze to the menu, let her think he wasn't watching her, gauging her reaction. "They have grits with cheese. I've never had them. Have you?"

"Of course." She wouldn't look at him.

He raised his brows. "Do you like them?"

"What?" She frowned.

"Grits? You said you'd had them."

She glanced at the menu, then pursed her lips. "I meant, of course, I will look for the real killer."

"Of course. What else would you do?" He held her gaze, or tried to. She looked away.

It was obvious she was lying. He'd pushed her enough. He'd worry about dealing with whatever were-wolves arrived intent on framing him for Russell's death later. For now he might as well use his time gathering other information.

He waved the menu in the air and called to a waitress.

After placing his order and waiting for CeCe to do the same, he returned to their conversation.

"Where do you call home?" Where is the pack located? How long before they arrive? Her answer could tell him many things.

She slid her menu back into place, then tilted her head. Her hair fell to one side of her face. Despite her height, she looked young and feminine, not at all like people envisioned a werewolf. And while she was muscular, it wasn't in an obvious way. More like a professional volleyball player than a weight lifter.

"I don't call anywhere home," she replied. "How about you?"

He smiled. She was smooth, reversing the tables on him. If this kept up, they would be dancing like this all night. And that would be fine with him. He was simply killing time now, waiting to see who showed up and what they would do when they did arrive, and for an opportunity to search her room.

"How were you turned?" he asked, suddenly curious.

Her eyes widened.

"I assume you were young. Since you obviously aren't old now."

"I…" She placed her hand against her neck, drawing his attention to her pale skin, reminding him of the tantalizing scent and taste of her.

His groin hardened. He ground his jaws together.

"I wasn't. Not all werewolves are."

"You're genetic?" He'd heard rumors of genetic werewolves, but never met one, never truly believed they were real.

"Yes." She glanced toward the kitchen. The warming shelf was empty and their waitress was across the room, refilling an older couple's mugs with coffee.

"There's no such thing with a vampire." Vampires didn't have children, didn't have families, not even the ones they had been born into. That was taken from them with the turn. There was no coming out of the coffin, no hope for acceptance. Nothing but a life alone, for eternity. It's why he guessed so many went insane, took out their rage on humans who had what the vampire himself had lost.

Her gaze shifted back to him. Her lips parted, a tiny puff of air escaped them.

He'd surprised her, but then he'd surprised himself. It was a small bit of truth he'd told her, but from the shadow that flitted behind her eyes, he could tell his tone had given away more than he had intended.

He snapped the menu against the table.

"And the treasure. How did you hear about that? What claim do the werewolves make on it?" Brusque.

Her head lifted and her expression changed, hardened. "It belongs to the wolves. What claim do the vampires make?"

Marc slid the menu onto the table. "Two of the coins pictured were vampire." Maker coins. Many vampires had coins made that they gave to each of their "children."

"Really? I didn't realize vampires had their own system of trade?" Her voice was coy, superior.

He batted back at her. "I am sure there are many things you don't realize about vampires." He paused. "And many I'd be willing to teach you."

She pressed her lips together.

The waitress approached with a glass of water in each hand. Seeing them, she took half a step back.

Marc turned and hit the poor human with a full force of thrall. Nodding, she placed the glasses on the table and shuffled away.

"You did something to her," CeCe commented.

Marc picked up his glass and took a sip. The water was cold, wet and completely unsatisfying.

He looked back at the female wolf. She appeared completely under control, but he could see her pulse moving at the base of her throat.

She was no more relaxed than he was.

Desire curled inside him like a live thing. Her blood called to him. She called to him. He'd told her he could teach her about vampires, and it was true. But what was more true, what he hadn't said, was how much he wanted to.

And suddenly, he had to get away. Without speaking, he stood and strode to the restroom.

Inside the small room, he stared at his reflection. A reflection many believed he couldn't cast. His features looked as they always did, no dent in the calm he wore like a B-movie vampire's cape.

But inside, behind that facade, a crack was forming,

a crack in the shell he'd used for two hundred years to protect himself.

And it was the female werewolf who was creating it.

Playing with CeCe, he realized, was like juggling stakes. If he didn't concentrate, keep his mind focused on who she was, what she was, he was going to get cut.

Then when her pack arrived, he would be weak and vulnerable. Nothing for them to do but gather around and lap up his blood.

CeCe dipped her fingers into the new sweating glass of water and trailed icy liquid down her neck. Following Karl's directions shouldn't have been difficult. Watch the vampire. Keep him occupied until the pack arrived.

And it wouldn't have been, if she could think of Marc as the vampire, but more and more she forgot what he was, on what side of the divide between the two groups he stood.

He was just Marc, a man who listened to her, had an interest in her. Of course, she knew the interest was false; it had to be. But then he'd give what appeared to be a slip, show her some hurt, and damn everything, she'd forget.

She stared ahead blindly.

Her fingers shook. She was losing it. She had to get back under control.

Probably even now Mar—the vampire—was busy doing something, calling someone to back him up, calling in more vampires. And meanwhile, here she sat like a duck waiting to be shot.

She picked up her glass and slammed the contents

back. Then she set it back on the table and went to do her job.

Watch the vampire.

The kitchen was directly across from the men's restroom. There was no way for CeCe to listen at the door without every busboy and waitress in the place seeing her and thinking she was…odd.

With just a glance at the closed door, she walked past and into the women's bathroom. With the door closed behind her, she moved to the wall that separated the two rooms and pressed her ear against it.

There was no sound from the other side, not even a flush.

She bunched her hand into a fist and pressed it against the wall.

She was getting nowhere, or worse she might be moving backward. Marc…the vampire…might have already escaped.

Her gaze shifted to the end of the room and the small window centered in the wall.

If she couldn't watch the vampire from inside the diner, she would have to do so from the outside.

Good intentions that ended poorly.

The window was painted shut. Standing on the sink, she broke the first layer of paint with her thumbnail, then shoved the window open.

Wood creaked and paint flecks fell, but within moments she was standing in an alley that ran behind the diner.

Ten feet down the wall, leading into what had to be the men's room, was a second window. And like the window in the women's room, it had until recently been painted shut.

The same bits of paint that she had left behind in the women's restroom dusted the ground here and the lower sash was open, far enough a body could easily have slipped through.

CeCe cursed.

She had lost him.

She stood for a moment, cursing her own stupidity. Then as she decided her best move was to go to the vampire's motel room—find him there or take advantage of his absence to search his belongings for evidence he was connected to Russell's death—a noise so soft she sensed more than heard it startled her out of her musings.

As if a cat had crossed her path, the hairs on the back of her neck rose.

She spun.

A male figure crouched atop a Dumpster. Not Marc. It was the only thought that registered as CeCe moved.

The figure stood and raced toward her. His feet seemed to barely touch the Dumpster's metal lid. He leaped and flew toward her, almost as if he had wings.

She stepped back, raising her arm in a defensive action while at the same time releasing her wolf.

She felt the shift coming, felt her eyes slanting and her senses increasing.

The man leaped on top of her, knocking her to the ground. Caught in the shift, she fell, but inside her wolf roared. Even falling, she smiled.

Let the fight begin.

She stretched out to make the change easier, swifter. Opened her mind and heart to the wolf.

Its power raced through her, filling her with excitement and the desire to hunt…to fight.

She was ready.

The man grabbed at her wrists, tried to pin her down, and she looked up.

Into the face of a monster…a vampire. She couldn't see past his open mouth, past his fangs…covered in silver and descending toward her.

Her wolf howled in recognition and rage.

And then his silver-capped fangs sank into her skin and her wolf froze…paralyzed by the bite of silver.

Marc approached the booth where CeCe should have been waiting. The waitress had come and gone, leaving two steaming bowls of grits with cheese sitting on the table.

But the bowls sat untouched; the werewolf wasn't there.

He grabbed the waitress by the arm and swung her toward the table. "The woman. Have you seen her?"

The waitress' eyes widened and her face paled. Shaking her head, she tried to pull free. Marc held on, but only for a second.

There was no reason for the human to lie to him. And no benefit in scaring her further.

With a growl, he pulled bills out of his wallet and tossed them onto the table. Then he stalked to the front door and into the night.

The werewolf had bolted. Where? Why?

Marc didn't have to ask. He knew. Her precious pack must have arrived. She must have left to be with them, to set up whatever trap they had planned to catch him.

* * *

Silver bit into CeCe, freezing her shift.

The metal was cold and cloying, its poison working its way through her body. She clawed at her attacker; her nails, those of a wolf, scraped down his back.

Material ripped, but the vampire didn't loosen his hold. Her blood ran, thin but hot down her neck.

Her wolf could smell it, but couldn't come out, couldn't fight back. She was trapped half human and half wolf…a werewolf's worst nightmare.

The vampire's lips moved. He was smiling, laughing at her pain and frustration, enjoying her failure.

She flung her arms to the side and groped for a weapon, anything that might dislodge the monster draining her life. Her hand hit dirt, debris…a paper cup…nothing dangerous, nothing that could save her.

She thought of the stake, wished she'd carried it with her, wished she had the power to bring it to her now.

But wishes were for fools. Action was all that could save her.

She gathered her strength and rolled to the side, managing to lift herself and the vampire six inches before crashing back down under his weight and enthusiasm. He was enjoying himself, feeding not only on her blood, but her pain.

Her eyelids fluttered.

She was weak…from the silver and loss of blood. She couldn't shift. She couldn't find a weapon.

What could she do besides die?

She opened her mouth and screamed—rage and pain mixing into one long soul-shattering howl.

Chapter 11

A scream tore through the night. Standing in the street across from the diner, heading toward CeCe's motel room, Marc paused.

A human in trouble. It had to be.

It didn't pay for a vampire to interfere in human affairs, no matter how dire things might be for the human. People didn't remember how the vampire had saved them. They only saw and remembered vampire—monster.

Marc lifted his foot ready to leave, but slowly he lowered it again.

Then he turned. The scream had come from the alley.

The alley that lay behind the diner and outside the bathroom where CeCe had seen him go. The scream still sounded…too long…then it shifted, no longer a scream. Now it was a howl.

With a curse, he began to run.

Twenty feet from the alley, he smelled blood. Ce-Ce's blood.

His fangs lengthened and his heart slowed to a deadly determined beat. The dark became light and as he turned the corner, the image of a man pressed on the alley floor with a woman…CeCe…beneath him almost glowed.

Rage, hunger, hate…they balled together into one blazing emotion that Marc couldn't control. Had no desire to control.

The man looked up. His eyes shone in the dark, like an animal caught in a spotlight.

But this was no animal.

This was a vampire.

Marc flew forward, his feet carrying him faster than his mind could process the facts of what was happening, where he was and what his best move would be.

The other vampire opened his mouth and hissed. Blood stained his lips and chin…CeCe's blood.

Marc hissed too. He hands rose at his sides. He could feel his fingers bending, feel the need to battle the vampire hand to hand, fang to fang, to establish his dominance, his rights to the female this interloper thought to take from him. Take…forever.

She lay limp, her legs and arms in awkward, boneless positions. Her body was twisted…caught in her shift. Blood streaked across her neck and her chest moved with dangerously shallow breaths.

Shallow, but there.

Not dead. Not gone. Not yet.

He stalked forward.

"Brother," the other vampire murmured. "I heard you were near." He ran his tongue over his lips.

Marc's hands closed, tight. He stalked closer.

"Not brother. Not friend." He kicked the vampire in the chest, sending the fiend sliding backward into the diner's wall.

The vampire stood and wiped his mouth. His eyes were slits. His fangs glinted…silver.

He'd worn caps. Come here hunting a werewolf.

"Did you kill the wolf?" Marc asked, as much to know the truth as to disarm the other vampire. "Have you been behind all of this?"

Had Marc been wrong? Had his arrogance, assurance that a wolf was behind Russell's death, cost CeCe her life? Cost Marc her life?

"Which one? This one?" The vampire licked his lips and tilted his head side to side. "Not yet. Those weren't my orders. But this job is so sweet, orders may need to be damned." He smiled.

White-hot rage blazed a hole through Marc's control. He heard each of the vampire's words, but could only focus on the last.

Sweet. And wild. And deserving of life.

Silent but swift, he raced forward. Hands out, he pinned the other vampire to the wall. Marc squeezed the bastard vampire's neck as if planning to remove his head from his body with bare hands.

The vampire gurgled and cursed. Spittle mixed with CeCe's blood dribbled from his lips. Marc squeezed harder, pulled back and slammed his head into the wall.

"A werewolf. You would fight me like this for a

werewolf?" The vampire's eyes were filled with disbelief, his words little more than a croak.

Marc didn't owe the bastard an answer. He didn't owe him anything…except death for what he had done.

He lunged forward, planning to rip the vampire's throat out with his fangs.

But the vampire bent his knees and collapsed, taking Marc down with him. On the ground they rolled, both grappling for control, both trying to attach their fangs into the other's neck.

To the side there was movement. CeCe struggling, shaking, but moving to a sit.

Marc shoved his opponent's face onto the pavement and held it there. "Leave. Run," he yelled. He had no intention of losing this battle, but if he did…

The werewolf stood. Her legs wobbled and her hand moved to her throat. Slowly, as Marc watched, her body morphed, back to human. She stared at Marc and her attacker as if she couldn't see them, couldn't process what was happening.

"CeCe," Marc yelled again. He was losing his grip.

The vampire in his grasp growled. "Her name? You know her name? How far have you strayed, Fringe? What side of the battle have you chosen?" He jerked to the side and slipped from Marc's hold. His fangs caught on Marc's shirt, ripping the material.

Marc gritted his teeth and grabbed the vampire again. Then he bowed his head and, praying CeCe listened, he found the other vampire's neck with his fangs.

He bit deep. Blood, thick and old, seeped into his mouth. He wanted to spit it out, wanted no part of the abomination that was this vampire inside him, but he couldn't. He had to hold on, had to bite more, continue until the vampire was too weak to fight, too weak to stand. Then Marc could take him out, remove his head or heart, ensure he never walked the night again.

To Marc's side, there was a growl.

CeCe.

She hadn't left.

The world was blurry. CeCe teetered to one side and then the other. Her shoulder knocked into the Dumpster and she tripped over something stretched across the ground in front of her.

Holding on to the Dumpster's side, she stared down. A leg…legs…four of them.

"CeCe."

At her name, she shifted her gaze. Up the legs, bodies…faces. Two, both familiar, both bearing fangs.

Marc…and…she growled.

"Run."

Marc telling her to leave. Talking to her the way Karl did, as though he was in charge. Telling her to leave him, alone, with the monster that had tried to kill her, was trying to kill Marc.

It wasn't going to happen.

She placed her hand against her throat. Her wounds, now that the vampire's silver-capped teeth were gone, had begun to close. Her body hadn't had time to regenerate the blood she had lost, but that would come. She was fine, was going to be fine.

There was no reason to run, but weak or not, there was every reason to fight.

The vampire who had attacked her bit into Marc's shoulder. Dark, almost-black blood leaked out of

Marc's body, slow but sure, staining his expensive white shirt.

The sight infuriated CeCe. She pushed away from the Dumpster and growled again. Shift or attack? Her body said to change, her wolf said to change, but CeCe knew she would do so at a cost, the cost of logic. Once wolf, the animal would take over, might not discern one vampire from the other, might attack both.

She couldn't risk it.

Instead, she spun and searched the alley, wished yet again she'd carried the stake, silver or not, with her.

The space was insanely clean, but inside the Dumpster, she found a wooden box, the kind peaches or other produce often came in. She tore it into strips with her hands.

Armed with her makeshift stake, she approached the vampires.

Marc could feel and smell CeCe near him. Could hear her breaths and feel her heartbeat. Her presence and his need to protect her were breaking his concentration, damaging his fight.

He had to block her out, concentrate on destroying this vampire as he had destroyed so many others. Although usually he went into a fight armed.

He snarled and pulled back, attacked the vampire's neck again.

"Roll. Damn it, roll!" CeCe stood beside them… too close. He could touch her boot. The other vampire could too.

He wanted to yell at her again, tell her to leave again, but he couldn't, not without lifting his mouth from her attacker's throat.

"Wolf. Don't leave. I won't be long." Even with his throat torn, the other vampire taunted her, taunted Marc.

"Don't worry, I won't." She moved closer.

Marc closed his eyes and flipped around, freed his hands from where they had been pinned beneath the other male.

Victory was near, but he had no time to gloat. He grabbed the other vampire by the head and jerked down.

With a snap, the vampire's neck broke and his jaw slackened. His hold on Marc's shoulder disappeared.

Marc shoved him aside and stood.

His chest barely moving, he stared down at the fallen vampire. Not dead. Left alone in the dark, he would eventually heal. Except he wouldn't, because Marc wouldn't allow it.

He turned, ready to comfort CeCe and tell her to leave.

But the werewolf was on top of her attacker, her legs straddling his incapacitated body and a wooden stake in her hands.

She slashed downward, so quick and strong the stake she held punctured the vampire's chest with barely a pause.

Marc stood frozen. For a moment the world seemed to twirl.

The vampire was dead, and the werewolf who had killed him was safe.

It should have been the wrong outcome. It should have sent Marc into a fit, bent on revenge, bent on killing the werewolf who had killed one of his kind, but his world had twisted.

His gaze moved to CeCe.

Her hand still on the stake, she stared up at him. Her eyes were hollow and confused. Filled with the same uncertainty that Marc knew filled his.

Their world had just changed, maybe forever.

Slowly, she released her grip on the piece of wood she had shoved into the vampire's chest and let out a breath.

Marc placed a palm over his own heart, wondered how seeing her with the stake, knowing how easily she had killed the other vampire, couldn't bother him, couldn't worry him.

He didn't know, but it didn't matter. He held out his hand. "Let's go," he said.

He'd get her away from here and come back. He'd have to destroy the body to make sure the Fringe had no way of learning exactly what had happened here.

If they did, CeCe would be as good as dead. Attacked or not, defending Marc or herself…none of that would matter.

A werewolf had killed a vampire. That was all they would see.

War. This would mean war.

And unlike the accusations the werewolves planned to make against Marc, any accusations against CeCe would be true. Her hand had delivered the final blow.

Marc's hand, so pale in the sparsely lit alley, reached out for CeCe.

A vampire's hand.

The vampire. She'd been trying to think of him that way, but now straddling the monster that had tried to kill her and staring at the man who had fought to save her, she knew she could never think of Marc that way again.

Yes, he was a vampire. She wouldn't, couldn't, deny that, but she also couldn't hate him for it. He was more than his fate.

He was Marc.

She slipped her fingers into his and let him tug her to her feet.

They both hesitated for a moment, both, she guessed, filled with similar thoughts and doubts. Then tired of thinking, tired of planning, she took a step forward and laid her head against his chest.

The slow steady beat of his heart was still there.

His hands rose and briefly ran down her back. His fingers traced her spine so lightly she almost thought his touch was only in her imagination. Then his arms closed around her and she was pressed against him, encircled by his embrace.

With a sigh, she wrapped her arms around him, closed her eyes, and just breathed.

Standing in the alley, holding CeCe felt right, too right. Marc knew they couldn't stay like this. Knew he had to pull away, separate himself from both the attraction and the connection he felt when near the female werewolf.

But not just yet.

He rested his forehead on the top of her head and let her warmth and scent surround him.

"The pack is coming. Or part of it," she murmured.

"I assumed," he replied.

She stepped back. "You did?"

He tilted his head. "Of course. You're a werewolf,

an important one. Your loyalty is to the pack. Nothing can change that."

Her gaze drifted to the dead vampire at their feet.

"I killed him." She looked up. "I'd do it again."

"Of course." And, he knew, if a choice came down
to him or the pack, she'd choose the pack. If the tables
had been turned, if a werewolf, a member of her pack,
had been attacking him, he would have been lying on
the ground now, a stake in his chest.

It was the way of wolves. Their own over all others. He had to remember that. He couldn't let it go.

"You go and meet them. I'll stay here…clean up."

She hesitated. "Are you sure?"

"Go." His patience was changing to anger. Anger
that despite knowing what she was, what her choice
would always be, he still wanted her to go, still wanted
to make sure no vampire learned what she had done.

Still wanted to protect her.

Unable to handle the onslaught of realizations any
longer, he shoved her toward the end of the alley. "Go."

Her nose lifting, she walked away…searching for
a scent. Searching for her pack—where she belonged
and he didn't.

Chapter 12

CeCe pulled her cell phone from her pocket and checked the time. Only an hour had passed. How, she didn't know. Too much had happened; too much had changed since she had met Marc at the diner for only an hour of time to have passed.

But the slow movement of time was her friend, assured her that the pack wouldn't be waiting for her when she returned to her motel.

She had time to clean the blood from her throat and destroy her clothing before they arrived. And come up with some story, a story that would turn their attention away from Marc. She owed him that.

Her steps slowed. Under a streetlight she came to a stop.

Stupid. She didn't have to turn their attention away from Marc. She simply had to give them something

else to concentrate on, something she already had—
the dead vampire.

It was obvious her attacker had been hunting werewolves. Why else would he have been wearing silver
caps on his fangs?

He had to be the vampire behind both Russell's and
Porter's deaths—assuming the humans were wrong
and Porter's death hadn't been natural causes.

Marc had been worried that accusations a vampire
had killed a werewolf would reignite the war, but with
the vampire behind the trouble dead, there would be
no reason for war.

Relief washing over her, she turned to hurry back to
Marc, to stop him from doing whatever he'd planned
with the body.

She needed that body. They needed that body.

The dead vampire was the answer to all of their
problems.

"CeCe! Stop!" The voice froze her where she stood.
Karl, but it couldn't be. Karl had to still be at least an
hour away.

The alpha stepped out of the shadows. "I found
her," he called.

Three more wolves appeared. All male and all
known to her, all members of her pack.

Her pack that lived two hundred miles away.

"How…? I didn't expect you, not yet." Her hand
flew to her throat, to the blood that still stained her
skin.

The alpha slanted his head and inhaled. "I smell
blood. Hers." He gestured to the others. Within seconds his three companions surrounded her, their backs
to her, scanning for any and all threats.

His body tense, Karl prowled closer. "What happened?" The always-intimidating alpha looked even more so tonight. Dark jeans, dark T-shirt and dark demeanor. Dark and deadly. Not in a mood, she guessed, to listen to reason.

She fought the urge to glance toward the alley. "How'd you get here so fast?" she spoke louder than necessary, hoping to alert Marc that the werewolves had arrived.

Go. Leave the body, she thought. If only Marc could hear her.

"You're hurt." Karl strode past the first werewolf, grabbed CeCe by the wrist, and jerked her hand away from her throat. "Blood. Dry, but blood."

It sounded like an accusation, made her wolf want to fall on the ground and beg for forgiveness. Instead CeCe lifted her chin. "I'm fine."

"The vampire. Where is he?"

"I…" Without thinking she reached for her throat. Karl's hold on her wrist kept her hand suspended, a foot from her face. There was blood on her fingers too, dark, thick…vampire blood.

Karl saw it, inhaled, then spat. His grip on her wrist tightened and he pulled her closer. She was forced up onto her toes. "Where is he?"

She didn't answer. She couldn't. Her mind was whirling, searching for some answer that would satisfy him, make him go away until she could talk to Marc, get their stories to match.

The alpha dropped her wrist and stared at her for a moment, his expression stormy. Then he spun and walked to a point just outside the circle that the other males had formed. Lines of tension ran down his back, clearly visible through the material of his tight-fitting T.

"I killed him," she stuttered.

"Killed him?" Karl's already dark expression grew darker.

"I thought you wanted him dead. I thought that's why you were coming here." She glanced at the males surrounding her. "Raced here." She rubbed her hands on her pants, wished she could kneel and rub them on the ground, get the vampire's blood off her, completely. "It's over. You didn't have to come at all."

Karl growled and turned back. "Didn't have to come?"

She flinched at his tone.

"Thinking isn't your job. We came here to get Russell, to get evidence that a vampire killed him, but if you've killed the vampire, what does that leave us? Nothing."

She wasn't following his logic, wasn't seeing where any of this was a problem. She had just told Karl that she had killed Russell's killer. What else did he need?

She voiced the question.

He made a grunting noise. "Evidence."

Of course, she should have realized that. She had broken one of the laws of peace. What proof now was there that doing so was justified? Was it justified? According to the black-and-white laws, maybe not.

"When did you kill this vampire? Where is his body? Is there something on it we can tie to Russell?"

The questions came quick and hard.

She latched on to the last one, the one that gave her hope. "Silver caps. He wore silver caps on his fangs. It's how I got…this." She tilted her neck, fully exposing the dried blood. "His body is there." Praying Marc was done and had disappeared out the opposite end of the alley, leaving the vampire and his silver caps behind, she pointed to where she had left her attacker's body.

"He wore silver?" Karl cocked his brow. "How are you alive?"

CeCe's nostrils flared. First judgment, now disbelief. She opened her mouth to defend herself.

"She lies. She killed no one." Marc stepped out of the alleyway. He was naked from the waist up.

CeCe's throat closed. She swallowed or tried to, her mind spinning.

Why was he still here? Why didn't he leave?

The werewolves around her closed ranks, formed a wall between her and Marc. She walked forward and shoved against them with flat palms, not hard enough to push them out of the way—just a test to see how determined they were to keep her in place.

They didn't move, not even an inch.

"So I see." Karl's voice shifted to the left, telling her though she couldn't see that he was moving closer to Marc.

Frustrated, she balled her fists and tightened her jaw. She considered shoving her way past the wolves, but to do so would be a blatant disregard of the alpha's wishes. Karl had, without words, given them their orders, and by their actions, hers.

To disobey was unthinkable.

She ground her teeth together and peered over the shortest were's shoulder.

"What do you know of what has happened here,

vampire? Of the wolf found dead? Of the blood on my destined mate's neck?"

Marc flinched, but his face stayed impassive. His gaze locked onto CeCe. She hadn't told him who she was, her place in the pack.

Why would she? He was a vampire, a stranger. She was a wolf. They were nothing to each other, could be nothing.

Her mouth dry, she licked her lips.

"I'm here, vampire, and I'm talking to you." Karl took a step sideways, blocking her view of Marc. "Are you taking responsibility? Should we haul you back for judgment?"

"Pack law has no jurisdiction here or over me. You know that." Marc's voice was calm and cold.

"That doesn't sound like a denial. In fact, it sounds like an admission of guilt. What do you think, Neil?"

One of the wolves in front of CeCe nodded. His hand moved to his back pocket. She had no idea what he might have concealed there, but she knew it couldn't be good, not for Marc.

As he reached, he stepped to the side, creating an opening in the wall of werewolves that surrounded her. She sprinted through it and into the space separating Karl and Marc.

"He's the liar. I did kill—"

Karl spun. He backhanded her. She fell to the ground.

Blood spurted from her lip. She pressed the back of her hand to the spot and stared at it. Anger and regret swirled inside her. Karl had hit her. Her human half fumed, but her wolf saw things differently.

He was the alpha and she'd stepped out of line, disobeyed what she'd known were his wishes. There was no excuse for that. She'd deserved the slap…deserved more. It's what her father would have said, but CeCe found she no longer believed that, not completely.

Her wolf and human halves circled each other, fought for the right to react, how to react. She flexed and unflexed her hands. Closed her eyes and bore the pain of the split inside her.

The wolf snarled…Karl had treated her as he would any other member of the pack, *as she deserved*.

Her human half screamed…he'd hit her, belittled her. She was tired of being third class in this pack, tired of being property.

As if sensing her struggle, Karl turned and leveled a gaze her direction that would in the past have caused her to curl into a ball.

As it was, she had to force herself to lower her gaze, remind herself of everything her wolf already knew. She closed her eyes and counted, prayed for the rage to pass quickly.

A chorus of growls sounded behind her. She opened her eyes. Marc had moved. He was standing six inches from Karl now, his fangs fully extended.

"Wolf. Is this how you treat those destined to you?" His skin shone white under the streetlight, and his pupils had narrowed to slits so small they were nothing but pinpricks.

A shiver danced up CeCe's back.

Her own situation forgotten, she leaped to her feet. "Keep her back." Karl roared, making a sweeping motion with one hand as if he would knock her aside like a gnat.

But CeCe couldn't let him. Not now. Not with Marc putting himself at risk.

"He lies," she yelled. "Would you believe a vampire over me? I did kill a vampire. He did wear silver caps. He is who you want, not—" she made a dismissive motion with one hand "—this whoever, whatever he may be."

Marc didn't move. He gave no indication he heard her claim or felt her insult, but the three wolves, who had stood around her, moved forward and grabbed him by the arms.

To her surprise, he let them.

Karl pulled her to her feet. He wiped the blood from her mouth with his thumb. "I'm sorry."

She raised her eyes.

"I should have thought before striking you in front of a vampire. They have no control when fresh blood is drawn."

Strangely shaken by Karl's words, she glanced at Marc, wondered if it was true, if the vampire's sudden change had been caused solely by the scent of her blood. Marc stared back, silent and unreadable.

Karl wiped his thumb on his pants, then turned his back on her, but Marc continued to watch her. Unable to meet his gaze, she began walking toward the alley. "The vampire, the one I killed, is back here." Her voice was shaking. She kept moving, hoping no one but her noticed.

As she passed Marc, she stopped. His tattoo was fully visible, was as she had guessed an exact duplicate of the design on the stake, if the stake's design hadn't been cut into two pieces. Noticing her interest, a question formed in his eyes.

"CeCe?" Karl's fingers wrapped around her wrist. She shifted her attention away from Marc and onto the empty street in front of her. Karl pulled her back so she was walking beside him. Then he motioned for the other wolves, with Marc, to follow.

"This vampire in the alley. He's the one I told you about."

She could feel Marc's gaze on her back. Her shoulders squared, and she lowered her voice. "I met him in the woods, then followed him here tonight. Once I was in the alley, he attacked, but I...fought him off."

"And the vampire behind us?"

She lifted her shoulders. "I told you, I've never seen him before." A quick decision, choosing to pretend to know nothing of Marc rather than say he'd tried to help her. Truth or lie, neither came without risk, but the entire truth, that she had jumped in to save Marc, couldn't be shared. No werewolf would understand what had driven her to do that. She didn't understand it herself, except that Marc had done the same for her and she owed him.

It was the only answer she could bring herself to accept.

Karl snarled. Unsure if he believed her or not, or what Marc might say when he heard her lies, she walked faster. Once she gave the pack the dead vampire with his silver-capped teeth, this would be over. Her life could go back to what it was meant to be, destined to be.

The thought, something she had accepted for so long, didn't bring with it any joy—just resolve....

The alpha moved like a jungle cat beside her. Any

female in the pack would have fought her for her future with him.

But she knew he'd accepted her as his future mate because of what her father had told him, promised him. Mate with a genetic wolf and gain genetic children who are born werewolf, stronger than a wolf that had endured the bite.

Was it true? She didn't know, and until today, she hadn't cared.

They entered the alley. The Dumpster was halfway down. A light shone from the diner's bathroom windows, indicating that someone was inside.

"There." She pointed to the ground below the windows where a body-sized lump lay.

Karl indicated for her to wait, then strode forward. He placed a foot on the dead vampire and pushed. The form tumbled over and collapsed into nothing but a pile of rags.

"But..." CeCe faced Marc. His body was tight, his muscles coiled, and his attention was on Karl.

The alpha picked up the strips of cloth and tossed them back down. "Vampire? Silver caps? What game are you playing, CeCe?"

Still watching Marc, she didn't reply.

"What would she gain from this game, alpha? It looks to me she has nothing to win...not with you."

Karl's eyes narrowed and his nostrils flared, but he didn't move forward. He held still. "A vampire attacked CeCe. A vampire killed Russell. And a vampire stands before me." He raised his hand. "Tie him up. We'll get his confession at dawn."

Dawn. Karl planned to roast Marc...perhaps inch

by inch. And if sun exposure didn't kill him as Karl expected, then what would the alpha do?

CeCe couldn't find out. Desperate and unsure what to do, what she could do to divert Karl from this path, she spun toward the alpha. "No—"

To her side, Marc lurched forward. With a hiss, he pulled free of the werewolves' grip. The three jumped, tried to grab the vampire, but he was too quick. He leaped out of their reach.

Then he grabbed CeCe, jerked her body against his and brushed her fangs against her neck.

"You're a fool, alpha, to treat something this sweet with disregard. But you fool yourself more if you think I would have stopped at one simple sip." His gaze on Karl, he dragged his fangs across her skin.

A tremor ran through her.

Karl dove forward, head and shoulders first, like a linebacker going for a tackle. Marc shoved CeCe to the side and let her fall on the pavement like a toy, broken and forgotten, like a possession he no longer wanted.

Chapter 13

The alpha's shoulder dug into Marc's gut. The pair flew backward until Marc's back slammed into the brick wall behind him.

CeCe lay on the ground where Marc had pushed her, to keep her safe, out of the battle he knew was about to rage. She rose onto all fours, then lifted her head and stared at him.

Her gaze was hollow and lost, but he had no time to consider what her expression meant, what she was thinking. The alpha grabbed Marc by the head and pummeled his head into the wall.

Marc's ears rang. The side of his face went numb. He lifted his hand and grabbed the alpha by the throat, or tried to…the werewolf stepped to the side, twisted around until he was behind Marc.

There, he dug his forearm into Marc's throat. A

move Marc guessed was effective when dealing with an adversary who needed to breathe. Unfortunately for the alpha, vampires didn't.

He twisted too, spun in the wolf's unwelcome embrace, until the two were less than a foot apart... the perfect distance for what Marc had in mind. He grabbed the other male by the hair and jerked his head back. With the werewolf's neck fully exposed, he lunged forward.

He would rip the werewolf's throat out—in front of his pack and his destined mate.

"Stop!" CeCe leaped between them, shoving herself in front of the alpha, blocking his neck with her own.

Marc's fangs brushed her skin. Her scent enveloped him. He jerked back. Shaking with unreleased rage and adrenaline, he dropped his hold on the alpha.

The werewolf didn't fall. He spun and shoved CeCe to the side, into the arms of the other three males.

Her eyes slanted, and nostrils flared, she inhaled a shaky breath. Then, with no warning, she shifted. Her hair grew; her body bent. She fell on all fours and a howl ripped from her throat. She went from woman to wolf in the space of two heartbeats. Marc had never imagined, never believed, the shift from human to wolf could be that fast.

But he didn't ponder the new discovery for long. He was too caught in the beauty of the creature in front of him. Her fur was silvery gray and glossy, and her eyes were gold. Her lips pulled up, revealing teeth that shone white in the night. She was menacing and strong...alluring.

Unaware of Marc's thoughts, she slipped from the male werewolves' grip like water. Her paws touched the ground with a whisper of sound, and then she leaped, landing between Marc and the alpha once again.

Her tail and head low, her lip raised, she snapped at both of them.

For a moment, the alpha didn't move, then slowly he held out one hand, palm up...cautious as if he too were amazed by the magic in her shift.

CeCe approached and sniffed, but as if she was afraid of being caught, she quickly danced back. Her eyes narrowed. She shifted her gaze to Marc and inhaled again, loudly.

He saw no recognition in her eyes. None. Beautiful, but all animal...all wolf.

Her head tilted side to side, then without warning she moved to a sit and a second howl broke free from her throat. Then just as suddenly, she was human again. Naked and shaking, she dropped to the asphalt.

Her skin was pale and smooth. Her muscles firm and defined. She wasn't wolf or woman; she was magic, art, everything Marc had ever imagined beauty could be.

She pushed her arms straight so her upper body was off the ground. "I don't... Stop. Just stop. This is getting us nowhere," she murmured.

Marc moved to kneel, to pull her into his arms, to hide her nudity and offer her comfort. Apologize for pushing the wolves, being headstrong...stupid.

Her gaze darted to him, warning.

He glanced at the alpha, remembered what the other man had said, the claim he had made. CeCe was his mate, not Marc's.

Then anger and tension balling together in his stomach, he stood back and watched as the alpha moved toward her instead, stood still and pretended he didn't care when the werewolf pulled her to her feet and handed her her clothes.

Silence had fallen over the wolves, a solemnity that despite his own angst, Marc didn't understand.

"Talk." The alpha held up both hands, giving CeCe the floor.

She pulled in a breath. "I told you this vampire isn't the one who attacked me. That I've never seen him before. Killing him will solve nothing. It will only make matters worse."

"You claim to have killed one vampire. Why would killing this one make anything worse?"

"I killed—" She glanced at Marc, then tucked her hands around the alpha's forearm and pulled him aside.

A muscle in Marc's jaw jumped. He stared at the wall, but his real attention was on the wolves and the words they were saying that apparently neither believed he could hear.

"I killed that vampire because he was trying to kill me. I had no choice, but this one...we don't know who he is or where he came from. Perhaps he was sent by others. Perhaps he's involved in Russell's death. Perhaps he can tell us what the vampires know of the treasure. If we let him go free, we can follow him. See where he takes us."

"We could find out what he knows and what he has done while holding him ourselves." A growl underlined the alpha's words.

CeCe's hands tightened on the alpha's arm. Marc's gaze locked on the spot where her skin touched the wolf's.

"We have no evidence tying this vampire to anything," she said.

The muscles in the alpha's arm, the one CeCe still held, tensed.

"We could kill him, but what if there are others? Why lose the opportunity watching him gives us?" she continued.

"Because he heard you say you killed one of his kind. If that gets back to the others, they'll mark you as a slayer and breaker of the law. They'll hunt you." The alpha shook off her hold. A bit of the anger Marc had sensed in him before CeCe's shift returned.

CeCe's lips pressed together. "I'll take that risk."

"It isn't your risk to take. As alpha, it's mine." The male wolf turned then, dismissing CeCe as Marc had seen him dismiss her before, and once again, CeCe didn't argue.

The alpha's treatment of her and CeCe's reaction to it gnawed at him. He longed for her to lunge at the alpha, to fight for her own voice.

But CeCe was a wolf and the alpha her destined mate. His treatment, of her, of any and all wolves beneath him, was the way of the pack.

The vampire balled his hands into fists so tight his knuckles popped.

The alpha faced him. Marc returned the other male's gaze.

The alpha raised one brow, then grabbed CeCe by the arm and with her by his side, walked from the alley. Two of the remaining three werewolves followed. The one the alpha had called Neil stayed behind, his arms crossed over his chest and his gaze never leaving Marc.

His attention on CeCe, studying her posture, looking for some sign he was mistaken, that she needed… wanted his interference, he ignored the wolf. He continued ignoring him until CeCe and the other werewolves had turned the corner and disappeared from view.

She didn't look back, not even once.

Still not looking at the werewolf, he moved to walk past him.

Like some third-rate bouncer stopping a gate-crasher, the werewolf's arm shot out, blocking Marc's forward movement.

Marc stopped and shifted his attention down. Then slowly he let his gaze travel up the werewolf's arm to his throat.

He stopped there; he didn't bother looking the man in the face. He wouldn't pay him the honor.

"You saw what I did to your alpha, how I bared his throat. Do you really think you will fare any better, underling?"

The wolf lowered his arm and stepped to the side, so his body blocked Marc's exit. "I saw my alpha let you go. Now I see a vampire with no one to protect him."

Meeting his gaze now, Marc laughed. "I stopped needing protection two hundred years ago, wolf."

"Are you denying the destined one's intervention? Denying that you watch her like a starving dog stalking a wounded lamb? My alpha may not see it, may not want to, but my job as his second is to see what he doesn't, act on what isn't worthy of his attention."

"Like me?" Marc cocked a brow. "I'm honored. Or did you mean CeCe?" He turned to the side and mimicked the other male's earlier posture, crossing his arms over his chest. "Why does he treat her the way he does? With disregard and disrespect?"

The werewolf dropped his arm and leaned forward. His neck was huge, like a bull's. The veins would be easy to locate, but Marc had no desire to sample the werewolf's blood, not for the pleasure of the taste at least.

"Pack business isn't yours." The werewolf's breath was hot on Marc's cheek. He glanced to the side, as if checking to see if the alpha and the others had truly left. "Tell me, did she tell the truth? Did she kill a vampire by herself with her own two hands?" he asked.

Part of Marc wanted to tell him she had, dislodge whatever misplaced belief the wolves obviously had about CeCe, her strengths and weaknesses, but a greater part of him still wanted to keep her safe. Which meant keeping the truth from making its way to the Fringe.

"A wolf, a single female wolf, kill a vampire? Surely you know better than that." His eyes focused on the other male's now. Again he laughed.

A line had formed between the werewolf's brows. At Marc's laugh, it smoothed. He nodded his head, and he stepped to the side, as if giving Marc permission to proceed. "It's been long enough. You can go, but keep away from the destined one."

"Or?"

"Or you may wind up like Russell, with a stake in your chest."

Apparently feeling that his threat had been properly delivered, the werewolf strode from the alley.

Amused more than annoyed, Marc watched him

go. Threats had no impact on him. How could they? He had no pack, no ties. He had nothing to love, nothing to lose.

CeCe walked beside Karl almost afraid to speak. What had happened back in the alley, her shift moving so quickly she'd barely been aware it was happening, could be seen as a challenge to Karl's position. No wolf changed that quickly, no wolf except an alpha, and only then if he had a full and strong pack behind him.

But CeCe had no pack behind her. She knew while she was accepted by the pack and guarded by the wolves, it was more as an asset, for her potential in giving the alpha and thus the pack offspring, genetic werewolves. More than one wolf might jump at the chance to call her move a challenge, take her down themselves, if Karl didn't.

Or worse, she might be accused of having hidden this ability from the pack, be plotting some kind of overthrow.

But overthrow was the furthest thing from CeCe's plans for herself, and the strangely fast change had surprised her as much as anyone else. She had to make sure Karl knew that.

"Leave," Karl ordered.

The four had reached CeCe's motel. Two trucks she recognized as the pack's were parked outside her room.

The other two wolves walked toward a room a few doors down from hers, and Karl turned to her, waiting.

Not wanting to have whatever conversation was coming in the public parking lot, she pulled the motel key from her pocket and twisted it in the lock.

Once inside, Karl roamed the room, his eyes cataloging everything from her open suitcase to the hairbrush she hadn't used since before finding Russell.

As Karl walked away, she picked up the brush and shoved it back inside her suitcase.

"We should have the ceremony soon."

She jerked. "Ceremony?" She'd expected the alpha to ask her about a number of things: her shift, Russell, Marc and the vampire she had killed—the original point of this trip, the treasure. But the mating ceremony tying her to the alpha? It wasn't a topic she had even considered.

"Things haven't gone as we planned. It would be best to move forward before the rest of the pack realizes this."

Before they realized she was not only what many had claimed, a freak, she was also a failure. Not fit to be the alpha's mate. She shoved her suitcase back. It knocked into the wall with a bang. The hairbrush she had placed inside fell onto the floor. She bent to retrieve it, then held it clenched in her hand.

"I didn't realize this trip was a trial," she replied. It was a lie. She had known. Every day since her father had convinced Karl of her assets as a mate had been a trial. The alpha bought what her father was selling, but many of the other werewolves, especially the females, hadn't.

He lifted one shoulder. "There was no reason for me to tell you."

"What about Russell?"

"What about him? We'll wait until day, when we know the vampires aren't active, then we'll go into the cave for his body. You don't need to be involved."

"What if I want to be?"

"You want to go into a cave?"

She straightened. Karl didn't know of her training. She'd endured her father's idea of growth long before she met the alpha, and she had shared the experience with no one. "Why wouldn't I?" she asked, testing.

He moved toward the bathroom. He emerged with her makeup and toiletries gathered in his hands. Her shampoo and conditioner were fresh from the shower. Still wet even though it had been over a day since she had used them. Water dripped on the floor behind Karl.

She felt each drip hit.

"Why would you?" he asked.

She bit her lip and forced calm onto her face. "I found Russell and I put him in that cave. I know where it is, know how I left him. I should be there when he comes back out." And she liked Russell, valued him, if not as a friend, as one of the few wolves who seemed to respect her as something other than the alpha's destined mate.

"We can find the cave without you. You can go back to the pack, get ready for the ceremony." Karl dumped her toiletries, water and all, into her suitcase.

"No."

Karl's head jerked toward her.

She covered her emotions by pulling the wet shampoo and conditioner bottles from atop her clothing and wiping them dry on her shirt. "If they are in there too long, things could mold," she offered.

"It's a two-hour drive."

A flat fact. No room for argument. The alpha pulled his shoulders back and stared at her.

She could feel him pulling on the power of the pack. The draw was slight, subtle, a warning, nothing more, but a move that in the past would have sent her scurrying to the parking lot with her bag in her hand.

But this time CeCe wasn't willing to give up the fight, not this easily. She placed the dry bottles on the dresser top beside the suitcase. Then she set the hairbrush beside them too. The three lined up like good little soldiers, awaiting their fates.

She turned her back on them.

"I started this. I want to finish it. I want to find the treasure and Russell's killer," she said.

Karl's gaze glimmered. For a second she thought he might force her, but that wasn't the alpha's way. Karl might reprimand with force, like the backhand he had delivered earlier, but he led with will.

CeCe, however, had never so openly defied Karl's will. She had angered him and been punished, but when asked to do something, no matter how distasteful, she had always complied. She had always known her place.

So, despite what she knew of Karl, she had no way of knowing exactly how he would react to her open stance against his orders. She dropped her gaze from his face to his chest. Let him know any challenge was unintentional.

He shoved his hands into the front pockets of his jeans and rolled back onto his heels. "Tell me your plan."

CeCe took a step back and bumped into the dresser behind her. The alpha had never asked to hear her ideas before, and quite honestly, now that he had, she had no idea what to tell him.

She licked her lips, searching inside herself for an answer, and as she stared into the alpha's steely gaze, she came face-to-face with the fact that she had no plan, nothing she wanted…except to stay here, near Marc.

Chapter 14

After waiting a few minutes to assure himself that the werewolf wouldn't return, Marc jumped on top of the Dumpster and grabbed hold of a drainage pipe that ran along the side of the building. Using the pipe and his upper body strength, he flipped himself onto the roof.

He landed lightly, like a cat. Then, silent as a feline, he padded to where he had left the vampire's body.

He'd been in the process of disposing of the corpse when he'd heard CeCe in the street, talking with her pack. Her rather obvious warning that the wolves had arrived had cut off his investigation. Now, he needed to complete his analysis, remove anything that might identify the remains and most importantly strip away any and everything that wouldn't, come morning, disintegrate into ash.

That part of the vampire myth was true. No matter the age, once life was removed from a vampire's body, contact with the sun would turn his remains to nothing but an innocuous pile of ash.

He started with the vampire's mouth and his silver-capped fangs.

After removing the distasteful weapons, Marc rolled them over his palm with his thumb. He hadn't seen a pair in years and unless he missed his guess this pair dated to even before the war. The silver was old and hand-beaten, and someone had bent them to fit more tightly.

The vampire lying dead on the roof, Marc guessed. The caps were not one-size-fits-all. Marc slipped the caps back onto the vampire's fangs. They fit, but it was easy to see that his guess was correct. Wherever the vampire had gotten the weapons, they had not originally been made for him.

Marc paused. Van Bom had said weapons from the war had been stored away—with the stake that the werewolves had feared.

What else had been stored there? Perhaps the two coins that the human Porter had allowed to be photographed? Was the treasure Marc had been sent to find no treasure at all, but a stash of weapons? If so, why hadn't Marc been told?

The questions slithered around his mind. There was, he decided, much more to this story than he had guessed…and this vampire was proof of it. He'd said something about carrying out orders. Whose? And for what?

Marc didn't like mysteries, but he liked the feeling that he was being used even less.

Another call to the Fringe was necessary. Perhaps this time Andre, his usual contact, would answer.

He pulled the caps off the vampire's fangs and rolled them over his palm again. Finally, he closed his fingers over them and slipped them into his pocket. Then he patted the dead vamp down. His back pocket revealed a surprise—another set of silver handcuffs.

Two sets of the cuffs in as many days.

Marc was not a big believer in coincidences. With a grimace, he shoved the set into his own pocket and finished checking the body. The vampire carried very little else, not even a cell phone or keys. After logging the information away, he stripped the vampire of his clothing and dragged him to a spot where the first rays of morning sun would be sure to find him.

Finally, with the vampire's personal items under his arm, he leaped from the roof.

He could leave the clothing in a Dumpster and head back to his motel, where he could contact Andre.

Or he could search out the werewolves. Search out CeCe. See if the alpha was with her; see what exactly being a destined mate meant.

Before his feet hit the ground, he knew where he was going, what his choice would be.

The Fringe could wait.

A quick trip to replace his shirt, and he would be headed to CeCe's motel.

CeCe placed her palm on the dresser behind her. Karl had asked for her plan; she needed to give him one. "You and the others leave. I'll stay and watch the vampire. He won't consider me a threat. He'll let his guard down." She said the words with confidence, hoped they sounded that way to Karl.

"And what? Lead you to the treasure? To evidence that he killed Russell? You have the stake and we will get the vampire. That will be enough."

It wasn't enough, because Marc didn't kill Russell, but she was past arguing the point with Karl. She'd faced that he would never accept Marc's innocence, not until she brought him the real killer, whoever that might be.

"And what about the treasure? That's why we came here in the first place."

Karl didn't answer; he paced to the side instead. "The stake. You do have it, don't you?"

"Yes, it's—" She turned, ready to motion to where she had hidden it inside her mattress, but the alpha closed his eyes and fisted his hands. His knuckles turned white. Stress showed in the lines around his eyes.

"You have it. That's enough for now. We will need it later, to prove the vampire was involved."

The stake. It was, in Karl's view, the major piece of evidence tying Marc to Russell's murder. She realized then she could move it....

She looked up. Karl was staring at her. "When you removed it, how did you touch it?"

"I used my shirt as a glove. I was careful not to destroy any evidence." And if there was evidence she couldn't see or smell... "Can we take it to a lab? There might be something on it. DNA."

"DNA?" His frame stiffened. "No. It's pack business, not human business."

"But surely, someone—"

"No." He growled. If he'd been in his wolf form, his hackles would have raised.

CeCe stepped back. The pack had connections, resources. And werewolves held all kinds of positions. Somewhere there had to be a wolf who could get the stake analyzed without raising suspicions, but Karl's expression was firm. There would be no arguing with him.

"What about the others?" she asked.

"What others?" The alpha ran a hand through his hair. His fingers shook. CeCe stared at them, sure she was seeing wrong.

"The vampires. They won't just stand by and let us take one of their kind. It won't be that simple. It could be war."

"It could." The lines around Karl's eyes had deepened. He looked older, tired. "But what about Russell? A killer has to be named and punished."

Not found. Named.

"If more vampires arrive…" He spun, thinking.

"If I can tie the vampire that I killed to Russell?" she prompted. "The pack would be satisfied." And Marc would be safe.

"We need a body."

"I'll find it." She could, she just had to convince Marc to take her to it. "The new vampire must have hidden it. I can follow him. As I said before, he thinks I'm weak."

"But you aren't." Not a question, a statement. As if suddenly Karl saw her differently.

He tilted his head and studied her. "What happened to the body?"

"I…" She'd left it with Marc, but she couldn't say

that. "I don't know. I left it in the alley. When we came back, it was gone." That at least was true.

"So, there were two vampires here." He sighed. "They're after it."

"The treasure?" She already knew Marc was here for the treasure.

Surprise shone in his eyes, but only for an instant. "Yes, the treasure."

"I can find it." She'd been sent to find the treasure. She could still find it and Russell's killer. She just needed more time.

"Maybe." Karl paced around the room. He stopped by the door, suddenly, as if he'd just made a decision. "The treasure isn't important, not any more. We stick with my original plan. Tie the vampire we have to the stake and Russell."

Frame Marc.

"Can you do that?"

Her world blurred at the edges.

"CeCe, can you do that?" Karl stood by the door, his hand on the doorknob.

Slowly, her head nodded. The movement felt distant and odd. As if she wasn't in control of it.

"CeCe, you didn't touch it?"

"What?"

"The stake. You're sure you didn't touch it?"

"No, I didn't touch it."

"Don't." He held up two fingers. "You have two days." Then he reached up and pulled something over his head—a chain. No, the chain of the destined mate. He dropped it over her head. The medal hung low between her breasts.

He grabbed her by the shoulders, pulled her toward

him and pressed a kiss against her lips. "Two days, then you return to the pack."

And with that, he left.

CeCe pushed the door shut behind him and stood with her palm flat against the wood.

She touched her lips.

Karl had made it official. Had made his claim. Soon her position would be more than destined; it would be real.

And if everything went as Karl planned, by the time the vows were spoken, Marc would be dead.

The alpha was inside the room with CeCe. Marc had seen him walk past the window and, as if sensing Marc's presence, peer out. Hidden in the upper branches of an older oak tree, Marc had no fear the werewolf had spotted him, and he doubted that, from inside the room, even the wolf's senses were strong enough to smell the vampire outside.

So, Marc crouched and watched, wished he dared sneak closer. But standing outside the door would only make it easy for the wolf or another pack member to discover him.

It had been an hour. The sky was turning gray.

Marc pulled a pair of sunglasses and his hat from his pocket.

Neither the alpha nor CeCe had walked past the window for the past ten minutes. He itched to be closer, to know what was going on inside the room. Were they arguing? Sleeping? Something else?

His fangs pricked his lower lip. He brushed the resulting beads of blood aside with his tongue, and forced his mind to concentrate.

He'd sat like this for days before, watching and waiting, not moving, but it had never been as difficult as this.

He adjusted his position and rearranged the leaves that sheltered him from detection. He had just settled back into place when the door to CeCe's room opened.

The alpha stepped out. CeCe stood behind him, fully dressed in the same clothing she'd been wearing earlier that night. The alpha glanced around, his gaze settling on the rising sun. He said something to CeCe; she nodded and spoke. Marc couldn't make out her words, but he could see she was on edge.

The alpha held up two fingers…telling her what? Warning her of what?

And that's what Marc thought it was…not a fond goodbye between lovers, not even a parting of friends…a warning, a deadline, some order the alpha expected completed or…what? Just what would the alpha do to CeCe? Just what had he done before?

A wind broke through the tree, lifting Marc's hair. He shifted his weight again, considered going with it, leaping from the tree and confronting the male wolf, asking him the questions pounding in Marc's mind.

As Marc leaned forward, the alpha reached behind his neck. Intrigued, Marc paused. The werewolf lowered his hands and held out their contents. A chain shone yellow in the sun.

Gold. Jewelry. A gift to make up for his treatment of her earlier?

CeCe lowered her head. The alpha slipped the chain around her neck and then he tilted her face up to his and kissed her.

* * *

Alone in her room, CeCe stripped off the clothing she'd worn for too long and stepped into the shower. Water beat down onto her. She grabbed the tiny bar of soap and lathered her body. Tried to pretend nothing had changed, but the kiss wore heavy on her mind and the chain Karl had given her pulled at her neck. Made of ancient gold, it grew warm under the stream of water.

The piece had been worn by the alpha or his mate for as long as this pack had existed. The words destined mate had become real. Too real.

She wasn't ready.

The chain, beautiful as it was, felt like a weight, dragging her down.

She touched the metal with two fingers and tried to push past the uncomfortable feeling of being bound, shackled to a life she was no longer sure she wanted.

She slipped her thumb under the chain and held it away from her skin, then dropped the links back into place. They fell against her…lay there just as heavy, just as impossible to ignore.

10:00 a.m. and Marc was still outside of CeCe's motel, still waiting for the female werewolf to appear. He pulled the brim of his hat lower. The alpha and three other werewolves had come out of their rooms and loaded themselves into two trucks an hour earlier.

Fifteen minutes more passed.

No movement.

He was growing impatient. Needed to do something.

He could do as he should have done earlier, return

to his room and call the Fringe, or he could stay here, letting the sun drain what energy he had left.

The sane course of action was to leave, but somehow Marc's feet didn't move. He waited more.

Finally, thirty minutes later the door to CeCe's room opened and she stepped out into the day.

In fresh pants and a white billowy shirt, she looked natural and fresh. Her dark hair glistened in the sun.

A cold spot in Marc's chest ached.

Then her hand rose and he saw the chain…hanging from her neck…proclaiming her as belonging to someone else.

This time, the spot of cold didn't ache; it cracked like ice.

Chapter 15

Marc followed as CeCe moved down the street. She pulled her hair to one side, baring her neck. Her fingers brushed the chain the alpha had given her.

She let her hair fall back into place, covering the chain, but Marc could still see it peeking through, catching the light.

At the diner, she paused. Then after a moment of apparent indecision, she pulled open the door and walked in.

Within seconds, she was seated in the same booth they had occupied the night before.

He strode through the door.

She didn't look up from the menu as he approached and he didn't give her a warning. He slid into the seat across from her and pulled the menu from her hands.

"Tell me, does the alpha strike all his pack members, or just the ones destined to be his mate?" It wasn't his business. He knew that.

Her eyes widened and her lips parted. No answer, but then he really hadn't expected one.

"Is it worth it? Being part of the pack?" He didn't know why his words came out so rough. He hadn't intended to start the conversation this way, but as he stared at her, remembered the alpha striking her, then kissing her...the little blood that flowed through his body boiled.

He dropped the menu onto the table. "Why are you loyal to that?" He wanted to understand. No, that was a lie. He didn't care to understand that kind of loyalty.

She didn't ask him what he meant; she didn't play dumb. She just turned her face away, displaying the skin that the alpha had struck. There was no mark, but there wouldn't be. She was a werewolf...like a vampire...no scars, at least not those visible on the outside.

"You're a vampire. You can't understand."

"Understand what? That he uses your loyalty to abuse you? Doesn't even believe you when you tell him the truth?" He kept his voice cool and uncaring, although inside he seethed.

She looked at him then, her eyes narrowed. "You could have helped. You could have told him what happened. We had the killer's body to show them, or would have if you wouldn't have made it disappear. This—" she waved her hands in the air "—could have been over, settled, but now it isn't. Russell is dead and Karl believes a vampire killed him. And guess who's the only vampire in town?"

She reached for a glass of ice water that sat on the table in front of her.

He placed his hand over hers, stopping her from lifting the glass. "Me? Let them." Let the pack come after him. Let the alpha come after him.

"No. I can't. You don't understand."

"What don't I understand?" He wanted her to tell him she cared about the truth…that she cared about him.

"Russell…he deserves better."

"Russell." Flat. No feeling.

"And you. I don't want you punished for something you didn't do."

Too little, too late. He didn't believe her.

"What if I told you I wouldn't be? What if I told you your pack doesn't scare me, can't touch me?" He was no lone vampire, no easy target. "Would you care then? Would you still want the truth?" Or would she follow her alpha's lead like a sheep, not a wolf?

She met his gaze. "Yes. I would."

It was something. More than he'd expected.

"And your alpha?"

She looked away.

He wanted to ask her to rip off the chain then, to leave with him, forget the pack, forget the alpha, forget Russell and the treasure, forget everything, but he couldn't.

It wouldn't work, he knew that.

And he had another mystery to solve. He had to find out who had sent the other vampire, find out if his guess was right and there was more to the treasure than he had been led to believe.

"What about the treasure? Are you forgetting it?" he asked.

His change in topic seemed to confuse her. "No…
yes…it doesn't matter, not with a pack member dead."

"Your words or your alpha's?"

Anger flashed in her eyes. "Both. I told you the
pack is important. Treasure is nothing compared to
that."

"Really." In two centuries, Marc had never seen a
being, werewolf, vampire or human, walk away from
riches he thought should be his. "So, the pack is giving up the hunt."

"Yes."

"Then either there is no treasure, there never was,
or the pack already has it."

"They don't. They can't."

"How do you know?"

"Because…" A frown, uncertainty.

"Why was Russell killed? You never told me that,
never told me who would want him dead."

"I did…no one. Russell was…harmless. It was
someone outside the pack."

"Outside the pack? A vampire? Me?"

"Yes. No. I don't know."

Treasure. This all started with treasure. If Russell's
death wasn't personal, the treasure had to be involved.

"Remember Russell's body, how there was no sign
of shift?" He'd pointed this out before, but she hadn't
wanted to listen. Maybe now she would. "He was
killed by someone he trusted."

"Or someone fast, someone who surprised him."

"A stake was driven into his chest. I'm sure it was a
surprise, but it wasn't delivered from yards away, not
even feet away. His killer was standing close, closer
than he would let someone stand he didn't trust.

"How well did you know Russell?" Marc thought he had solved the mystery now, or part of it.

She lifted one shoulder. "As well as anyone. He was new. He'd only been in the pack a couple of years. This mission was an opportunity to prove himself."

"Maybe he didn't want to prove himself. Maybe he wanted to be free."

She shook her head, hard. "Wolves don't want to be free, at least not like you mean. Being free for them is being part of the pack, knowing others are there to back them up. Being on your own…being rogue. That's every wolf's nightmare."

Hers too? He wanted to ask.

"Besides, we didn't find the treasure to steal."

"*You* didn't," he corrected.

"Russell didn't," she insisted. "It wasn't in Porter's house. You saw us leave. Neither of us was loaded down with treasure."

"Maybe he went back later or found something that told him where it was."

Her eyes widened.

"The woods. Russell had no reason to be in the woods."

"Except…"

"The treasure."

They looked at each other.

She pulled her hand away. The glass she'd held tilted; water spilled across the tabletop. Both ignored it. Both knew they were sitting on top of a decision… trust or fight. Look for the treasure together, see where it led them, or continue the age-old rivalry between vampires and wolves.

He wanted to trust her. He wanted her to trust him.

He held out his hand, palm up, fingers curved.

She stared at his fingers for a moment, a moment that seemed to last five lifetimes. Then she slipped her hand onto his, so her fingers curled around his and they hooked together.

After a second, she murmured, "We should go... look near where I found Russell, maybe go back to his room. See if I missed something." She stood.

Marc followed her example, but he wasn't interested in searching for the treasure, not yet. He leaned forward until his face was inches from hers.

Her lips parted. Fear flickered in her eyes.

He pushed his advantage and leaned in more. The cook came out of the kitchen and motioned toward them. Others stopped their conversations to stare.

With a growl, Marc blocked them out, threw up a thrall to divert their attention away from them, then whispered in CeCe's ear. "Your alpha doesn't value you, but I do. Trust me, CeCe."

Her lips parted. Afraid she was going to say something to stop the rush of passion surging through him, he shoved his hands into her hair and pulled her lips to his.

His kiss was savage...primal...he couldn't help that. Maybe it was the wildness in her, maybe it was the memory of seeing her kiss the alpha or maybe it was the length of time since he had kissed a woman, done anything with a woman aside from feed on her, but his need to kiss CeCe, to have her pressed against him, was so intense he couldn't pretend at civilized.

And he didn't want to.

At first he thought she would pull away. He trembled at the thought, with the need for her to stay, meet his passion with her own.

But then, slowly, her hands slipped up his chest and around his neck, and her lips met his, hard and crushing. Filled with every bit as much need as was roaring through him.

Her tongue thrust into his mouth.

Around them the noise of the diner dimmed. People moved around them, lost in the thrall he had cast, their gazes dancing over the two of them, and to Marc the diner disappeared all together.

All he could hear was the beat of CeCe's heart and the soft pants of her breath. All he could taste was the sweet honey of her lips. All he could smell was the wild earthiness of her skin. And all he could feel was her, her tongue touching his, her face soft beneath his thumbs.

And that was all he wanted. He placed his knee on the table and pulled CeCe up with him. Chest to chest they kneeled on the table as if no one else existed.

Glass crashed…the water glass slipping from the table and onto the floor. A waitress exclaimed and hurried forward, broom in hand.

CeCe pulled back. "I…" She looked around, panic in her eyes. "What…?"

He touched her cheek, tried to turn her face back to his. "They don't see us."

"None of them?" Uncertainty…reality seeping back into her consciousness.

He nodded, but her attention wasn't on him. It was on the waitress, sweeping the last few pieces of glass into a dustpan. The unwelcome human left, but still CeCe hesitated.

"I…" Her hand drifted to the damned chain the alpha had hung around her neck.

She was thinking, realizing what she had done.

And for the first time in Marc's long life, he cursed logic. Being with her had taken him to a new place, a wild place, a place where he felt free.

He wanted the same for her, but as she pulled farther away, lowered one leg and then the other back onto the booth's seat, he knew that he'd lost her, knew she was slipping back into the werewolf she thought she should be rather than the woman she was.

He couldn't let that happen. He wouldn't.

He pulled her from the booth and down the short hallway, into one of the small bathrooms. Then he spun her around and kissed her again, pressed her back against the closed door and reveled in their differences. She was pack; he was a loner. She was soft and warm; he was hard and cold.

They had nothing in common, but he wanted her more than he had wanted anyone or anything in his undead life.

She stared at him, uncertain, but not fighting him. Letting him touch her, appreciate her. She wasn't pushing him away.

It was, for the moment, all he wanted.

He ran his hand up her side, beneath her T-shirt. Her skin was silky and smooth, but solid muscle lay beneath it. Strength the alpha didn't appreciate, didn't deserve.

The alpha.

A rock formed in Marc's stomach. He didn't want to be reminded of the wolf; he wanted to pretend he didn't exist, that the pack didn't exist. At least for a while.

He grabbed the chain that hung from CeCe's neck and lifted it over her head. It caught in her hair, but he pulled the necklace free and dropped it onto the floor. Then he kicked it to the side and out of his sight.

CeCe raised her hand to her throat. Her lips parted. Guilt shone from her eyes. Marc grabbed her fingers and held them tight in his, then slowly he kissed each finger pad, willed her to give him this time…to pretend along with him that their differences didn't exist.

Slowly, her eyes drifted shut and her head tilted back. He folded her fingers into his hand and stretched out her arm. He kissed her wrist where the blood ran strong beneath her skin, then traced the blue lines of her veins with his tongue. A tremor ran through her.

His groin tightened and his nostrils flared. She had asked him about other places for vampires to drink. There were many: the neck, the wrist, the elbow…. He worked his way up, placing tiny kisses along the line of her vein until it disappeared from view. Then he swirled his tongue over the bend of her arm.

She stared down at him, her gaze open and curious. He knew then she would let him bite her, and he wanted to, but not yet. There was more he wanted to do, more he wanted to share.

He moved back against her, crushing her body with his, crushing her mouth with his. His fangs were extended; they dragged over her lower lip.

A bead of her blood dripped into his mouth, giving him a taste, a promise he could hardly resist.

Finally, her hands moved too. Her fingers wove into his hair, pressed his mouth closer to hers until blood coated his tongue, made it hard for him to concentrate, to keep himself from plunging his fangs into her throat.

But this wolf wasn't just a midnight snack. Wasn't a meal to enjoy and leave. This wolf was special, this time they shared special. He couldn't waste it, couldn't risk that she'd misread his actions as being something so base as just filling his need for blood.

He pulled his mouth back so his fangs no longer pierced her lip.

She murmured an objection and his body tightened.

She was under no thrall. She could walk away at will, but it seemed she wanted to be here…with him, vampire though he be.

He cupped her face with his hand and kissed the corner of her lips. Her fingers trailed down his chest, slow, unsure as if she too were worried that he would misread her actions.

But he wanted her touch, wanted her. He placed his hand against the small of her back and pulled her pelvis against his, let her feel the desire there, let her know he wanted her in every way.

Her hand moved lower. She pulled his shirt from his pants and ran her fingers under the material, across his bare skin. Her fingers dipped lower, beneath his waistband, brushing sensitive skin.

A hiss escaped his lips; he could feel his eyes changing, the pupils disappearing.

The taste of her, her scent and now her touch… it was too much. The vampire in him wanted more, wanted everything now.

Chapter 16

CeCe brushed her fingers over the skin beneath Marc's waistband, heard him hiss. She could feel his sex through their clothing, hard, pressing against her, making her insides tighten and her breath come in pants.

He'd bitten her earlier, not on purpose and not deeply, but enough that her lip still bled. She licked the blood from her lip, wondered at how the taste didn't repel her, how the reminder that he was a vampire didn't fill her with revulsion.

It should; she'd been raised to think of vampires as monsters…murderers. One had killed her mother.

No one, she guessed, not her father, not the pack… not Karl…would understand what she was doing with Marc and why.

Karl…the thought of him should have filled her

with guilt, but she couldn't feel shame, not for being with Marc. The experience, the emotion, was too freeing, too uplifting.

Everything she was doing was wrong, by every standard she had been raised to uphold, and she didn't care…didn't give one tinker's damn…at least not right now.

Afraid that thinking too much, going too slow, might change that, she slid her hands up Marc's chest and began popping buttons through holes. His chest was bare under the dress shirt. His skin was pale and cool as she had come to expect. She brushed her cheek against him, then pressed kisses against his chest.

His fingers wove through her hair and trailed down her back, as though he was memorizing each bump of her spine. She arched her back like a cat and dug her fingers into his sides.

He responded by pulling her more tightly against him, cupping her butt, kneading.

She was hot, flushed, and his skin was so cool. She needed to feel it against hers. She pulled her shirt over her head, then unsnapped her bra and dropped it onto the floor.

Nudity was nothing for a werewolf. They shifted from wolf to human and back again, at times not bothering with getting dressed in between.

So nudity had never been sexual for CeCe, but standing before Marc she suddenly felt shy. He wasn't a wolf, hadn't seen her a thousand times walking in front of the fire or into the woods.

The bathroom was warm. She hadn't noticed it before. She placed her palm on Marc's chest. His heart beat slowly but steadily, while hers seemed to race, threatened to jump out of her chest.

Again she ticked off their differences, and again it didn't matter. If anything, the list made him all the more appealing.

"You're a creature of magic, CeCe. You deserve to be free." He whispered the words against her neck. A tingle moved down her spine. Her core tightened.

The tips of her breasts brushed against his chest… hot against cold. She shivered, and desire like she had never felt before wrapped around her, squeezing until she thought she would yelp from the pure uncontrolled pleasure pouring through her.

His fingers moved to her pants. She wiggled her hips, desperate to be free of the confinement. She reached for the waist of his pants too, pushed them down until her fingers found his firm buttocks.

Every inch of him was muscle. Slim, but strong. A secret strength the werewolves wouldn't guess at, and that CeCe would never reveal to them.

Marc and his strengths were her secret. Not something she would share with anyone.

"Magic," he murmured again.

"All shifters are," she whispered. It was true. Some blamed a virus, but a virus alone couldn't explain changing from wolf to human. Magic was in all of them. It had to be.

"Not like you." He ran his hand down her back and over her buttocks, lifted her up so her thighs parted and his sex bumped against hers.

She tensed again, her body calling for him to enter her.

"There's nothing about you that isn't magic," he continued.

Her breaths came quick, barely controlled. She dug her nails into his back, scratched him. "You too. Your thrall...you have magic, can use magic. I can't do that."

"No." He shook his head and pressed a tiny kiss against her neck. "Vampires have no magic. Vampires have only a curse."

Then he lifted her off the ground, braced her back against the wall and drove his erection deep inside her. She gasped and clawed at his shoulders. Not to be free, but to help him, to intensify the delicious wild sensation of his cool hard erection moving inside her.

He leaned forward, his fangs brushing her neck. She tilted her neck, giving him access, knowing what was coming and wanting him to know she agreed.

His fangs teased at her skin, their touch light like fingernails, trailing up and down.

His hand moved to her breast. His thumb circled one nipple.

With so many sensations happening all at once, CeCe couldn't keep track of the tiny explosions of pleasure inside her body, like an electrical charge traveling from one spot to the other, lighting some new previously unknown frisson of excitement before moving on to another.

Then his fangs sank into her skin and everything froze for one crazy pleasure-soaked moment, before racing up again, so fast, so intense, CeCe could barely process the feelings washing over her.

Her sex tightened around his. Her body moved up and down...the wall scraping her back, her breasts brushing his chest. His lips covered the spot on her neck where he slowly sucked blood from her vein.

Every touch, breath, color and smell intensified

until the world was awash with them all, one no longer identifiable from the other…all of them coming together in one big sensation that was just Marc.

She whispered his name and clawed at his back again. Her body tightened more and he drove harder and faster inside her. Then everything fell away, like bits of a curtain dropping, and she found herself back in the bathroom, her legs wrapped around Marc's waist, her back against the tile wall, and her heart beating as if it, like she, were about to explode.

"Magic," she whispered to him. "You are magic." He had to be; there was no other explanation.

Marc slowly, reluctantly pulled his fangs from CeCe's neck and swiped his tongue over the twin wounds he had left there.

"When will the wolves be back?" He'd seen them leave, didn't know if it was a short trip or if they'd left for good—although he doubted the latter.

He didn't want to think of them now, didn't want to remind CeCe of them either, but he needed to know, needed to warn her about the place on her neck.

She wouldn't want her pack to see it. A truth that made him sad, sick, and reminded him how alone he was and would always be. CeCe would walk out of this bathroom away from him and what they had shared and back into her life with the pack…and its alpha.

As he feared, awareness flashed through her previously sleepy eyes. She clapped her hand to her neck. "I don't know when I'll see them."

"Werewolves heal fast, right? You should be fine." She unwrapped her legs from his waist. Cool air replaced her warmth. He pressed his lips together and tried not to care.

Her feet touched the ground and he turned away. He couldn't watch her pull on her clothes, witness her eagerness to cover herself, to put what they had shared behind them.

"I…" With his back turned, he couldn't see what she was doing.

"We need to go to the woods…."

"Ah, yes. The treasure." They couldn't be forgetting the treasure. Once they had it, she could leave. His jaw tensed. They'd made love, but nothing had changed. Nothing could change.

Her hand touched his shoulder.

Realizing he was still undressed, he bent and pulled on his clothes.

He couldn't stand to feel her warmth now, knowing how fleeting it would be. He'd been stupid to allow himself this hour of weakness. It would just make her leaving later all that much harder.

"We can go now. I just need…" What? A moment to forget her touch? Her taste? To remind himself that she didn't belong to him or in his world?

The sun was high in the sky, a time of day he avoided, but there was no time to waste. Every minute he spent with her would make it that much harder to walk away.

Confused and embarrassed, CeCe hurried down the hall and past the table where she and Marc had sat. The waitress, who had stood a few feet away as CeCe kissed Marc, was kissed by Marc, glanced at her as if surprised, then moved out of her way.

Feeling cold, then hot, CeCe pushed open the door and stepped outside. The streets of Cave Vista were empty. Seeing them made CeCe feel empty too. Empty and alone.

She was a werewolf and Marc was a vampire. He was right to be distant. She had, selfishly, put him at risk. The pack would go insane if they learned of what she had done. Karl would…her hand rose to the chain Karl had given her, but touched nothing but cloth. No lump under her clothing, no heavy weight around her neck.

The chain was missing.

Marc had removed it. He'd slipped it up and over her head, then dropped it on the ground.

And she'd let him.

Karl would never understand that. The pack would never understand that. How could she expect them to? It was wrong. What she had done was wrong.

And if the alpha found it missing, if Marc was found with it— She turned and rushed back through the diner. She pushed past the waitress and jumped in front of a man in overalls as his hand reached out to push open the bathroom door.

"Excuse me," she muttered, wishing she had a vampire's skill of hiding in plain sight.

The man blinked but didn't comment and she hurried past him, into the bathroom.

The window was open and the small room was empty—no Marc and no chain.

She'd lost it, and it appeared she had also lost Marc.

Marc sat in his pitch-dark motel room, waiting for the ache in his heart to heal.

He'd let himself get close, let himself taste a dream.

He knew better, and now he was paying the price.

He gripped the alpha's chain in his fist, wished he could squeeze the metal to bits, wished that would change what it symbolized.

He would have to return it to CeCe, he knew that. He should have gone after her when he found it lying on the floor after she left, but he couldn't…couldn't hand her another man's promise, another man's claim.

By taking it, though, he had endangered her.

Her bites might heal, she might wash his scent from her body, but the alpha wouldn't miss the fact that his chain no longer hung from her neck.

Marc should take it to her now, brave the sun and the throbbing pain in his head it created.

He picked up the chain and flung it across the room. It smashed into a lamp. The light's pottery base exploded, crockery and chain crashing to the floor.

With a growl, Marc jerked his laptop from under the bed, opened his internet calling service and clicked on the Fringe account.

No response.

He slammed the laptop's lid shut and let the dark engulf him again. CeCe would be looking for him, wondering why he hadn't followed her, wondering why he wasn't going with her to find the treasure.

He didn't care about the treasure. Didn't care about anything but forgetting.

He would take CeCe's chain back to her, and look for the treasure, but not now, not yet.

When night fell, he'd be stronger, ready to pretend

he didn't care, that the chain and what it symbolized meant nothing....

Maybe by then he'd even believe it.

Marc awoke to shuffling footsteps in his room. Someone...a number of someones, he corrected... stealing through the dark room, trying to find him, he guessed, without flipping on a light.

Unfortunately for them, he had only been resting, not lost in a vampire's dead sleep. He lay still, keeping his eyes closed until he could pinpoint where the would-be slayers were, how many and what species.

Species hit him first—werewolf, and not CeCe. No, this scent lacked the special spice.

Besides, these were males. The alpha and his thugs, Marc guessed.

Unsure of how well the wolves could see in the dark, he kept his eyes closed and relied on his vampire hunger to assure him of the number. Their heartbeats called out to him...one, two...three in all. One missing.

The alpha, Marc had to guess.

Did he wait outside? Or was he with CeCe? Had he noticed the missing chain, Marc's scent on her? Was she being held? Punished? Worse?

Anger and fear for the female werewolf swelled inside Marc. His fangs lengthened and his eyes flew open.

Dark was as clear to him as bright light was to a human; he spotted the intruders immediately.

The alpha was with them and he and two of his minions were almost on top of Marc.

He surged to a sit, then bounced and rebounded onto his feet.

"Grab him," the alpha yelled.

Marc kicked the closest wolf in the head, then spun and jumped, clearing the others as they bent forward thinking the vampire was still lying on the mattress waiting patiently for their attack. He landed on the floor behind them.

"Uncover the windows." The alpha again, this time his voice cold and determined.

Wood popped as one of the wolves pried at the boards Marc had nailed over the large front window.

Marc laughed and searched for the wolf who had given the order. The light wouldn't hurt Marc, but the alpha didn't know that. He'd given his command with every intention of watching Marc disintegrate into ash in front of him.

But Marc was happy he had. Happy because it gave Marc permission to do what he'd been wanting to do since the alpha had backhanded CeCe in front of him.

Fangs extended, he rushed the wolf. He shoved the other male back against the wall, but the alpha was ready. His hands wrapped around Marc's throat, holding the vampire back, keeping his fangs from making contact with the werewolf's throat.

Not caring how tightly the wolf held his neck or how long, Marc took a step backward, then plunged forward again, smashing the werewolf into the wall a second time.

The alpha's head crunched into the concrete-block wall. He growled, and his thumbs dug into Marc's throat.

"Try again, alpha. I don't need air," he muttered.

"How about light? How do you feel about that?" One of the wolves working on the window jerked a board free. It clattered onto the floor and light streamed into the room.

All of the wolves froze, waited, and Marc used the moment to his advantage. He surged forward again. His fangs scraped across the alpha's neck, tearing his skin and leaving twin trails of blood streaming down his neck.

The alpha cursed and swung, struck Marc in the temple. Crazed with the need for revenge and fed by the scent of the wolf's blood, Marc barely felt the blow. He hissed and leaped.

A board smashed into his chest, another wolf swinging at him, like a baseball all-star going for the fence.

Marc staggered backward and hissed. Then he charged again. All three wolves faced him now. He knew he didn't have a chance, knew they would capture him, hold him and most likely drive a stake through his chest. His only goal was to take one or more of them out too.

And his sights were set on the alpha.

The werewolf saw him coming. He bent at the waist and rushed forward, catching Marc in the middle. The vampire flew up and over the other male's back, tumbled onto the floor, and just as quickly somersaulted onto his feet.

He spun again. The light from the window caught him in the eye, blinding him. A board zipped past his face…a swing, but a miss.

Marc threw out his hand, grabbed the strip of wood and jerked it from the werewolf's hand, then he flung it into the far corner of the room, onto the broken lamp and the alpha's chain.

The alpha's fist smashed into his temple, knocking

Marc sideways. He grabbed the closest werewolf by the arm and twisted his body, so Marc's back was to the werewolf's chest and his fangs were descending toward his wrist.

"Now," the alpha yelled.

Used to such games, Marc didn't look up. He stayed focused on the prey he had in hand. Something cold and heavy wrapped around his throat. A chain, iron, and based on its stench, coated with garlic.

Marc's eyes watered; bile rose in his throat. Trying to ignore the smell of garlic, he pushed against the binding. His skin burned where the herb touched him. Not a flaming burn, but an annoyance.

An annoyance he could ignore, but the werewolves were ready now and working together. As he pushed against the pull of the chain, tried to reposition himself to take down the werewolf whose arm he still held, another length of chain fell past his face. A hand grabbed his hair and his throat was pulled back. He hissed…a mistake and exactly what the werewolves had wanted.

The chain tightened against his open mouth. The wolf pulled on it, wedged the metal links between his jaws. He jerked his head side to side, but couldn't dislodge the mass.

The werewolves had him muzzled, made it impossible for him to bite, impossible for him to do anything

Within seconds, he was pulled onto his back and more chains were wrapped around his arms and legs. Shackled head to toe in garlic-drenched iron chains, he could do nothing but lie there and await his fate.

Chapter 17

The alpha stepped over Marc, stood with one foot on each side of the vampire's body.

"What do you know of this, vampire?" He pulled a cloth-wrapped object from his pocket.

Unable to do anything else, Marc waited.

"This is how you killed Russell." The alpha unrolled the cloth, let the object inside fall onto Marc's chest. Silver flashed in the sunlight that now leaked into the room, and metal clinked against metal.

Marc didn't look down. He didn't have to; the weight told him the object was metal. The smell told him it was covered in the werewolf Russell's blood.

Russell's murder weapon, and Marc guessed the legendary stake the werewolves' feared.

The iron chain pressed against his tongue. The bitter taste of metal and garlic made him gag. But most importantly the chain kept him from speaking…from defending himself in any way. Not that anything he said would have changed the alpha's plans, whatever they were.

There was desperation in the werewolf's eyes.

He needed Marc to be guilty.

To save face with the pack? To believe in his own right to be leader?

Whatever the reason, Marc had no doubt that the alpha wasn't here searching for the truth.

The alpha pulled on a leather glove and crouched beside him. He picked up the stake and stood it on its end, so the pointed tip was balanced over Marc's heart. Still Marc didn't look, not at the stake or the werewolf. Unwilling to give the wolf the satisfaction of his anger, he stared at the ceiling with bored insolence.

"This stake isn't new. It's been around since before the war. Some say it caused the war. Did you know that, vampire? The vampires wanted it for a long time. Then they stole it and hid it away."

The alpha looked up, at one of the other wolves. "The mallet." He held out his hand and an ancient wooden mallet appeared in his grip.

Still wearing the glove, the alpha edged the tip of the stake inside Marc's shirt, onto his bare skin. The metal seemed to sizzle.

The werewolf cocked a brow. "Do you hear that? Like Pop Rocks. It's the magic inside the stake, asking to be fed. Do you know what it likes to eat, vampire?"

He didn't wait for Marc's reply. He jerked his head and addressed one of his wolves. "The recorder."

One of the males pulled a small digital recorder from his pocket. He sat it on the floor next to Marc's head.

"Admit your guilt, vampire, and I won't have to feed the stake."

Marc snarled. It came out muffled and weak. He bit down on the chain, thinking of what he would do to the alpha if released. He could feel his eyes narrowing and his body hardening, could feel the most lost part of his soul rising up.

He had never hungered for blood as he did right then…werewolf blood.

The door to the room slammed open. Light streamed into the space, hitting Marc in the face.

He blinked, the light, the pain of it, knocking him out of his state like a bucket of water in the face.

He turned his head to see what new hell had joined them.

Framed in the doorway, backlit like an angel in some church window, was CeCe.

The door smashed into the wall. It had been slightly ajar, alerting CeCe that something was amiss. She had charged in without thinking, but now as the musky smell of anger fed by testosterone rolled over her, she paused.

The room was cast in shadows. Someone had removed a few of the boards that had covered the window. They lay splintered on the floor.

Her gaze dashed past them, searched for Marc. She found him too soon, not dead, not impaled by some vampire hunter, but in a situation almost as bad.

He lay on the floor wrapped head to toe in chains.

The light streaming through the open door landed on his face. His eyes were nothing but slits and his brows bulged. He looked like the monster that had attacked her in the alley, but he wasn't.

He was Marc.

Karl crouched beside him with the silver stake CeCe had pulled from Russell's chest poised, ready to thrust into Marc's.

Her heart lurched.

"Stop." She stepped into the room, crunching one of the boards under her foot and shutting the door enough to block some of the sun streaming into the room.

She'd come to find Marc, to talk about what had happened and to, hopefully, retrieve Karl's chain. She hadn't decided what she was going to do with the chain when she found it, but she couldn't risk Marc being found with it.

But apparently he had.

The wolves were here…attacking Marc… Her gaze shifted to the weapon in Karl's hand…the stake.

It had been hidden in her room, inside her mattress. How did Karl get it?

Marc's attention was on her, his eyes distant and unreadable.

She shifted her gaze to Karl. What she saw in his eyes caused the hairs on the back of her neck to raise. He wasn't bluffing. He held the stake and he meant to use it.

She froze, held as still as a rabbit hiding in the snow. One twitch and the predator would be on her. Her only choice was to stay calm, pretend calm.

"I thought you were gone," she said.

"We left the motel for a while." Karl ran his thumb over the mallet's handle, caressed it.

"I…" The stake glinted at her…winked…as if speaking to her, guiding her. Her heart thumped. "I went to my room and saw the stake was gone. I thought perhaps the vampire had taken it. It appears I was right. How did you find out?" She knew Marc hadn't taken the stake, knew Karl had for some reason broken into her room while she was gone and taken it instead, but now was not the time to challenge him. Better to feign ignorance.

"Did you? When was this?" Karl's thumb moved back and forth, rhythmic, lulling…terrifying.

"Just now." Ten minutes ago. It was the time it had taken her to walk from her hotel to Marc's. She had spent some time before that asking around the diner, searching for any sign someone other than Marc had taken Karl's chain. Left with no other option, she'd gone back to her room, showered and built up her courage to face the vampire again.

"And where were you before?"

It was a simple question, but like the rabbit, CeCe smelled a trap. She glanced around, noticed one of Karl's three companions was missing. "Where's Neil?" she asked.

Karl's lips pressed into a thin pale line. A vein throbbed at his neck. He looked down at Marc. "Perhaps we should ask the vampire."

"The—?" Her attention shot around the room. The wolves, she realized, were all too still, too quiet. Something had happened. "Where's Neil?" she repeated.

Karl shifted his grip on the mallet, so his fingers wrapped around its head. "He's in the truck."

The truck. A bit of air left her lungs. Not what she had thought.

Karl moved the stake from Marc's chest to his neck, wedged it against his throat. "Dead, drained, by a vampire."

A thick, dark line of Marc's blood swelled onto the silver.

CeCe stared at it and swallowed. "When? When did you see him last?"

Intent on pressing the stake harder against Marc's throat, the alpha didn't answer.

"When did you see Neil last?" she repeated. Her voice was harsh, rough with emotion.

Karl looked up at her, his brows lowered. The other wolves moved but with no real purpose, just a physical expression of the alpha's annoyance and their awareness of it.

But CeCe didn't back down. She waited.

Finally, Karl flicked a hand toward one of the others—Robert, one of the wolves who predated CeCe's acceptance into the pack. The golden-haired wolf glanced at his watch. "Been four hours now since we saw him alive, an hour and a half since we found him dead."

"Marc didn't do it."

He couldn't have. He'd been with her during that time.

"Marc?" The stake shifted again, lifted as Karl rolled back onto his heels to stare at CeCe. "You know the vampire's name? Are you close?"

"No. Of course not." She didn't hesitate in her answer. She couldn't afford to. Marc couldn't afford for her to.

Karl narrowed his eyes to study her. "Where's my chain, CeCe?"

Even knowing that the chain was missing, she moved her hand to her chest. Her mind whirred. Marc had it, she knew that now, had really known it all along, which meant odds were good the wolves would discover it eventually.

She hung her head. "I lied. I didn't come here looking for the stake. I came looking for the chain. I took it off while I showered. When I came out, it was missing, but I recognized the scent in my room."

"The vampire?"

She nodded.

"When was this?"

She bit the inside of her cheek. "Ten minutes ago. It's just the chain I noticed was missing, not the stake."

"So, you believe he's a thief, but not a murderer. Interesting." Karl moved the stake up and down, causing it to bob over Marc's neck like a wobbly guillotine.

"But I'm right, aren't I? He is a thief—he had the stake." A push to see if Karl would admit he had taken it from her room. She wondered what else he and the others had been doing since leaving her.

"It's here."

Not an answer, not to the question she had asked. A new anxiety clawed at CeCe.

Marc lay stiff and unmoving, incapable of doing anything else, but she felt energy emanating from him, knew he wanted to say something, tell her something.

"And my chain?" She walked farther into the room, hoping it would distract Karl from what he was doing, or was about to do.

The other wolves blocked her. She walked up to

them with confidence, as if she had every expectation that they would step out of her path.

Karl rose. Another knot of tension loosened, allowed her to breathe a bit more freely.

"Have you looked around? Searched for clues?" she asked.

"Clues? We don't need clues. We have a werewolf drained of blood, two holes in his neck, and we have a vampire. That, plus the confession the vampire was about to give us is all we need."

"Confession?" She noticed a box then, the size of an MP3 player, lying on the floor next to Marc's head.

Karl was being thorough, covering his bases to satisfy both the pack and any vampires who questioned his decision to kill Marc.

"He hasn't given it to you yet, and he won't." She knew Marc would never admit to doing something he hadn't done, not even to save his own life.

"You don't know that." Karl turned the stake so it shone in the light. Fresh blood stained the tip.

"He won't."

"Then there's no reason to wait." Karl moved back toward Marc.

CeCe grabbed him by the arm. "What's wrong with you? You aren't thinking."

He turned on her. "There's nothing wrong with me. I'm not the one defending a vampire."

"So, you kill him with no evidence, then what? What about the others? Do you expect them to take your word of his guilt?"

"I'm the alpha." His attention shot to the other wolves. All lifted their chins, agreeing.

"Not the pack." She knew the pack would follow

him. He was all they had; the string that held them together.

"The other vampires," she added.

"They don't need to know. He disappears. I'm sure vampires have disappeared before. No one will know. No one will care."

No one will care. It wasn't true. CeCe would care, surely someone else would too. The words cut her; she didn't look at Marc to see if they hurt him too.

Her gaze dropped to the stake in Karl's hand. The incised figure eight was toward her.

"Are you so sure?" she asked.

"Vampires aren't—"

She shook her head, cutting off Karl's lecture. She pointed to the symbol. "When I first saw this I thought it meant vampire. Now I know it does. Look at his arm." She pointed at Marc.

The wolves turned, but none moved to touch the vampire. "He's chained," Karl replied, as if that nullified her claim.

Frustrated, she stepped closer. "Then trust me. He has that mark, without the break." She pointed to the stake. "On his arm. I don't know what it means, but it means something. It means he's important to someone."

Her. Marc was important to her.

Anger flashed in Karl's eyes. "You don't know that." But she could see her claim had struck. The alpha's life was protecting the pack. If she was right and the vampires did come forward to enact revenge for Marc's death, he'd be putting each and every wolf at risk.

Karl stared at her for a second, his expression unreadable, then he jerked his head toward Marc. The other wolves trotted to the vampire and pried the chains apart. Then with Karl standing over them, they worked his sleeve up, far enough that the lower half of Marc's tattoo was fully visible.

Karl nodded, giving them permission to step back, and returned his attention to CeCe. "He has a tattoo. The same as on the stake. It doesn't mean the vampires have a connection among them. It doesn't mean this one matters."

But he did. More than CeCe had imagined anyone could. "He's part of something. I don't know what, but he is." She put as much certainty into the words as she could.

"It's why he's here," she muttered, working things out for herself, but aloud.

"Why?"

Lost in her own thoughts, CeCe looked up. "He was sent here, like me. Why else would he have come? Which means the vampires have to have some kind organization, some kind of leadership."

"Meaningless," Karl replied. "He saw something on the news, like we did, jumped at the chance to steal our treasure. Vampires are like that."

She frowned, frustrated. "Two vampires? He wasn't the only one here. And now…with Neil…" She looked up. "There are more. Who knows how many?"

"Now you want me to free this one because others are here too? That's an argument to eliminate what we can." His gaze went back to Marc.

She shook her head. "Not until we know what is going on—how many vampires are here, what they know, how this vampire—" she avoided using Marc's name "—fits into all of it. Killing him could restart the war. You know that. You don't want that."

"You still sound awfully sure." Karl's gaze was assessing.

She didn't waver. "I am." Karl was tough and at times, yes, abusive, but he loved his pack. She couldn't imagine him doing anything that would put them at risk—to do so would tear him up inside.

"So, you're suggesting what? We let him go? Undo his chains, dust him off and send him on his way?"

"No." She knew the wolves would never agree to that. "We—"

A wolf howl sounded from Karl's pocket. With a frown, he pulled his phone free. The conversation was one-sided and brief.

"How many?"

"Are you sure?" Karl walked to where Marc lay and stared down at him. He nudged the vampire in the side. Marc's upper lip rose. His eyes glowed with hatred.

CeCe could feel it, knew the other wolves could too. She didn't know what she expected from Marc. He had been chained and prodded with a stake. But the snarl felt all encompassing, delivered to every wolf in the room.

She might trust Marc, might even manage to save him, but it didn't mean he would trust her in return, not after hearing her conversation with the alpha.

"Ten minutes." Karl shoved his phone in his pocket and motioned to the others. Without questioning, they moved toward the door. After they had exited, he walked back to where she stood unsure and anxious. "Prove I should trust you. Stay here. Watch him. I'll call you if I need you to do anything." He dropped the stake onto the bed and held out the glove he'd been wearing. When she didn't take it, he flapped the leather.

She let him drop it onto her palm, curled her fingers around it, felt it bunch in her palm. "What is happening?" And what might he need her to do? She was afraid to ask, afraid to hear the answer.

"Nothing. I'll call you." His expression told her not to ask questions.

Knowing she'd pushed him too far already, she bit back her response.

He turned as if to leave, then looked back. "What you were looking for, what you came here to retrieve, is over there."

She glanced to the side and saw Karl's chain lying in a pile in the corner of the room. It was surrounded by broken pottery, what had obviously once been a lamp.

She made her way through the debris, pottery crunching under her feet. Then she did as she knew was expected—she picked up the chain.

It was heavy and warm, although the room wasn't. She moved her hands up and down as if testing its weight against her palms, then she turned, her hands raising to slip it over her head, but Karl had already left. The door to the room was closed, and she was alone...with Marc.

She lowered her arms, let the chain swing from one hand. Then she threw it onto the bed. It landed next to the stake.

Shaking inside, she walked around the mattress and stared down at Marc. His eyes met hers. She couldn't see what he was thinking, couldn't even guess.

Prove I should trust you. Karl's words burned through her mind.

Prove it by leaving Marc as he was, by making sure he didn't escape, that he was still here when the pack returned, waiting for their justice.

"He'll kill you," she murmured. The words were soft, but she knew Marc had heard.

He closed his eyes as if he didn't care.

But he had to. He had to want to live.

Almost as much as CeCe wanted him to, but she wanted the pack, too. And saving Marc would cost her that, would cost her the only thing any werewolf really valued, the only thing that kept them sane.

Physically, she could save Marc, but could she really? Could she give up everything she was and ever planned on being?

To save a vampire?

The thought was beyond ludicrous.

Chapter 18

The alpha and his minions had been gone ten minutes. CeCe had done little besides stare at Marc since. His eyes closed, he waited for her to decide her next move.

She stepped closer. She knelt and ran her hands over his body, over the chains. He opened his eyes; she was watching him.

"The pack is my world," she murmured…apologized.

She'd decided, then. He kept his eyes closed.

"Without them, I'm nothing."

He opened his eyes again. The statement was absurd. He couldn't believe she believed it, but he could see by the stress pulling at her face that she did. He rolled his eyes upward and stared at the ceiling.

He was in no position to play counselor.

Her fingers slid under the chains across his chest.

He glanced down, not knowing what to expect. She found the lock the werewolves had used to secure the chain and jiggled it. When it didn't give, she changed tactics and tugged on the chain.

The metal links pulled tight across his back and dug into his shoulder blades. Her lips formed a line and she pulled harder, managed to pull the loops an inch, maybe three, away from his body.

"Hold still."

She cursed and gripped the chain tighter. Her knuckles white, she jerked again. After a second, she rolled back onto her heels.

"I can't get it loose enough. I thought with slack I could get it over your head." She was mumbling, more to herself than him. Aware of that, he didn't try to reply. Not that his reply would have been understood. Not with the chain still gagging his mouth.

"There must be something we can do. Try to get on your knees." She rolled him onto his stomach. He wormed his way to his knees. The process was awkward and uncomfortable, and under other circumstances, when his life wasn't at risk, would have been embarrassing.

"Now the bed." She grabbed the chain from behind and used it as a handle to help him stand. Soon, he was facedown on the bed. He rolled over and she pulled him to his feet.

Upright, but still draped in chain. He couldn't fight; he couldn't run. The entire exercise felt worthless.

He growled.

She ran her fingers through her hair and scanned the room. Her gaze stopped on the bed, on the stake.

She slipped on the leather glove the alpha had worn

when handling the stake and picked up the weapon. Then she kneeled at his feet and looked up. "Don't move."

She positioned the stake, then struck the head with the mallet. With the first hit, he felt the chain loosen. With the third the iron gave and the garlic-laced restraints clattered to the ground.

He spit out the strand that had been shoved into his mouth.

CeCe rose to stand beside him, the stake in hand. The weapon that had almost been the instrument of his death was instead the instrument of his release.

He held out his hand to take it.

"What now?" she asked.

He rolled the stake so the broken vampire symbol was on the top and ran his thumb over it. A chill raced through him, a cloying chill, the kind you couldn't shake off. No, he decided, fighting off the need to drop the thing, the feeling was worse than a chill…it was empty and hollow…a lack of feeling, but then the feeling shifted. Elation shot through him.

It was death and power. He was strong…invincible. He wanted to prove it, wanted to kill…

He looked up, at CeCe.

Her eyes widened. She slapped his hand…sent the stake sailing across the room.

Marc felt as if he'd been sucker punched. He gasped and bent at the waist.

"What?" CeCe placed her gloved hand on his back. "What happened?" Her voice was edged with panic.

She'd seen…

"It was designed to destroy us." The words were difficult to get out. He wanted to lunge across the room and grab the stake, wanted to touch it, to own it, to master it. But the feeling wasn't normal, wasn't right.

He couldn't look at CeCe, not yet. For a moment, he had wanted to kill her, destroy her, see her blood coating the stake. He couldn't face her yet; couldn't stand to realize that the thoughts had gone through his mind.

"The vampires?" she asked.

"No." He shook his head. "All of us, the werewolves and the vampires."

"But it saved you."

"You saved me. The stake wanted to use me." He closed his eyes and stood. He felt shaky and drained… dirty.

"You haven't touched it, have you? With your bare hand?"

She shook her head. "It was in Russell's chest when I found him. I pulled it out, but with a cloth."

"Don't." It was all he could say, all he could think.

They stared at the stake as if a viper had just entered the room.

Finally, CeCe spoke. "What do we do with it?"

They couldn't leave it behind, couldn't risk another vampire or werewolf finding it.

"It needs to be destroyed." He pulled his gaze away from the glistening silver. He still longed to touch it. He curled his fingers into a fist. He understood now why the werewolves feared it.

"The stake pushed someone to kill Russell, didn't it?" CeCe asked.

"Yes." After holding the thing, feeling the swell of need it created, the need to kill, Marc understood what had driven the killer—far better than he liked. "What we don't know is where it came from."

"Did Russell or the killer bring it?" CeCe added.

"And why was it left behind? If you hadn't knocked it from my hand, I don't know if I could have let it go." He clinched his jaw.

She ran her fingers down his arm, light and gentle. "I don't believe that."

"You don't believe I would have killed you?"

"No."

Trust, pure and clear, shone from her eyes.

Marc relaxed. He believed it too…but still the desire had been strong, nearly impossible to fight. If he hadn't known CeCe…loved CeCe.

He faced the word. He loved her.

"We have a…connection. If we didn't…" He glanced at the stake.

"You'd have killed me." Flat truth. It didn't seem to bother her, not as it bothered Marc. "You've said whoever killed Russell knew him."

"I still think they did. They just didn't—" he stopped himself from saying the word "—care enough to overcome the stake."

"But maybe that's why it was left behind. Maybe the killer cared enough to run when they realized what they had done."

"Maybe." It made sense. Because while a part of Marc wanted to hold the stake again, a bigger part of him was repulsed by it and what it had tried to make him do.

They took the stake with them when they left. Not wanting to touch it, Marc had watched as CeCe wrapped it in a cloth and tucked it into a bag that she slung over her shoulder.

While she was doing that, he had grabbed his laptop. He had no time to check in with the Fringe now, but as soon as he could establish an internet connection he would. He needed to find out what was going on, who had sent the vampire he'd left on that rooftop and why.

He was afraid, however, he already knew. Russell's killer knew the power of the stake, but who else did? Who else might be out there hunting it? And how far would they go to get it?

Marc didn't bother locking the door behind them when they left the motel. There was nothing of value inside, and odds were good that he wouldn't be coming back.

CeCe had slung the bag containing the stake over her shoulder. She ran her hand up and down the cord. "I have a car at my hotel. You can use it."

"Me?"

"It's old and not worth much, but it should get you away from here. I'll tell Karl…something."

It was dark now, had been for a half an hour. As was typical of Cave Vista after dark, the street was quiet. Maybe a hundred yards away, a dog sniffed around a car, but there was no other sign of life.

She stepped off the curb and headed toward an abandoned side street.

Marc grabbed her by the arm and spun her around. "I'm not leaving. Not until we figure out how to destroy that." He pointed to the bag. And he wasn't leaving without CeCe.

She shook her head. "I found it—I brought it back here. I'll figure out how to get rid of it. You need to leave. If Karl discovers you've escaped—"

"Your alpha will have to catch me to kill me. Besides, this is what I do." He shoved his sleeve up so his tattoo was fully visible. "You want to know what this is?"

CeCe's lips parted.

"I'm a regulator, part of a group of regulators. If my guess is right, that vampire you killed isn't alone. There will be more, all searching for that." Again he looked at the bag. "I'm not leaving until it's destroyed or put far out of any werewolf's or vampire's reach for good." He understood now the drive of the vampire Van Bom had told him about, the vampire who had taken the stake and disappeared. Perhaps he had been the hero of the story, not the villain as Van Bom believed.

"But Karl, the pack…they will…"

"This isn't a werewolf problem." Not solely.

He lifted his laptop case. "I need to check in, and do some research, see if I can find anything that tells us how we might destroy that thing. There's a coffee shop down there." He gestured to a building not far from where he'd seen the dog. "They have Wi-Fi. With any luck it's an open connection and strong enough I can tap in from the alley. I'll see what I can learn, then we can decide what to do next."

He left CeCe standing in the street, knowing that if he did make contact with the Fringe and a contingent was dispatched to Cave Vista, he would have to send her back to her pack.

There wasn't a single member of the Fringe who would understand, tolerate even, what he and CeCe had between them. Sending her to her pack would be his only choice.

* * *

As Marc walked off, CeCe wandered farther down the street. Marc's motel was in a sparsely populated part of the town, not that any part of Cave Vista was booming.

She stared into the window of what had once been a souvenir shop, but now seemed to be a storage area for some kind of junk store. Or maybe it was a junk store. It was hard to tell.

She pressed her hand against the glass and leaned closer, trying to decide for no good reason what the business actually was.

From above her there was a noise, a rock or nut skittering across the flat asphalt roof.

The junk shop forgotten, she stepped backward, out into the street.

Standing on the roof, silhouetted against the moon, was a man. He raised his arms and moved to the edge. Then he smiled. Silver fangs shone from his white face.

A vampire.

And based on his choice of dental work, not one friendly with werewolves.

Her wolf growled and moved forward, but CeCe kept her at bay. The opportunity to talk would be lost with a shift, and this vampire might know something she and Marc could use. She had killed one vampire in human form; she had to believe she could kill another.

The vampire walked to the edge of the roof and kept walking. Without pausing his steps, he dropped down in front of her like a spider on a strand of web, slow and controlled, his arms extended and a fang-revealing smile on his face. "Where's the stake, wolf?

We checked your room, checked the other wolves we've found and left…but we haven't checked you. Not yet."

Other wolves. Karl. Robert and Logan. Were they safe? Dead, drained, like Russell and Neil?

She stepped to the side and let the bag that held the stake slip down her arm, until the cords were in her hand. "I wouldn't think vampires would be fond of stakes," she replied.

He laughed. "No, but they can be useful, and I've come for the one you have."

"Why?" And how had he known about it? Even Marc hadn't known she had it, not until a few minutes earlier.

She let the bag sway as she spoke, tested its weight and estimated her aim. She needed to be closer, but if she moved, the vampire would attack. She had to be certain she was ready, and she had to get as much information as she could first.

The vampire prowled to the side, circling her like a lion waiting to pounce. "Is that it? There in the bag? Give it to me and perhaps I'll let you live. Perhaps I won't drain you completely." He smiled again; she couldn't miss the flash of silver covering his teeth.

He was getting too close.

"That is a tempting offer," she murmured, then she sprang forward, whirling the bag as she moved. The vampire moved too, but she was ready. She smashed him in the face with the bag. His fangs caught in the material, slicing it. The stake fell to the ground. Bare-handed, CeCe grabbed the weapon. Her hand wrapped around the leather-covered hilt, and her thumb brushed the silver. A shock shot through her, reverberated along her bones. She held on.

"You look comfortable with that, wolf. Too comfortable."

The vampire was right. As CeCe held the stake, energy snaked around her wrist, seemed to hold the weapon in place. She didn't know that she could have dropped the stake if she had wanted to, but for now she had no desire to be free of the weapon.

She lunged. Her arm swung up and down, striking at the vampire. He dropped and hissed. One of his silver caps fell to the ground. CeCe danced forward and smashed it under her shoe, then just as quickly dashed back.

She smiled. With the stake, she had the upper hand. She was strong, stronger than a thousand vampires. She could kill this one. She would kill him, for no other reason than to rid the earth of one more of the parasites.

Parasites. The word her mind had pulled out shocked her.

Marc was a vampire. She didn't think of him as a parasite...a monster.

Her hand trembled, the stake shook. She gritted her teeth, tried to organize her thoughts, separate fighting this one vampire that had attacked her from hating all vampires.

But she couldn't; her concentration wouldn't hold. She would think of Marc, then her hand would burn, itch with the need to taste vampire blood.

She stared down at the stake, horrified. Marc and Karl had both told her not to touch it with her skin and now she knew why.

The stake wanted this death, wanted the death of all vampires.

And werewolves too.

It wasn't just the symbol for the vampires that was incised on its side. The sign for werewolf was too.

The stake was working with her now, helping her, but it could just as easily turn, perhaps even urge her to use the thing against herself.

The vampire, seeing her indecision, rushed forward. Afraid now of both the stake and the vampire, CeCe swung with her unarmed hand. She caught the vampire in the mouth.

Silver sliced her skin. She flinched and jerked back. A jagged line of blood marked the silver cap's path down her arm. The sick feeling that always accompanied any touch of silver wound through her.

She swallowed, tried to force back nausea and sudden lethargy.

"First taste," the vampire whispered. Her blood streaked across his cheek. He ran his finger through it, then sucked the digit clean. "Wolf. I've never tasted it before. I want more."

And the stake did too. Her palm sweated and her hand shook. Energy fed by hate flowed into her; the nausea disappeared. The lethargy did too.

She stood frozen, confused and torn. There was no doubt this vampire meant to kill her, no doubt he had zero reservations about her death. A week ago she would have felt the same about him.

But the stake changed that, knowing it wanted her to make this kill, knowing it was screwing with her mind, made her reluctant to do what any other wolf in her situation would, what any rational being in her situation would.

She was tired of being controlled by what others and now this thing wanted of her.

"Give it to me," the vampire demanded again. For a second she considered it. For a second she wanted nothing more than to rid herself of the hideous weapon, but as her fingers loosened, as she imagined handing the stake to the vampire, a new realization hit her.

If touching the tool with her bare hand did this to her, filled her with hate and the desire to destroy, it would do the same to the vampire.

And he would have zero qualms about using the weapon against her, against all werewolves.

She had to stop him, but she couldn't do it with the stake, not the way the stake wanted her to.

For her new plan to work, she would have to be strong and she would have to be quick.

She sucked in a breath and tossed the tool in the air. She caught the stake by its wedged silver end. Then before she could think again, before the magic or curse of the stake could put more thoughts into her mind, she jumped forward and rammed the weapon's butt into the vampire's temple.

He staggered, and she lunged again, struck again.

He wrapped an arm around her waist and held her close. Sank his now unadorned fangs into her neck. A cry escaped her lips, but she didn't let the pain stop her. She slammed the stake into his temple again and again, continued until her arm ached and she knew she had lost. Knew if she wanted to live, she had no choice but to let the stake have what it wanted, to let it taste blood.

Chapter 19

Marc strode into the dark. The buildings blocked the moon's light, and the alley was quiet—peaceful with no sign of life, not even the dog Marc had seen earlier.

Dark and quiet, a vampire's dream. He felt his body and mind relax.

Feeling more under control, he found a deserted box and flipped it over to use as a makeshift desk, and then he turned on his computer.

As he had guessed, the coffee shop's wireless was available here, and they hadn't bothered to turn it off for the night. He logged in to his internet call service.

To the right, he heard sniffing. The dog. He clicked on the Fringe account. "Marc?" Van Bom.

Toenails scratched over concrete. The dog was growing brave.

"Where are you?" the older vampire asked. There

were noises in the background. The vampire wasn't alone. The screen, however, gave no hint as to where Van Bom was. The scene behind him was only a blank wall.

Marc frowned. Van Bom wasn't in the Fringe office, or, based on the flat white paint, in his home. The older vampire had more opulent taste than that. Marc doubted there was an unadorned wall in his mansion.

"Where are you—?" Marc began.

The smell of woods and wet leaves flowed over him.

Not a dog. A wolf.

Marc spun as the animal leaped. It landed on Marc's chest, its teeth flashing toward his throat.

"Delacroix!" Van Bom's voice boomed from the computer.

Marc grabbed the animal by the neck to keep its teeth at bay. Its eyes were amber. Its intent clear.

He rolled, flipping the creature onto its back. It snarled and struggled, used its hind feet to push at him, but he held on, ignored the swipes of its canines over his face and chin. Ignored the blood that flowed from the wounds. He placed a hand on each side of the wolf's head and slammed it back onto the concrete.

The animal twisted and pulled itself free. It staggered to the side, snarling. Back on his feet, Marc snarled as well.

Blood stained the creature's gray fur. Marc didn't know if it was vampire or werewolf, his or his attacker's.

"Silver, Delacroix. You will never beat him without silver. Use the stake." Van Bom's disembodied voice coming from the computer.

The stake? How did Van Bom know he had found it?

The thoughts sped through Marc's brain, but he didn't have time to pursue them. The werewolf had come back to itself.

It leaped again.

Marc swung and made contact with its snout. The animal went down. Its tongue hung from its mouth, but it stood again.

Silver. Marc had silver—the caps he had taken from the vampire he'd left on the roof.

He pulled them from his pocket and slipped them onto his fangs.

The wolf growled with a new intensity. Then it tilted its head and raced past him.

Marc spun, unsure whether to let the creature go or chase after it. Adrenaline raced through him. He wasn't ready to give up the fight, couldn't understand why the wolf had been either.

A howl sounded from the street, from where he had left CeCe.

Van Bom yelled from the computer, demanding to know what was happening.

Marc ignored him, ignored everything except the burning instinct to get back to CeCe now.

CeCe's blood flowed from her neck. Even without the use of silver caps, the vampire was weakening her. Maybe the stake was working against her, punishing her for not giving it what it craved.

Or perhaps she was…did the damned thing care whether the blood it dined on was vampire or were-wolf? CeCe guessed not.

She tried to open her hand and drop the thing, but

her fingers wouldn't uncurl. The stake seemed to cling to them.

Then suddenly she went down, the vampire falling on top of her. His fangs pulled from her neck. He screamed.

She heard growls and smelled fur...wolf.

She rolled onto her knees, and then staggered to her feet.

A werewolf clung to the vampire's throat, jerked and tore, seemed determined to rip the creature in two.

The vampire fought him off, or tried to. He punched the animal in the head. The werewolf flew sideways, landing on its feet.

Karl, come to save her. Karl, whom she had stopped trusting.

The alpha charged again. And the vampire met that charge.

The stake in her hand pulsed...laughed. The thing was enjoying this. It's what it had wanted all along... what it craved.

Blood and fur spattered the street.

Both creatures were tired; both bled more than seemed possible.

The stake pulsed...reminding her of what she held, the power she held. She could stop this. She could save Karl, but at what cost?

"CeCe!" Marc raced toward her, his clothing torn and bloodstained too. But that isn't what held her attention, isn't what she focused on. No, her gaze locked onto his mouth and the silver caps that covered his fangs.

The stake laughed again.

Who can you trust, little wolf? Who can you trust?

* * *

CeCe stood in the street, her clothing soaked with blood. Marc raced toward her, relief blinding him to everything except the sight of the female he loved.

She took a step forward and lifted her arm.

Gripped tight in her hand was the stake. Indecision clear on her face, she took another step.

"CeCe?" He slowed and looked past her, saw the wolf that had attacked him caught in a vampire's embrace.

The animal bucked and tore at the vampire's arm.

"You're wearing silver caps."

CeCe's words pulled his attention back to her.

He moved his hand to his mouth, felt the caps on his fangs.

"The wolf attacked me," he said, not sure why he felt the need to explain himself, and not liking it.

"It's Karl. He came back for me, came to save me."

He'd come while Marc lagged. She didn't say it, but he heard the censure. Knew the alpha had proven something to her, something important.

"You're his destined mate." A fact, nothing more. If the alpha hadn't given up his fight with Marc to save CeCe, Marc would have hated him all the more. As it was, that hate was turned inward, was another sign of how ill-suited he and the female werewolf were for each other. He hadn't heard her cry; he hadn't been drawn to her side. The alpha had.

"I have to help him—I have to kill the vampire." She took another step, but toward Marc.

"CeCe?" He jerked the caps from his mouth and tossed them onto the ground.

She took another step.

Behind her a third werewolf appeared. It raced forward, but didn't get far. A vampire dropped out of the sky, and then another. A line of them ran along the roofs of the surrounding buildings. One after another they launched themselves and landed in a crouch on the ground.

More wolves appeared too, charged from the darkness, their fur bristling and their feet eating up the ground.

The war had begun and CeCe was standing seemingly lost in the middle of it.

Marc ran toward her. Her eyes were glazed, and her skin was pale. She lifted her arm and slashed downward, caught him in the shoulder with the stake.

The void he'd felt when he'd touched the metal himself flowed into him, filled him, but multiplied tenfold.

His fangs extended; a hiss left his lips. He spun, ready to attack, every instinct telling him to attack.

CeCe stared back at him, her eyes empty and confused. "Kill," she muttered.

He fisted his hands and pushed back against the monster inside him, threatening to come out.

This wasn't CeCe. The woman he'd made love to couldn't have acted that well; he couldn't have misplaced his trust that thoroughly. It was the stake.

She lifted the weapon again.

He walked into her strike, grabbed her around the forearm and forced her arm above her hand. She fought back, her free hand swinging toward him, her nails scraping over his face.

She snapped at him, her teeth even and white, 100 percent human, but her eyes slanting and all wolf.

If she shifted she would drop the stake, but he

guessed she would lose something else as well...her humanity.

She took a step backward and leveraged her body forward. The stake dipped lower.

The broken vampire symbol caught his eye.

Whoever created the thing had done so to break them, the vampires and the wolves, but that person had failed before. One vampire had stopped them before.

Another could again.

He had to get her to drop it. Had to force it from her hand.

Knowing he couldn't control whatever magic had been forged into the weapon any better than CeCe, he forced her arm straight...away from their bodies, so it looked as if they were engaged in a tango.

CeCe snarled and tried to bend her arm. Marc held tight and jerked her closer to his body, until he could feel her heart against his chest, smell the shampoo she'd used on her hair.

Then he bit her. Not the savage bite of a vampire unleashed. This bite was the seductive bite of a vampire intent on putting someone under thrall.

Her werewolf blood precluded her from falling under his powers completely. But he hoped he was strong enough to relax her, to remind her he wasn't her enemy.

He just needed to get her to trust him once more.

Behind them the vampires and werewolves continued their battle. Wolves screamed and vampires hissed. The heady scent of blood filled the street, but to Marc it was all background—his only focus, his world, was CeCe.

She stayed stiff and unyielding at first, struggling

against him, but slowly some of the rigidity left her frame and her body began to slump. He lapped his tongue over her skin, healing her wound, and hopefully, healing her, wishing they were alone and not stuck in this insane magic-created nightmare.

Her head tilted and her empty hand crept up his back. She caressed his muscles. He pressed a kiss against her throat and murmured an apology for what he was about to do.

Then eyes closed, he slammed her hand against the brick wall. She sucked in a breath and her eyes flew open.

"Drop the stake, CeCe."

She stared at him, no comprehension of what he was asking on her face.

He gritted his teeth and smashed her hand against the wall again.

Anger flashed through her eyes and relief washed over him. The stake's power was weakening.

"The stake—"

Her gaze shifted, her expression shifted, from anger to horror. Her hand opened and the stake fell, clattered to the ground, where it lay winking up at them.

Luring them to pick it back up and continue the fight.

CeCe bent. He wrapped his arm around her waist and jerked her backward.

When he looked up, three wolves were bearing down on them, mouths open, muzzles stained with blood.

He grabbed CeCe by the waist and slung her over his shoulder. As he did, the vampires moved in and one did the unthinkable, at least in Marc's mind.

He picked up the stake.

Marc stared at him, memorizing his face and frame. "Drop it," he yelled.

The vampire rolled the thing over in his hand. His face creased. His mouth opened. He shook his arm, seemed to be trying to drop the weapon he had picked up of his own free will.

Marc hesitated, remembering the feeling of death when he had touched the stake, thinking to help the vampire.

A wolf knocked into the vampire. The male turned and his lips pulled back. He hissed and then he drove the stake into the canine's back.

The creature shrieked.

CeCe murmured something, reminding him he had his own werewolf to protect.

He glanced at the vampire one last time, then his grip on CeCe tight, he ran.

The stake had won. The war was on.

Chapter 20

The world zipped past as CeCe hung upside down over Marc's shoulder. She relaxed against him, strangely relieved to have the job of thinking, sorting out what was happening, taken away from her.

But when they entered the woods, she knew she could go no farther. She pounded on his back with a closed fist.

Without questioning, he set her upright on her feet.

Their clothing was torn and they were both covered in blood. She wrapped her arms around herself. She'd attacked Marc. She'd seen him coming and something inside her had snapped.

"You were wearing caps," she murmured.

He nodded. "And you were holding the stake." His eyes were hollow. She felt the same, dazed and confused…lost.

She stared past him, at a tree. "We both looked the part, didn't we?"

"Played it pretty well too."

She glanced at him, looking for some sign of censure, but his gaze was clear and honest.

"I'm sorry. I saw you with the caps...I should have known—"

He placed a finger under her chin and lifted her face to his. "It's the stake. The stake is causing all of this." He blinked as if clearing his mind. "I saw a vampire pick it up, saw him use it."

Her eyes widened. The stake was in a vampire's hands.

She doubted anyone, wolf or vamp, could resist its magic. The energy snaking around her wrist. She shivered.

"Where is it?" she asked.

He shook his head. "Back there still in the battle."

She stepped to the side, ready to push past him. "We have to get it, destroy it."

His fingers wrapped around her arm. "Not now. Whatever damage could be done has been." His lips pressed together. "Going back this minute will solve none of that. We have to think, and wait...for daylight."

"Daylight? What will that do? You've proven vampires can walk in the day."

"Some," he corrected her. "The older ones, but older vampires aren't what I saw tonight. They were all new, under twenty years turned. They will be hiding soon, or paying the price for ignoring the need."

"But the werewolves—"

"Won't find them."

"But you can?"

"Of course."

"So, we're going vampire hunting?" It seemed wrong to voice the question, but Marc was unfazed.

He smiled, a grim pull of his lips. "Yes, we are."

CeCe followed Marc into the woods. She knew where they were going—the cave. Her heart clutched at the thought, but still twenty yards from where they had left Russell, Marc veered another direction. They left the path.

A gibbous moon hung in the sky, but the canopy of the trees was thick here and blocked most of its light. She hooked a finger through a loop on Marc's waistband and let him guide her.

"We have two hours before the vampires will be looking for a hideout," he murmured. "The entrance we found is for a small cave, little more than a hole in the ground, but there's another not far away, bigger and more tempting to vampires looking to hide from the sun."

A bigger cave would be better, less like the well she'd survived as a child. She could do this.

She focused on the thought, did her best to convince herself, but she found herself walking closer to Marc and still stumbling. Her fear was getting in her way. She knew that, but despite that knowledge, she couldn't control it.

Twenty minutes later, they stopped. Marc pulled her around to face him and tilted her face upward. "It's another hundred feet; you don't need to go in. I can do this alone." He pointed somewhere to their right. "I've been here before. There's a path, it leads to a gas station on the highway. Take it and get a ride somewhere. Be safe."

"No—"

Howls sounded. The hair on CeCe's arms stood. "Werewolves."

Marc placed his hand on her back and applied pressure, nudging her toward the path she couldn't see.

"If the wolves are coming, the vampires will be behind them. You need to leave."

She shook her head. "I can stall the wolves so you can get inside." She gestured the direction he had been going, where he said the cave was located.

"No."

More howls, but the howls aren't what worried CeCe. Wolves didn't howl when they hunted. It was the silence around them, the same stillness she had noticed the first time she stood in these woods when Marc, a vampire, first entered.

Perhaps the forest sensed him again, perhaps that explained the quiet. Or perhaps there were vampires around them. Perhaps the war had followed them into the trees.

She didn't want to go into a cave and she didn't want to face the vampires, but she had zero intention of doing as Marc asked, either. She wouldn't leave him here, tuck her tail and run away. She would stay and face the vampires or she would go with Marc and face the cave, but she wouldn't leave him here alone.

"I can call the pack. I'll be fine." But the pack, she feared, might have already morphed into something she didn't know.

"CeCe." Karl stepped out of the trees. He was naked and covered with blood. In his hands was a stake, not the stake, but another made of wood. "Step away from him." He motioned for her to move to the side.

Marc stilled.

"Where's the stake, CeCe?" Karl held up the one in his hand.

"I—" She stopped herself from looking at Marc, but it didn't matter. Karl cursed and spat on the ground.

"You released him, didn't you? Did you give him the stake too? A vampire? How stupid can you be?"

Her jaw tightened. "What about you? What didn't you tell me? You stole the stake from my room, didn't you? Then when you used it, you wore gloves? Why?"

"In case you've forgotten, I'm a werewolf. I thought you were too."

The barb hit, but didn't hold. "Yes, it's silver, but the handle is wrapped. Why the glove? Is it because you know what the stake does? Know about the magic inside it?"

A new realization hit her. "My God, you left it so I'd pick it up, didn't you? You meant for me to be taken in by its spell. You meant for me to kill…" She didn't finish. She didn't have to—all present knew what Karl's intentions had been.

He stared at her, no remorse and no explanation. "Your father warned me, but I took you in anyway. I thought I could overcome your bad blood. Was I wrong? Are you a wolf or an abomination?"

She flinched as if struck. An abomination? She'd always known her father didn't love her, that he saw her only as something to be used, but he'd never gone that far, never cut that deep, not even when he left her in that well, alone, cold and hungry for days.

Karl slapped the wooden stake against his bare

thigh. "I promised the pack. I'm committed to making this work. How about you, CeCe? How committed are you? Where's my chain?"

Her hand rose to her chest while her mind drifted to the motel and the bed where she'd left the symbol of her bond to the alpha…or the promise of their bond.

He lifted his arm. "This is for the pack. They're all that matters." The stake flew through the air. CeCe turned, leaned toward Marc, tried to cut off the trajectory of the alpha's missile with her own body, but the vampire pushed her aside. She fell and the stake hit. She heard Marc's grunt.

"No!" She jumped to her feet.

Marc was bowed over. She couldn't see the stake, couldn't see his wound.

"Let him die, or better, finish him. Show your loyalty. It isn't too late." Karl stood still and straight, commanding.

Too late. It had been too late long before she was born. She realized that now. Her father had never loved her. The pack had never accepted her. She'd been a possession, nothing more, and there was nothing she could do to change that. Nothing.

She had never had a chance.

Karl raised a hand. Robert, dressed in jeans and a T-shirt, stepped from the trees.

"We searched the vampire's room. Did you know that? Do you know what we found?" Karl asked.

Robert held up one hand. Dangling from his gloved hand were the cuffs Marc had used on her that first night.

"Laced in silver. This vampire isn't innocent, but if

you won't believe that now…" Karl motioned toward her. A third wolf appeared; both moved toward her.

She grabbed at Marc, tried to get him to stand, to move.

"Forget the vampire. He's dying. Time to remember who and what you are."

The wolf with the cuffs walked toward her, unsnapping the restraints as he moved. The click was loud and foreboding. She didn't know where to look, where to turn.

"Time to go home, CeCe. Time to fulfill your destiny."

Her destiny. A destiny she had no part in choosing.

Marc's blood congealed on her fingers, made her hand stick to his shirt. She wanted to curse and scream.

Then Marc's fingers found hers. He edged backward, away from the wolves. He was still alive, but he was wounded, and in this state, didn't stand a chance against the three male werewolves.

CeCe clutched at him, unwilling to let him go. There had to be a way out of this, had to be a way to save them both.

"A cave," Marc murmured.

A cave? She realized then why Marc had chosen the spot where they had stopped. Another opening, not as big as the one they'd used to dispose of Russell's body, but still an opening big enough for her, big enough for Marc.

He wanted her to jump.

But she had no idea what lay below them, how deep the hole went, what would be at the bottom…if Marc, injured as he was, could survive, if she could survive.

The last wolf to arrive pulled a second wooden stake from his back pocket. "Should I finish him?"

Karl lifted his chin. "CeCe, step away. You need the pack. Don't make this hard."

Robert was beside her now. He held out the cuffs.

Marc sucked in a breath. She could feel him waiting, wanting to jump, but refusing to leave her.

He would stay beside her, let himself be staked. Her own father wouldn't have done that. Her supposed destined mate wouldn't either.

She stared at Karl; new strength and anger swelled inside her. "You got something wrong. My father needed the pack and he needed me to get back in your good graces. But me? I don't need anything, not from my father, or you, or your pack."

The werewolf with the cuffs dashed forward, tried to tackle her. She stepped to the side, then spun and kicked him in the chest. For a moment hope washed over her. She could do this. She could take Karl and his minions out .

The werewolf fell backward, but so did CeCe. Her foot slipped from under her. She tensed for the coming impact, but it didn't come. She didn't hit the ground. Instead she stumbled backward, slipped on the grass hiding the cave's opening and then tumbled into the never-ending darkness of the cavern. Her back hit something hard, a ledge. She grabbed wildly around her, tried to cling to bare rock, but it was hopeless. She fell.

The werewolves were gone, Karl was gone, the world and life she knew was gone.

The cool air hit CeCe first, then the smell of damp earth. It was like falling into a grave, and she realized she was. The fall was too far, the bottom when she reached it would be too hard. Even a werewolf couldn't survive this.

She closed her eyes and tried not to scream. She wouldn't give the werewolves standing at the top of this hole even that.

Unexpectedly, fingers tightened on her hand. Her heart jumped and she was jerked into an embrace. She collided with a hard masculine body. She wrapped her arms around the form and eyes squeezed closed, she hung on. The body pressed to hers was cool, the words murmured against her ear calming.

Marc. He had jumped with her; he was falling with her.

"Hold on," he murmured, his hand cradling her head, his lips brushing against her ear. And she did. Her arms wrapped around his body, she clung to him as she had never clung to anyone before. He turned in midair, shifting so when they hit the ground, his body broke the impact.

The landing was hard and jolting. Her jaws snapped together, her head jerked backward and she tasted her own blood.

But as she lay atop Marc, her heartbeat slowing and her mind cataloging each ache, she realized she had survived. They had both survived. They had fallen from God knew how far and she had only a bleeding tongue and aching head to show for it.

Marc had said he had no magic, but he was wrong.

She pushed herself up, off Marc, and slid onto the earth beside him. "We're okay." She stared blankly for a moment, still processing. Then she leaned over him and bunched the front of his shirt in her fists. "We're okay." She pulled him up toward her, laughing.

He brushed a strand of hair she couldn't see from her face and tucked it behind her ear. "We are." But his voice was strained.

The stake.

The elation she had felt at surviving dissipated. She lowered him quickly, jerked herself upright and ran her hands over his chest. The stake was still there, protruding from his pectoral muscle, but it had missed his heart by six inches. "Who knew Karl was such a lousy aim?" she asked, trying for light…to keep the fear that had crept back over her from showing.

Marc grunted. "Not a bad aim. Slow. At least if he wants to hunt vampires." He grabbed the stake and jerked it free.

CeCe flinched. Then she grabbed the weapon from Marc's hand and threw it into the darkness. She never wanted to touch or see a stake again.

"What now?" she asked, shivering. With the elation of their surprisingly easy landing behind them and the too-obvious reminder of the danger they were in still fresh and bloody, the temperature of the cavern hit her. She rubbed her hands over her arms.

"We wait for day and continue with our plan." His voice sounded tight and he hadn't moved since they had landed. She wished she could see his face.

"Look for another exit?" she asked.

"Look for other vampires."

As she started to speak, he held a finger to her lips.

She realized then that the werewolves were talking…about her.

* * *

Marc moved his finger to CeCe's lips, hoping she'd read his silent signal and know to keep silent. He didn't want her pack deciding to come down in the cavern and investigate what had happened to them. Better they think both CeCe and he were dead.

Of course, CeCe, despite what she had said to the alpha aboveground, might not agree. She might still want the pack. He ran his thumb over the back of her hand. The bones were fine and delicate, but right now she was the strong one. He was wounded, severely enough that he wasn't sure he could move without resting or feeding.

"Do you think she survived?" The voice of the wolf who had approached CeCe with the cuffs drifted down the channel through which they had plunged.

"How far is the drop?"

Marc's lip rose at the new voice—Karl, the wolf who was supposed to be CeCe's destined mate, supposed to be dedicated to her.

A pebble skittered down the through the hole and landed on the flat rock next to CeCe. She watched it bounce, then closed her eyes and began rocking back and forth on her seat.

Nerves or regret? Marc feared it was the latter.

"Can they hear us?" she whispered.

Still lying on his back, he reached up and ran his fingers down her spine.

"Can you understand them?" he asked. He didn't know how good a werewolf's hearing was.

She nodded.

"Can't tell." From above again. "Didn't hear the rock, or for that matter, them, hit."

The tone was cold and analyzing, as if they were talking of inanimate objects lying at the bottom of this chute, not another wolf, one supposedly a valued part of their pack.

But then, Karl cursed. "The vampire did this. He turned her mind somehow." More rocks and debris fell through the opening. For a moment Marc thought the alpha might fall in too—or jump.

One of his men must have pulled him back. There was the sound of low arguing voices.

"Fine. We leave. We'll come back after we've destroyed the others and regained the stake." There was silence for a second. Then low, almost inaudible, a whisper. "I never desert my pack, CeCe, and despite what you might think, you are pack." The words were followed by the noise of something else falling. Two objects hit the ground beside Marc. One landed on his chest.

He grimaced and reached for it.

A flashlight.

He handed the light to CeCe. She stared at its unlit end. "As if this fixes anything," she muttered.

"He cares. In his twisted way, he cares." Marc hated saying the words, hated believing them even more, but CeCe deserved to know the alpha and his pack did care for her, even if it was in a completely sick way.

He didn't know if that made what the wolves had planned for CeCe any easier to swallow. It might even encourage her to forgive them completely, but she had earned the information.

She looked up, but nothing else fell. After a moment she moved onto her hands and knees and shuffled through the dark to see what else the werewolf had dropped.

She held an old canteen out to him. "Water. With your wound you can use some."

He closed his eyes. The werewolves were gone; the immediate threat was gone. If he concentrated, he could rest for an hour, use that time to heal before daylight came fully and he needed to start hunting for the vampire who had taken the silver stake. "Water isn't what I need."

Back beside him, she placed a hand on his chest. She flipped on the light and pointed it at his wound. He kept his eyes shut, but he could feel the warmth of the bulb and could see it shining through his closed eyelids.

"It isn't healing. Shouldn't it have healed some by now?"

"Perhaps werewolves heal without aid, but vampires need rest or…" He didn't want to tell her he needed blood. Didn't want to sound as if he was asking for something she might not be willing to give.

"What? Not water… Oh." She flipped off the light and laid it down beside him.

He sighed. "I'll take an hour to rest. It will be enough."

"Will it?" she leaned close; her hair brushed over his neck. "Are you sure?" Her breath teased at his skin. She smelled of blood too, hers, the vampire's she'd fought, others that she had encountered, but all he could concentrate on was her.

"You were wounded too," he reminded her. "You should rest."

"Only silver keeps us from healing. There's no silver touching me." Her lips trailed over his neck. She nibbled at his skin. He'd never had a female bite him like this, not teasing and playful.

His groin tightened and his fangs lengthened.

"If you're too weak—"

He rammed his fingers into her hair and pulled her mouth to his. She tasted wild and sweet. He slipped his tongue past her lips; her tongue met his, both demanding, both trying to prove they were the strongest.

He rolled over, so she lay beneath him. "Never too weak…" he murmured against her lips. He ran his fingers down the front of her shirt, then jerked it over her head. Dried blood was caked on her neck. He ran his hands over it, massaging it away. "I'm sorry I wasn't there. I'm sorry he bit you." No one would ever bite her again, no one except Marc.

He lapped at her skin, cleaning away every hint of her hurt, every hint of someone else having touched her…harmed her.

She shivered and pulled at his shirt, jerked it free from his pants. Her hands were warm on his back, and when he tossed his shirt to the side and lay on top of her, her body was warm against his. He could feel his wound healing already, could feel his soul healing too.

Being with CeCe did that to him, reminded him of being alive, made him strong enough to allow himself to feel.

He wanted to do the same for her.

"Do werewolves ever exchange blood?" Vampires did when the feelings were intense on both sides. It showed they trusted each other enough to bare their throats, risk everything even their immortal existences.

"We…bite."

He felt her blush.

"Like you just did?" he asked, honored and intrigued.

"More." She opened her mouth and bit down softly on the muscles that ran from his neck to his shoulder. "And…during."

Sex. He finished the sentence in his head.

Vampires did the same.

"It's a sign…" Her words drifted off again.

"A commitment," he guessed.

"Yes," she whispered against his neck. Her breath was warm and stirred his hair, stirred his interest in stopping their discussion and moving on to something much more physical.

He didn't want to ask about Karl, didn't want to think of he and CeCe together, but he needed to know…. "Have you made a commitment like that?"

She shook her head. "No. I haven't."

It was all he needed to know. The alpha might have given her his chain, but she hadn't taken it with her when they left the hotel, and now she had admitted she'd never really committed herself to the werewolf, to any werewolf.

He murmured words of appreciation into her ear. Kissed the side of her face and down her neck. She was beautiful. He wanted her to know that, wanted her to realize how special she was. He didn't care if she was a werewolf, didn't care that the rest of their kind was at war. CeCe was meant for him and he was meant for her.

He could never be happy, never be whole, not without her by his side.

* * *

Marc's tongue trailed down CeCe's neck. A shiver danced up her spine. She clutched at him, grabbed the firm muscles that ran up his sides. He shifted so his mouth moved lower. He kissed her breasts, swirled his tongue around one nipple.

Her back arched. She pulled his face closer. Her thighs parted and he ran one finger between her folds, found the tiny nub there. She wriggled beneath him, desire and excitement building until her breath left her mouth in tiny pants.

She moaned and he moved again, dropped his mouth even lower, to her inner thigh. His fangs grazed her skin. He whispered something she couldn't hear.

Her breasts ached, her core tightened. Something was coming, her body knew it, was ready for it, craved it.

Then his fangs pierced her skin, and he suckled at her thigh, blood flowing from her body, slow and rhythmic as if he had somehow matched the beats of her heart.

She cried out and wrapped her fingers in his hair. Pleasure so intense she could never have imagined it existed coiled around her. She squirmed, wanting this strange new experience to never stop but also longing for what she knew would come next.

Slowly, delicately, he pulled his fangs from her flesh. She gasped and pulled at his hair again, desperate now to feel his fangs at her neck and his sex deep inside her. To join with him completely.

As if sensing her need, he walked his hands up the rock beneath her, let his naked body brush over hers, inch by inch, slow and deliberate.

With his mouth next to her ear, he whispered, "And now you know one more place a vampire may bite. Do you approve?"

She moved his hand to her heart, let him feel the rapid beat of it. "Judge for yourself," she answered.

With his lips against her cheek, he smiled. "And what about the neck? Does it deserve another try?"

"To be fair, before I decide my favorite," she murmured.

He smiled again, then he lowered his mouth to her throat and pierced her skin again. The feeling was just as intense, the euphoria like nothing she had felt before.

Her core tightened. She shifted her body, so his thigh fell between hers, so his sex, hard and ready, lay against hers.

He groaned and pulled back, stared down at her with eyes that she knew were nothing but pupil. Dark and dangerous, but she felt no fear, no trepidation at all. She knew that what awaited her would be welcoming, make her feel safe…no, more than that—strong.

She lifted herself to him, opened herself, and when he plunged inside her, she gripped his shoulder with her teeth and held on, let herself fall, forgot about hiding her wolf, forgot everything except being, living, experiencing this moment.

With the holds on her wolf loosened, the creature crept forward, snarled and tried to retreat, but CeCe didn't let it. She pushed that half of herself forward, until she could no longer separate the two parts. She was no longer wolf and human. No longer wild and contained.

She just was.

Then she wrapped her arms around Marc and lost herself in being with him, lost herself in the taste of strength he gave her, and she stayed with him, moving her body to meet his every thrust, nibbling him, encouraging him until they both lay exhausted and fulfilled on the cold rock.

Marc traced CeCe's face with two fingers. They should be moving now, looking for the vampires, but he couldn't get himself to stand up, couldn't get himself to vacate this moment.

He kissed the corners of her eyes. Even in human form there was a hint of the wolf in her eyes, almond-shaped and golden hazel. No human he'd met had eyes such a color, and few such a shape.

"How does it feel?" he whispered.

"What?"

"Shifting."

Her lips parted, and he could see her surprise. "Exhilarating, at least for me. I've heard the other wolves say it hurts, watched them scream and grimace the first few shifts. But for me—" she lifted one bare shoulder "—it's like running through the woods, chasing a rabbit. It's...what makes me feel free."

"And you don't feel that way human?"

She shook her head. "No...I haven't."

"Then why...?" Why be human? Why not stay wolf? He couldn't voice the question; even after what they had done, it felt too personal.

"Why not stay wolf? That would be giving up, wouldn't it? Be like killing half of myself. How could that be the answer?"

She sounded sad. He didn't want her to be sad, and he didn't want her to shift and never shift back.

"It isn't." He pressed a kiss against her lips, soft and gentle. He wanted her to feel free whichever shape she was in, wanted her to be free, and he swore right then to himself that no matter what it took, no matter how this all ended, he would somehow make sure he gave her that.

CeCe and Marc had left the safety of the place where they had fallen and made love twenty minutes earlier. Marc had talked of sending her back up the sides of the chute, out of the cave, but the channel walls were too steep and the hole they had fallen into too deep. Even the vampire had been unable to gain a foothold.

Besides, CeCe had no intention of leaving him.

"What now? Do you think it's dawn?" The dark was too all-encompassing, the depth they were at too deep. CeCe had lost her normal feel for the moon. She had no concept if it was still visible in the night sky or had been outshone by the first bits of sun.

"It's close enough that the vampires will have taken refuge."

She ran her thumb over the flashlight's switch, but resisted the urge to flip it on. She was with Marc and safe. She didn't need light now to assure her of that, but she didn't know what might come later. She needed to conserve whatever battery power was left.

"That's good though, right?" She knew the best situation would have been to arrive in the cave before the vampires so she and Marc could have looked for entrances, exits and a place to watch unseen, but if the vampires were already asleep…that would have to be the next-best situation.

"Only if all the vampires are new." He stopped.

Wanting to see his face and be able to read what he was thinking, she flipped on the light.

They had redressed earlier, but he'd given CeCe his shirt. He walked through the fifty-degree tunnels naked from the waist up as if they were still above ground in the hot Kentucky heat. She, on the other hand, even with the extra layer of his shirt over her own clothing, fought not to shiver.

As the light played over his back, he turned. She lowered the beam to keep from blinding him. His hand rose to the spot where Karl's stake had struck and massaged at the spot, as if it were stiff and painful.

The wound was healed now, but the skin was discolored and puckered. She pulled his shirt tighter around her body and tried not to stare, tried not to show her concern.

Seeing her expression, he smiled. "We don't heal as quickly as some stories would have humans believe, but we do heal. By tomorrow, this will be almost normal."

She nodded and lowered the light's beam even farther, and hoping what he said was true, waited for him to explain his comment about the vampires.

He lowered his hand as if realizing his touching the wound was keeping her from forgetting what had happened.

"All I saw were young vampires. That doesn't mean no older ones are around."

She twisted her lips to the side. "But they wouldn't need the caves."

"Not for safety from the sun," he agreed. "But if the invasion was organized, an older vampire might have come along, might be standing guard. Werewolves may think we don't work together, but they are wrong. We may not have a pack, we may not like one another, but we were each created by another vampire. We take that seriously. We don't just leave the young to die."

"But you'll kill another vampire." He'd attacked the one who had attacked her. She had certainly thought he meant to kill the other male.

"If we have to." He turned away then, abruptly.

Afraid she had gone too far, she fell into silence.

His face strained, he looked back. "From this point on we need to keep the light off and move as silently as possible."

"Do you sense them?"

He shook his head. "But I can smell fresh air. There's another entrance and this is the cave I spotted the other night. They will be in here somewhere."

Now that he had mentioned it, she could smell the world beyond the cave too. It was hard to discern through the scent of damp rock and earth, but it was there—grass and sunshine. She longed to be walking there, away from the underground world of this cave.

Marc's lips parted; he stared the direction he had pointed, down the channel that he said led to the cave's main entrance. "I can walk you there. You can find the highway from there."

"No." She shook her head. She wasn't leaving. She clicked off the flashlight. He'd said no light. She could do that.

They stood in complete darkness, the kind of dark you couldn't experience aboveground, not even during the darkest night alone in the woods. CeCe began to shake. After a few moments, she felt Marc's hand reach for hers.

She wove her fingers through his and held on. In the distance she heard water dripping. When she'd been in the well, left there by her father, there had been water. The underground creek that had fed it had all but dried up, but there had still been water at the bottom. She'd stood in it up to her knees for days. Her feet had turned soft and sore, been numb from the cold. She'd tried to climb the walls—made of brick, built by slaves a hundred years earlier—but she had slid back down, landed in that damn stagnant pool.

Her father had told her how her mother had died in such a pit, how the vampire had tortured her. He'd told her experiencing it now would make her stronger—ensure she didn't repeat her mother's mistakes.

And for a while she had believed him. But then she had met Marc. And now she realized her father was wrong—worse. He was insane, so focused on his hatred of vampires and his desire to make her strong, that he'd twisted her view of things too, could have destroyed her.

As memories washed over her, she shook. She closed her eyes. Her jaw clenched and her hold on Marc's hand tightened. His fingers squeezed back. She held on, focused on Marc. His touch kept her from dissolving.

She wasn't alone. She could leave when she liked.

"Let's go," she whispered.

She could feel Marc's hesitation. She placed her hand on his back and kept it there, let him know she was okay and more importantly, she wasn't leaving.

After a second, he started walking.

Eyes open and heart pounding, CeCe followed.

She would welcome finding the vampires. Would welcome anything that brought this torturous trip through the dark to an end.

Chapter 22

They had walked another twenty feet before Marc found where the path intersected with the one that led to the cave's main entrance. The scent of vampire was strong here. Vampire and something else.

He pulled CeCe against him and whispered as softly as he could into her ear. "Do you smell that?"

She nodded and mouthed "Human."

"What does it mean?" CeCe moved her lips without uttering the words.

He shook his head, then realized she couldn't see him as he could see her. He pulled her closer and shook his head again, this time with his chin pressed against her head. It could mean nothing. Humans came to this region to explore caves. He just hoped none were inside now.

She sighed. He could feel the tension running

through her frame. She'd been tense since they'd started walking, grown more so when they'd turned off the light. He didn't know what had happened to her, why she feared the cave, but the fact that she did, and still refused to leave when he asked her to, meant something, made him hope that he'd found a tiny bit of what the wolves had...pack, loyalty, belonging.

They kept walking. Another five yards and the channel widened. They were in a room with three passages leading off it. He held out his hand and felt the air currents. One passage dead-ended; the others went deeper.

The vampires would be deeper. Which meant that is where he would have to go, but he didn't have to take CeCe with him. While he loved that she refused to go back to the surface without him, he couldn't take her any farther. Taking her into a room full of vampires, sleeping or not, would be foolhardy. Both for her and his safety.

He grabbed her by the shoulders and spun her around, pressed her back up against the wall. "Do you trust me, CeCe?" he whispered in her ear.

Her nails dug into his chest. Her heart pounded and his body reacted, hardened. His vampire senses reacted too. His fangs lengthened. He could hear her blood leaving her heart and returning, feel her body flush as the blood flowed faster through her veins. He brushed his face against her hair, inhaled her scent. "I need you to stay here. Wait for me. Don't leave."

She shook her head.

His hands cupping her buttocks, he pulled her closer. "If there is a vampire awake, he'll sense you. Let me go first."

She hesitated this time. He rested his cheek on the top of her head. He knew she was afraid of the dark, but fear and threat were two different things. The vampires were threat, a real threat to a werewolf who sneaked in while they were sleeping.

"You have your flashlight. This tunnel dead-ends. Go to the end and turn it on. Wait for me there."

Still she didn't reply.

He squeezed her. "I need you to do this. If we want to succeed it's the only way."

Finally, he felt her nod.

He waited a moment longer, as reluctant to let her go as he sensed she was to be left behind. Finally, he unwrapped his arms and nudged her toward the dead end.

Her hands on the wall, her feet walking sideways, she crept along. When she turned the corner and was out of sight, he heard the flashlight click on. A spot of gray showed from the turn in the tunnel, but it was okay—where he was headed that spot would soon disappear.

The vampires would have no idea he was coming and no idea CeCe had been left alone only a few yards away.

Guilt lanced through him. Alone and afraid of the dark. Was he no better than her alpha? He moved to go after her, but stopped himself.

She had a light and she was strong, stronger than she realized. As long as she stayed where she was and waited for him to come back, she'd be fine.

Now he had to do his job…steal the stake and come back.

If he didn't, if he messed up, got caught or killed, CeCe would be on her own, in a cave filled with angry vampires.

The hard rock wall behind CeCe was damp. Cold leaked through Marc's shirt and hers onto her skin. Her flashlight shone on the blank rock face across from her. This tunnel was narrower than the others. Two people could walk abreast, but no more.

She held the flashlight in both hands, so tightly her knuckles ached. Every instinct she had said to go with Marc, and not just because she didn't want to be alone, didn't want to risk her light burning out. No, she realized, it was more than that…it was her pack instinct telling her to go with him, fight with him.

Wolves didn't let their pack members face a threat alone. They attacked as one.

Marc had no pack. He was walking into the vampire nest by himself. She should be there with him, helping him, but he had asked her to stay behind, had told her it would be safest for her *and* him.

Afraid she'd weaken and race after him, she crouched in the dirt and closed her eyes, tried to think of all the reasons what he'd said was true, all the reasons she should listen to him.

None came to mind.

She stood. Her feet crunched on gravel as she turned. Realizing she hadn't heard the sound before, that the rest of the cave had smooth floors, she paused and flashed the light around.

The ground here was softer, a combination of sand and fine gravel. She ran the beam over the walls and realized the rock here wasn't like what she'd seen of the rest of the cave. This tunnel wasn't natural; it appeared to have been formed by man—mining of some sort was her guess.

She stepped into the middle of the path and looked down. Footprints, a number of them, pointed deeper into the cavern and headed back out.

How long would footprints last in a cave? Forever, she guessed, if they weren't disturbed by water or some animal. So, these easily could have been made by miners one hundred or more years earlier.

But somehow she didn't think so.

Somehow she thought this dead-end tunnel had been visited recently, was related to the vampires, the werewolves and the stake.

Stepping to one side, where the ground was harder and her own footprints wouldn't be as visible, she started walking. At the next curve she paused and listened.

Nothing. No sound of life…or death. A vampire sleeping would make no noise.

She glanced at the light. She couldn't stand the idea of walking around the corner blind, and if a vampire was there, the light might be her best protection. She'd seen Marc avoid direct glare.

But the light might also wake a sleeping vampire, create a problem for her rather than fix one.

After a second of indecision, she pulled off Marc's shirt and pulled it tight over the flashlight's bulb. The light dimmed. She could see, but it was unobtrusive. And best, if she needed to, she could easily drop the shirt.

Feeling as prepared as she could be, she stepped around the corner.

Silver, jewels and gold glinted in the flashlight beam. The treasure. She'd found it.

Excitement lanced through her. She took a step forward. Something hard rolled under her foot. She flashed the light down and froze.

Mixed in with the coins and jewels were weapons—stakes, guns, bullets and silver vampire fang caps.

She stood frozen, her mind whirring. What kind of treasure had she been sent to find?

The remainder of Marc's journey was quiet. No sound except the slow, steady drip of water somewhere deep in the cavern. The tunnel he'd chosen narrowed and widened, went from no more than two feet wide to fifty and back in again. It twisted around columns formed over the years from stalactites and stalagmites joining together.

He placed his hand on one, wishing the vampires and werewolves could blend as easily.

Paused, he heard movement. The whisper of wings… bats settling in like the vampires. He inched forward a bit more. Past a second column, the path widened again. This time, though, he knew he had reached his destination.

The room, a shelf actually, extended for fifty yards before jutting out over what from Marc's position appeared to be a giant abyss. Closer in, stalagmites dotted the floor like spears shooting up from the ground. Scattered around them, passed out, was an army of vampires. All young and all dead to the world still alive around them.

Finding and taking the stake would be no problem at all.

"Hello, Marc." Van Bom stepped from behind a column, a revolver in his hand.

CeCe ran the flashlight beam over the treasure as she inched deeper into the space. Coins slipped under her feet and her fingers tightened around the flashlight's base. She placed a hand on the cold wall beside her to keep from falling.

She'd found the treasure. It was real. She had begun to doubt that the treasure she had been sent to find truly existed. But this…these weapons mixed in with jewels and coins…she didn't know what to make of it.

Taking a step forward, she ran the flashlight's beam over the floor and the treasure scattered across it. There were perhaps a thousand coins. None were familiar, and although most at least looked human, some bore the same sideways-eight snake as Marc's arm.

So, his story was true too. The vampires did have a claim on the stash. She knelt to study a coin more closely, even reached out a finger to trace over the upraised design…but as she did, a chill crept over her. She glanced around, halfway expecting someone to be peering out at her, but there was no sign of life, no scent or sound.

She returned her attention to the coin. Vampire, not werewolf.

Where was the werewolf claim to this treasure?

She looked up slowly, raising her light as she did. The snake-embossed coins, the guns, the silver bullets and the fang caps were all vampire.

But the stakes…those could be from either.

What about the stake that had killed Russell? Which side had created it?

She stood.

Why had Karl sent her to Cave Vista? Had he known what she would find? If so, why hadn't he told her?

She spun and swiped her hand to the side. Coins and weapons cascaded to the floor. The noise was deafening. She stood still, letting the sound knock into her body. She made no attempt to stop the slide of gold and silver that flowed across her shoes, buried her feet. The treasure felt angry; she felt angry.

Behind the disappearing stack, something moved… teetered.

As the last few coins skittered to a stop, her beam shot up, into an alcove she hadn't noticed before, and onto the death-hollowed face of a vampire.

She sucked in a breath and leaped backward, out of the creature's reach. Her foot slipped and she fell. The vampire fell too…on top of her.

Her muscles clenched and her wolf jumped forward. She lashed out with her fist, ready to fight, ready to grab whatever weapon her hand touched first to survive.

But the vampire didn't move, didn't hiss. He did nothing but lie on top of her, a dead—and she quickly realized desiccated—weight. He even smelled of dust.

This vampire was dead and had been for a very long time.

She closed her eyes briefly, willing her wolf to relax and her heart to slow. Then she pushed the vampire's body off hers and scrambled to her knees.

Light in hand, she studied him. It was hard to tell his age or how long he had been here, but, by the light weight of his body and the brittle feel of his skin, she guessed his death hadn't been recent. She shone the light onto his face. His eyes had been closed when he died and his face peaceful, as if he had accepted, even welcomed his end.

She shifted the beam lower, onto his chest.

What she saw was both expected and shocking. His hands were positioned directly over his heart, or where his heart would have been, but they weren't laid flat in the peaceful repose of death. Instead they formed two circles, one stacked on top of the other, as if he had been holding something—something large that had protruded deep into his chest…deep into his heart.

The vampire had been staked, and by the angle of his elbows, CeCe had to guess, by his own hand.

The question was why?

Her hand shaking, CeCe placed her fingers lightly on top of his. His skin was dry and hard, giving no clue as to what had happened here, what had driven this vampire to take his own life.

But CeCe didn't need an explanation. There really was only one.

The stake. It had to be. This vampire, whoever he was, had brought it and all these other weapons to the hidden part of this cavern.

And then he'd killed the only being who knew where they were hidden—himself.

She squeezed his fingers, wishing she could tell him how brave and right he had been.

"Van Bom." Marc folded his fingers against his palm. "You're watching over the young ones. That's good." He'd known an older vampire might be in attendance, but he was surprised to see the senior member of the Fringe.

He glanced around, looking for any other familiar faces, but all the vampires passed out in the cave were strangers. He walked to one and stared down at him, checked the pallor of his skin, the rapidity of his heartbeat. As vampires aged they lost the glow of life and their hearts beat slower.

The vampire before Marc looked as if he had just fallen asleep, and his heart thumped like a rabbit.

He was freshly turned.

How fresh?

Careful to keep his suspicions from showing, he turned back to Van Bom.

"I didn't realize the Fringe was sending reinforcements."

The vampire moved his finger so it was no longer pressing on the revolver's trigger, but he didn't set the weapon down. "We haven't talked...in depth."

"So, this..." Marc motioned to the sleeping vampires around them. "Was a recent decision?" There were twenty to thirty vampires in the chamber. Gathering that many of their kind quickly would be near impossible, unless you had a personal connection to each, unless you were tied by blood, had made each.

Van Bom had been very busy, and not in a way the Fringe would approve.

"The Fringe doesn't always know what is best." Van Bom flicked his fingernails against each other. His nails were long and curved at the ends, like a hawk's talons. His eyes were like the predatory bird's too, cunning and containing zero emotion.

"Where's the girl, Delacroix?"

"The girl?" Marc slid his hands into the front pockets of his expensive pants. "What girl?"

"The half-breed. Alfred's bastard."

"Alfred?" Marc no longer had to act confused; he had no idea what the older vampire was rambling about.

Van Bom waved the gun. "The idiot who hid the stake from me before."

The stake. Van Bom was after that stake. That Marc had expected. The rest… "You mean the vampire you told me about who hid the stake and other weapons after the war, who *stopped* the war."

"Yes, him…the hero." Van Bom snorted. "His bastard. Where is she? You didn't let the wolves get her too, did you?"

"Too? What are you talking about, Van Bom? You're making no sense." But he was. Van Bom's half statements were adding together, drawing a picture in Marc's mind, one he would never have guessed could be true, knew CeCe would never guess either.

"Yes, too. They took the stake. If they have both…" Van Bom waved the gun more.

Marc wanted to ask about CeCe, confirm that she was the girl the vampire had spoken of, but he knew better than to tip his hand, to let the older vamp see their connection.

"A vampire had the stake when I left."

"We…don't you mean, we? The others told me you left with the girl."

So, it was CeCe. His unspoken question answered, he ignored Van Bom's. "Where is the stake now?"

"The wolves have it. The damn kit had it in his hands and he lost it. He couldn't handle its power. He went berserk, attacked everyone around him, vampire and wolf."

"The vampires turned on him." Statement, not question. When the scent of blood was in the air, young vamps had no control. Van Bom had been a fool to think his children would react otherwise.

Van Bom sighed. "Yes, and the wolves moved in. The sun was coming, and down to the last man, they panicked." He walked to one of the sleeping vampires and brushed a lock of hair from his face. "They weren't ready."

He looked up. "But you have the girl. We can use her to get back the stake."

Marc held out both arms. "No, I don't." He glanced around the cavern, debating his best move. Obviously, the older vampire had to be stopped, but confronting him here, in front of his sleeping offspring, would be suicide. Even a freshly turned vampire would awaken if his sire called to him in this close proximity.

Van Bom dropped his hand from the sleeping vampire's face. His finger returned to the gun's trigger. "Do the wolves have her?"

"No—"

Van Bom's shoulders lowered and his head moved forward. He inhaled. "Wolf," he murmured. He motioned for Marc to step behind a column.

Afraid CeCe was about to enter the room, Marc hesitated. Van Bom lifted his lip, revealing his fangs. He pressed his will outward, toward Marc.

Marc stiffened, but realizing his best move was to keep the older vampire off guard, he slipped behind the column and waited.

Ten werewolves crept into the space, all male and all wearing belts loaded down with stakes.

No, Marc corrected himself, not werewolves…slayers.

Across the cave, Van Bom hissed. Then he fired.

A werewolf screamed and fell. He clutched his shoulder and writhed on the ground. Those with him cursed and dropped.

Van Bom fired again.

The space smelled of gunpowder and fear, whose, Marc wasn't sure.

One of the wolves shifted. A slow grinding process so unlike what Marc had seen CeCe go through at first he thought Van Bom's bullet had struck him too, that the wolf was convulsing from contact with the silver. But then, fully transformed, the male stood on all fours and shook himself from tail to snout.

Then he leaped.

Van Bom fired again, but his bullet missed. With a curse, he spun and screamed, a harsh screeching noise that vibrated off the rock walls and shot through Marc's core. Werewolves bent at the waist, or staggered to the side, and all slapped hands over their ears.

The sound was unearthly and unmistakable.

Van Bom had just called the dead to wake.

En masse the sleeping vampires stirred.

Chapter 23

CeCe left the treasure as she'd found it. There was nothing there for her. Nothing she wanted to take back out into the world.

She didn't know who the vampire she'd found was, but she knew after feeling the magic...the poison... in the stake that he'd done the only thing he could to stop it.

And even that hadn't worked. Porter had found the treasure and carried the stake back out into the world.

With all the gold and silver there, why had Porter chosen the stake to carry out? She was sure he'd meant to come back for the rest, but why take the stake first? Because it was obviously valuable, being heavy and made of silver? Because he'd found it buried in the vampire's chest? Or because the stake wanted him to?

She swallowed the unease that rose at the last

thought and hurried her steps. She'd followed the path back to where she had left Marc, then turned, going in the direction she guessed he had gone.

The path was crooked and uneven. She slipped in the dark and clawed her way back to a stand, but she didn't stop and she didn't turn on the light.

She'd seen the power of the stake, knew now she had something bigger to fear than a simple absence of light.

The werewolf who had shifted landed on a vampire fifteen feet to Marc's left. Before he or the waking vamp could move, the wolf had torn out his target's throat and was leaping to a new body...a new victim.

With a curse, Marc grabbed the two vampires closest to him and jerked them to their feet. "Run," he urged. "Deeper into the caverns."

It wasn't advice he would normally give another vampire, but these vamps were too young to fight unrested.

The werewolves would slaughter them.

Van Bom yelled, a sound that to Marc had no meaning, but the vampires he held reacted. They reached to the small of their backs. Pistols appeared in their hands.

The weapons were old, the type used sixty years earlier, the type Marc had once used too...when fighting the vampire-werewolf war.

Van Bom might not have the stake, but he had found the rest of the cache, and he'd outfitted his freshly made army accordingly.

Bullets exploded from gun barrels. Werewolves shrieked and fell, but as quickly as they did another wolf was beside them tearing the bullet from their companions' bodies and shoving the wounded wolves back to their feet.

Half shifted. Half stayed human. Those in full wolf leaped forward, teeth bared and their brethren's blood from ripping out bullets staining their muzzles.

Van Bom fired again. The bullet whizzed past Marc's ear and lodged into the dirt wall behind him. "Fight!" the older vampire yelled.

But for the first time in Marc's life he stood frozen and unsure. Which side did he defend, which did he try to destroy?

There was no side here he believed in. No side that he wanted to win.

Fire burst to life around the chamber—the werewolves tossing flaming flares into the chamber.

The energy in the room exploded.

The vampires hissed and covered their eyes, but the wolves had something to lose too. Smoke clouded the space. The werewolves coughed as it found its way into their lungs.

Both were hampered, but both continued to fight.

Marc stood to the side, still undecided.

"Delacroix!"

A wolf hit Van Bom in the chest and the older vampire went down.

With a curse, Marc leaped. He might not agree with what he thought the vampire had done, but he was Fringe. Marc couldn't stand by while he died.

The wolf on top of Van Bam was huge, over two hundred pounds. Marc grabbed the creature by scruff and tail and flung him to the side. The wolf hit the cave wall with a thump, but barely seemed to notice…he jumped to his feet and raced back toward Marc.

"The gun." Van Bom, bleeding from the neck, motioned to the revolver he had held earlier. It was within Marc's reach, but as the wolf barreled closer, he couldn't bring himself to pick it up.

He wouldn't be part of this war, not until he was given no other choice.

And the werewolf seemed determined to do that for him.

The animal surged forward, his teeth bared. Marc stood with his hands open and ready to grab the creature around the throat. The wolf plowed into him, knocking him onto his back, but he kept his grip and arms locked, held the creature's flailing teeth away from his face.

"Karl!"

CeCe had arrived.

The wolf on top of him stilled.

The alpha. Marc should have recognized him.

"She's alive, alpha. No thanks to you," Marc pulled the wolf close and muttered in his ear. "What kind of alpha are you? What kind of protector? You let her fall…but then, that isn't all, is it? What do you know of Russell's death?"

The wolf rose on two legs, taking Marc to a stand with him. The creature lashed side to side, his teeth dragging across Marc's chest, digging into his flesh.

Marc lunged forward and grabbed the creature around the neck, held on like a cowboy clinging to a bull. "Was it worth it, alpha? What did you hope to gain? What do you still hope to gain?"

The wolf twisted; its teeth clamped on to Marc's arm.

Marc winced in pain.

With Marc unarmed, the wolf had the advantage. His massive fur ruff protected his neck and his strength matched the vampire's. The wolf landed on all fours, taking Marc down with him. His back smashed against the hard floor, but he held tight. The wolf twisted, tried to pull Marc's arm from his body. Marc moved with the wolf, his free hand landing on the dirt, supporting his weight.

His fingers touched metal…cold and reassuring…a knife. He picked up the blade and, praying it contained silver, plunged it into the wolf's neck.

The werewolf loosened his hold and Marc pressed the advantage. He twisted the knife and slammed his knee into the creature's throat. The wolf let go and with the knife still shoved in his neck, he stumbled backward.

Marc staggered to his feet. "Where's the stake?" he asked. He knew if Van Bom had told the truth, if the werewolves had the stake now, Karl would know.

The alpha snarled and shook. The knife Marc had shoved into his neck flew free. With a roar, the werewolf began to shift. Within seconds, instead of the moments it had seemed to take some of the other wolves, the alpha stood before him, naked and human.

"You know nothing, vampire." He turned and began loping away, toward CeCe's voice.

Marc wouldn't let him get to her. He threw himself on the werewolf's back and sank his fangs into his neck. The werewolf cursed and his knees bent, but he didn't fall. Five wolves descended on them and tore Marc from their alpha's back. They dragged him across the ground, his heels leaving twin trails in the dirt with each step.

"Drop him over the side. See if he is like a bat. See if he can fly," the alpha called over his shoulder and loped away.

Marc jerked against his captors' hold, but there were too many of them. They held him by arms and feet and swung him back and forth.

Then they let him go.

From a ledge overlooking the cavern, CeCe stared, shocked, at what was happening below. The chamber was filled with bodies, werewolves and vampires thrashing and snarling. Guns fired and spots of fire glowed. Smoke rose from the flames, clung to her hair and clothes, and worked its way into her lungs.

Her gaze had jumped from body to body, searching for Marc, and then she'd found him…on the ground under the weight of her once-destined mate, Karl.

At her call, Marc looked up. She couldn't see the expression on his face, couldn't say if he was glad at her appearance or enraged.

At the moment, it didn't matter. What did was stopping this fight.

But she was twenty feet above the chamber, twenty feet from being of any help to anyone.

Without pausing to consider what she was going to do, she turned and jogged back the way she had come. Then she turned again and raced forward, and seconds before running out of ground, she leaped.

"CeCe!" She heard Marc curse.

She didn't look in his direction. She couldn't afford

to; she had to focus on where she was about to land...
on top of three werewolves, all in wolf form.

She hit them hard, knocking all three to the ground.
Her jaws snapped together. She bit her tongue, and
blood filled her mouth.

The wolves she had landed on snarled and whipped
around, their mouths open and their teeth bared.

From the ground, she snarled back, balled her fist
and smashed the closest in the snout. "Back off," she
yelled.

The wolf pulled back, but she could see his indecision. He was lost in his animal and in the fight. She
lifted her foot and kicked him in the side of the head.
"Goddamn it, Robert. Back off."

Hoping that would be enough to remind the werewolf who and what she was, she spun. She had to find
Marc, had to get Karl off him.

With the pair in her sights, she charged forward,
knocking against vampires and werewolves alike.

Ten feet from her target, a body stepped in front
of her.

"Ms. Parks."

A vampire holding a gun blocked her path. His neck
was torn. Skin hung in a loose flap over ragged flesh.

He'd battled a werewolf, but he was still standing,
still moving. So, he must have won.

Lucky for him. Not so lucky for her.

"Does silver kill a half-breed miracle?" he asked.

"I..." CeCe tried to look past him to see Marc and
Karl, but the world around them had disappeared into
the smoke of newly lit flares.

"No matter. I can assure you it would hurt. Not that

I want to use it on you." He wiggled his finger over the trigger. "Where is the stake?"

"The stake? The vampires have it." And she wanted it back. She turned her attention on him full force.

"No. I'm afraid we don't. Not any longer." He cocked the gun. "But we will…as soon as you get your pack to give it to us."

"My pack?" He said that as if she had some control over what the wolves chose to do.

"Yes, your pack. Don't tell me you didn't come here with them to get what your father stole."

"My father?" Her father was, last she'd heard, curled up safe in front of his TV watching sports and drinking beer, secure in the knowledge that he had traded her fair and square for a place back in Karl's pack.

"Yes, the stake. He stole it."

"Porter? Porter wasn't my father."

The crazed vampire laughed. "The human? No, of course not. Oh, dear, you don't know, do you?" He shook his head. "To be a miracle and not know. How does that happen?"

A chill crept over CeCe. "What miracle? What are you talking about?"

The vampire tilted his head, revealing more of his wound. "You get me the stake, and I'll tell you. I'll tell you more about your father and your mother than you ever wanted to know. Who knows, you may decide giving me the stake was the best thing you've ever done."

CeCe seriously doubted that, but she did want to hear whatever secrets the old vampire thought he held.

"CeCe!"

The voice came from behind the vampire. She lifted her flashlight and shone it into the darkness. At first only smoke was visible, but slowly it cleared.

Karl, in his human form, stood at the far end of the cavern, naked and bleeding. "I need you, CeCe. The pack needs you. You can end this. You can end all of this."

Around her the fighting continued, but the pace seemed to slow as if the world were waiting on her response. But what response? How could she end this?

"Where's Marc?" she asked, no longer caring if Karl knew she used Marc's name.

"The vampire? He's gone." He jerked his head to the side.

CeCe flashed her light in that direction. There were two columns, then nothing, nothing that she could see.

"What do you mean? What happened?" Her voice rose, she knew her panic showed, but she couldn't contain it. Marc was all she had now, all she could trust.

She could feel the older vampire's eyes on her, could feel him analyzing her reaction, but she couldn't focus on him. She could only think of Marc and why she couldn't see him any longer.

"Vampires can't fly. They only think they can." Karl picked up a rock and threw it over his shoulder.

It fell, but it didn't hit…at least not that CeCe could hear.

"It's a pit," the vampire hissed. "He threw Delacroix into the pit. It's deep—too deep for even a vampire to survive. What do you think now, half-breed? You and Delacroix grew close, didn't you? The stories are true. It's the vampire half of you…recognizing your own kind. Don't let the wolf win. Fight. Get revenge…

bring me the stake. Together we can dominate the were-wolves. You can be alpha, if you choose."

"Take the stake, CeCe. You're the only one who can." Karl now, talking and holding out the stake. It was wrapped in leather, but she knew what it was. She could feel its pull. It wanted her to touch it, to hold it, to feed it.

Confused and still thinking of Marc, she stared at the leather-wrapped end of the weapon Karl held out to her.

"Take it, girl. Take it and use it for the vampires," the vampire whispered. She felt his energy, like a nudge in the back pushing her forward.

She ignored it. "Where's Marc? What did you do with him, Karl?" Her hands fisted. Her wolf's ruff rose.

"I told you—he's gone. He was bad for you, confusing you. Remember who you are, CeCe, what you are, where your loyalty lies." Karl waved the stake.

Marc couldn't be gone.

She rushed forward, past the werewolves and away from the vampire. Her flashlight beam bounced over the ground, giving her no real guidance as to where she was going. Then suddenly an arm shot in front of her and she was jerked backward, against Karl's bare chest.

"The pack needs you," he murmured against her ear.

He pressed the leather-wrapped stake against her hand. She leaped away and walked backward.

"CeCe," Karl warned.

She stopped. Behind her the air grew cold, colder even than the rest of the cavern. She felt empty and exposed…alone. A chill crawled up her spine and she turned. There was nothing behind her, no cave walls or floor, nothing but a vast open pit.

"He's in there. You dropped him in there." She muttered the words, anger swelling up inside her so strong, so filled with despair, that she couldn't contain it. The werewolves had thrown Marc into this pit, thrown him away like trash for what? A stake? For power?

Her gaze shifted to the leather-wrapped bundle in Karl's hand.

"Why?" she asked.

"He was clouding your judgment. Changing you."

Karl was right. Marc had changed her; he'd changed her for the better. She turned to face the cavern and ran the flashlight's beam over the opening. It bounced from wall to wall. She could see nothing.

Her body shaking, she closed her eyes.

She couldn't lose Marc.

But she had.

Chapter 24

Marc clung to the cavern walls like a cat clinging to cloth. When he fell, he'd hit a ledge that jutted into the main opening like a bridge to nowhere. He'd crawled across it until it dead-ended into the wall. There he had found a two-inch lip protruding from the otherwise sheer rock. Barefoot, he'd continued on. Using his toes and fingernails to keep from plummeting into the pit.

He was maybe twenty feet below solid ground now. He could hear the voices above his head, but he couldn't get to them. Positioned as he was, clinging to the rock, he couldn't even call to them, assuming that would have been a wise choice.

He rested his forehead against the wall and did the only thing he could for now. He waited.

* * *

Marc couldn't be gone. CeCe wouldn't believe it.

Pulling strength from some reserve she hadn't known she had, she leaned over the side of the cliff.

"CeCe." Karl ordering her back. He moved toward her as if to grab her. She scurried to the side. As she did, her flashlight caught a shape, a human shape clinging to the rock below her.

Marc.

He was alive.

She turned, ready to order Karl to help her, but her lips closed in silence.

Karl and the werewolves had thrown Marc into this pit. If they knew he still lived, they wouldn't help her save him. They would do the opposite.

She had to get rid of them.

She glanced at the vampire holding the gun; he'd followed her along with Karl. The three of them— her, the vampire and Karl—were separate now from the others. Briefly she considered asking for the vampire's aid, but what would that mean? Shooting Karl? She couldn't do that. If Karl was wounded, the other werewolves would sense his trauma and react too. Her problems would only increase.

"What do you want, Karl?" she asked.

"I told you, to give you the stake."

The vampire's eyes shifted in his face. "Remember what I told you, girl."

"Why? Why would you want to give it away?" It was obvious now everyone wanted the stake. So, why did both Karl and the vampire seem intent on her taking it?

"I can't control it." The alpha's response was low, almost a growl.

She froze, realization dropping over her like an icy net. Russell.

"You killed Russell." She closed her eyes. She felt sick.

Marc had been right. Not a vampire. Someone close. Someone Russell trusted and wanted to impress. "He just wanted to be accepted." The anger swelled again. "You're the alpha. You should have protected him."

"It wasn't supposed to happen. It was supposed to be an easy assignment for him."

For Russell. "What about me?"

"You too. Only you were supposed to find the stake. Russell was just to come along and gain some confidence."

"How'd it happen?" She wanted him to explain it, to tell her something that would make what had happened if not okay, understandable.

"He called me. He found the stake in Porter's basement. It was wrapped up and he could tell it was valuable. He wanted to give it to me himself."

"So you met him."

Karl nodded. "I'd planned on your finding it and bringing it to the pack. It would have sealed your place. No one would have questioned why I chose you once you had the stake in your hands."

Why her? That question had yet to be answered, but first CeCe needed to hear more about Russell's death. She needed to hear all of Karl's story. Needed to hear why he killed one of the werewolves that needed his protection the most.

"I knew the stories, knew no wolf had been able

to handle the thing without going berserk, but when Russell unwrapped it and held it out, I had to take it."

If he hadn't, if he'd told Russell he was afraid of the thing, he would have lost face, risked not only his standing in Russell's eyes but potentially his very position as alpha.

"So you took it."

"Bare-handed." Karl looked away.

CeCe could see the pain on his face, knew he regretted what came next, but it didn't matter. His regret couldn't make up for the loss of Russell's life.

"I thought I could touch it for a minute and wrap it back up, but it didn't give me that time. It was as if the thing got stuck to my hand. I could feel its energy wrapping around my wrist, snaking up my arm…into me. The next thing I knew Russell was dead."

"You killed him." She wanted him to say the words, couldn't let him evade the complete ugly truth of what he had done.

He met her gaze. "I did. I didn't mean to, but I did."

"And then you left him." Alone in the woods, food for any animal that came that way.

"I had to. Once I got my hand free from the stake, I couldn't touch it again, couldn't risk being near it, at least for a while."

He'd overcome that though, when he'd sneaked into her room and stolen it. How much longer before he weakened completely and wanted to keep it for himself?

As if reading her thoughts, he shook the stake, urging her to take it. "You can handle it. No one else can."

Why did everyone say that? Why did everyone

seem to want her to take the stake…and be on their side? The last part couldn't be forgotten.

"I touched it. It affected me too," she said, keeping her hands at her sides.

"Did you kill anyone you had a duty to protect?"

"No." But it didn't mean she wouldn't have. She didn't believe Karl's vague claims that she could control the stake better than anyone else. She didn't believe anyone could control the stake. It was evil, plain and simple.

She blew out a breath. "Why me?"

"Your mother created it." The vampire had crept closer. He stood to her side, away from Karl and out of her reach. "And your father hid it."

"A vampire hid it." She'd seen his body.

The vampire's eyes gleamed. "Yes. You understand now."

Karl shook his head. "Don't listen to him. You're a wolf. You know that."

Confused, CeCe ran her fingers through her hair. She wanted Marc there, needed him. She glanced toward the pit.

He was okay. He was a vampire—he could cling to that wall for hours, eternity even.

She willed herself to believe the thoughts while fighting the need to rush back to the cliff and check to see if they were true.

"He's gone," Karl said, noticing the direction of her gaze. His tone was flat, leaving no room for argument.

Which if she was a wolf, she'd respect, but she was tired of respecting the alpha for no reason other than him being alpha, and suddenly she needed to show that fatigue. She walked to the edge of the pit and stared down. But she didn't dare use her flashlight, didn't dare risk illuminating Marc.

She inhaled. Deep, dark and black. Nothing but black.

"CeCe." It was just a whisper, so soft it could have just been in her mind, but it wasn't—she knew it wasn't. Marc was there. Out of reach for the moment, but there.

"Get the stake away from them."

She closed her eyes and took in Marc's voice like lifesaving oxygen.

Stronger, she turned. It was time for answers. Real answers.

"Why won't the pack accept me?" She didn't look at the alpha when she asked. She didn't need to. Besides, she asked the question as much for Marc as herself. He'd pushed her to ask it; he deserved to hear her finally question her lot.

"You're an outsider. It takes time."

"Twenty years?" She suppressed a snort. Russell hadn't been accepted either, but he had only been in the pack two years.

"You—" Karl's voice grew tight "—smell different."

Surprised, she did look at him then. "How?"

He shook his head. "It's hard to say, but you don't smell like a wolf, not completely."

"Vampire," the old vamp murmured.

"No." Karl denied it, but she could see the uncertainty in his stance. He didn't want her to consider that she might be something other than wolf, didn't want to risk her loyalties being split.

No worries for that. He'd lost any loyalty she had left to give him when he threw Marc into the pit.

"And if that's true? If I am half vampire?" she asked, curious to hear his response.

"It won't matter, not once you're my mate."

He was fooling himself. As she had been fooling herself. If the story was true, if she was half vampire, the pack would never accept her. In fact, declaring herself as the alpha's mate would just make things worse.

"They don't have to know." Karl's expression was earnest, as if living a lie so she'd be accepted would be in any way palatable.

But she wouldn't say that to him, not when she needed him to give her the stake.

She held out her hand.

"Remember," the vampire whispered. "He killed your friend, and Delacroix. You can't trust him, and his pack doesn't want you, but the vampires do."

Wrapped in its leather casing, the stake felt like nothing more than a lump of metal. She felt no vibes from it at all.

She motioned to Karl and the vampire. "Leave and I'll decide. I need time alone." Time to save Marc.

The alpha shook his head. "There's nothing to decide. We leave together."

"Or not at all?"

His silence was answer enough.

"My mother made this?" she asked, buying time. She should have lied to Karl, gone with him, but the vampire wouldn't have stood for that either. She was trapped; Marc was trapped. All she could do was string the werewolf and vampire along until she saw some escape. "Why?" she asked.

Karl crossed his arms over his chest. "Because of the vampires. They twisted her like they tried to twist you."

The older vampire laughed. "Don't lie to the girl. She's too smart for that." He lifted the gun and pointed it at Karl. "Tell her the real truth, or I will. I'm not afraid of it."

Karl jutted out his jaw.

"Tell me, or I toss it over." CeCe glanced to the right, into the pit. How deep was it? If she threw the stake, how long would it stay hidden this time?

"Tell her." The vampire cocked his revolver.

Karl glanced at the vampire with cool indifference. "Threats, vampire? With this cave filled with my wolves?"

"Karl?" CeCe asked.

He let out a breath, deflated. "Your mother was a werewolf. Your father...the father who raised you... turned her, but he did it by force. She didn't know and she didn't forgive him."

"There's more," the vampire prompted.

"She was in love with a vampire."

"Your real father," the vampire explained.

"But after she was turned, after he learned she was a wolf, he walked away from her."

"It was during the war. A werewolf would have done the same."

Karl stared at the older vampire. "But we didn't. CeCe's father, the one who raised her, knew what she was. He didn't abandon her."

No. He just tortured her and then traded her for what he really wanted, a place back in the pack.

"The pack kicked him out because of what he did to my mother."

"He put the pack at risk. Your mother wasn't like other humans."

"She wasn't powerless, he means. She had magic and could fight back. If she'd been normal, the wolves wouldn't have cared. Isn't that right, alpha?" The vampire tilted his head.

Karl growled.

"So, my mother made the stake. Then what? Where is she now?"

"She killed herself." Van Bom offered this. "Alfred, your real father, found her. She made the stake, and then she used it on herself. Alfred went crazy. He took the stake and all the other weapons he could find and hid them." Disgust colored Van Bom's words.

"And then he used it on himself." She ran her thumb over the stake's covering. It had taken both her parents' lives.

"Did he? How sweet. Like Romeo and Juliet." The vampire tapped one long nail against the revolver's trigger guard. "You've heard the story. Now choose. Vampire or wolf?"

CeCe lowered the stake so it hung by her side. She could feel Marc below them, listening, encouraging her.

"You still haven't explained why you think I can handle it." She couldn't control the stake. She had tried before. If Marc hadn't interceded, she would have killed and killed again. She was no more resistant to the stake's power than anyone else. And more importantly, she didn't want to handle it. She wanted to fling the thing away, rid herself and the world of it forever. But if she did that now, with the vampires and the wolves here, the fighting would start anew, and this time it might never end.

"Where vampire and werewolf meet, will the stake know defeat," the vampire quoted. "Your mother's words. Her curse. She created the most powerful weapon of all time, one she knew both vampire and werewolf would kill to control, then she cursed it so only one being in all the world could—you."

"Where vampire and werewolf meet." If everything Van Bom and Karl had told her was true, she was that place.

"A miracle," the vampire murmured. "That's what your father called you when he learned of you. Vampires can't procreate, you know. We can only create." He waved his hand over his shoulder, where the other vampires waited. "I hear it isn't the same."

"A miracle that he left," she murmured.

Her father, her vampire father, could have chosen to take her instead of the stake.

But he didn't.

She hated the stake, hated everything about it, and at that moment she hated the vampires and the werewolves too. She could feel her mother's anger. Felt her own anger, too.

Half werewolf and half vampire, wanted by neither, at least not until they realized they could use her.

"How long did it take you to figure this out?" she asked. She pointed the question at Karl.

"I didn't know about you or the stake until your father told me."

And then he'd taken a gamble, accepted her father's

terms in the hopes the story was true and the stake would turn up. And if it hadn't?

"You never meant to give me that chain, did you?" she asked.

"I gave it to you and you left it behind."

Not an answer, at least to her question, but she was done with the werewolf. More than done.

She shifted her gaze to the vampire.

He lifted one shoulder. "I've always known you existed. I just didn't know where you were. I even thought perhaps my dear friend Alfred might have—" he sighed "—killed you. But happily he didn't." He smiled, but CeCe felt no warmth.

"I realized who you were after speaking to Marc. The signs were there. I'm surprised he missed them."

"I think I understand." And she did. She knew what she had to do. She unwrapped the stake.

It glistened at her, called to her. As much as she didn't want to admit it, she understood why Karl had picked it up.

Then she leaned over the edge of the cliff and she dropped it.

Chapter 25

Clinging to the wall, Marc had heard every word of Karl's and Van Bom's explanation.

CeCe was half vampire. He should have guessed. The signs had been there: her scent, her choice of sun-blocking clothing despite the heat.

And now both sides wanted her...wanted her to take up the stake and fight on their side.

An obvious choice. She'd been raised as a wolf, shifted like a wolf. How could she choose anything else?

He steeled himself, waiting for her to make her declaration, waiting for her to either walk away or reveal his presence to her alpha.

Instead he heard a noise, something sliding down the rock wall toward him. Instinctively he raised his hand to block its descent, to keep whatever the object was from knocking him from his perch.

Cold metal met his grip.

The stake. CeCe had given him the stake.

He'd no sooner had the thought than the world above him exploded. Yells and hisses.

Van Bom and Karl both realizing what CeCe had done. Both, he knew, now intent on revenge, on getting to her…killing her.

He couldn't let them. He grabbed the stake and slammed it into the rock. Then slowly, painfully, he used it to pull himself up, an arm's reach at a time.

CeCe wasn't sure why she had dropped the stake. She had just known she had to. As long as she held it, the vampire and Karl were in a standoff, waiting for her choice, but once it was out of play, the lid was popped off.

There was no reason for them to pretend anything, but more importantly there was no reason for them to stay either.

Except it didn't work that way. They didn't leave. Instead their anger erupted so loud and violent that it called the other vampires and werewolves into the space with them.

Soon the battle they had left briefly behind raged as loud and large as ever. A werewolf in wolf form rushed a vampire and pinned him to the wall with his jaws. A vampire dropped from an overhang onto another wolf's back. As he bent forward, toward the animal's neck, CeCe caught a flash of silver.

They were going to destroy themselves. And over what? A stake that no longer existed.

Van Bom turned to her, his gun again pointed at her chest. "You are like your father—stupid."

She smiled. "My father, for his mistakes, seems to be the only being in your little tale with any sense, any desire to save what he loved."

"Your mother? She was already gone."

"No, you and them. He gave up everything to save you from yourselves and you are too stupid to appreciate his sacrifice."

Done with the vampire, done with all of them, she returned to the edge of the cliff.

She couldn't wait for the vampires and werewolves to leave, not any longer. She had to save Marc.

When she'd seen him, he'd been at least twenty feet below ground level. Too far for her to grab him. She needed a rope, but she couldn't risk leaving the cave to get one.

She would have to use something else.

A naked werewolf grappled with a vampire, knocking a gun from his hand and kicking it into the void.

Naked.

The werewolves had arrived wearing clothes, but as they shifted, they dropped them.

CeCe jogged to the nearest pile and gathered it up. Then she ran to the next. Her arms full, she rushed back to her spot and began tying jeans to shirts and shirts to jeans.

"What are you doing?" Karl stared down at her.

"Go away," she replied. "You have no use for me now."

"You're still a genetic wolf."

Oh yes, her other great value for the pack.

"You're making a rope." The alpha glanced at the pit to their side. "I told you, he's gone."

"Either help me tie or get out of my way."

He stared at her, his gaze flat. Then he picked up her pile and tossed it over the side. "He's gone and he's going to stay that way."

She leaped to her feet.

"Don't count on it." The stake appeared over the edge with Marc's hand wrapped around it.

"Marc." Karl forgotten, CeCe lunged forward, but the alpha was there. He held her by the waist.

"He's a vampire, CeCe, and he has the stake." He threw her to the side and stalked forward. He grabbed Marc by the wrist and shook, tried to shake free his hold on the stake.

"No!" CeCe jumped onto the alpha's back and sank her teeth into his neck. With a curse, he reached over his shoulder and jerked her over his head.

She landed hard; spots drifted in front of her eyes. The alpha moved again, his foot flying out as he tried to kick the stake free of the earth.

CeCe flipped over and propelled her body forward. With her bare hand, she grabbed the stake and forced it deeper into the ground. Her fingers touched cold metal, but her hand also touched Marc's. It gave her hope.

With her free hand she reached for him and their hands met again.

Their arms formed a circle. For a moment they just lay there.

Relief poured through CeCe. She had him. He was safe, or would be as soon as they pulled him onto solid ground. Marc's head appeared over the edge, then his elbows and upper body. He smiled at her and she leaned forward, ready to press a kiss to his lips.

Behind her Karl snarled. He kicked, aiming for Marc's head.

Power shot through her—magic. It electrified her. Her hair rose and her body tingled. She looked at Marc and saw the same shock on his face that she knew was visible on her own.

Karl's foot froze mid-kick, seemed to hit some kind of barrier and bounced off. He fell backward onto the ground.

A gun fired. CeCe couldn't see by whom, but it didn't matter. The bullet met the same barrier as Karl's foot—froze, then fell.

Marc flipped his body onto the cave floor. Then he pulled her down, so her body lay across his.

He raised their intertwined hands. A blue light blazed around them. "See, you are magic," he murmured.

She shook her head. "Not me. Us."

"Where vampire and werewolf meet, my life will be complete," he murmured.

"That isn't the quote." Her words were soft. She was afraid to speak too loudly, afraid all of this would go away.

"But it is true." Then he rolled over and captured her lips with his.

After witnessing the protection the stake gave CeCe and Marc, it wasn't hard for Marc to convince the vampires and the werewolves that it was in their best interest to give up the fight.

He'd allowed himself one more kiss with his wolf

before pulling her to her feet and turning to face them. Van Bom had tried to play hero, claiming he had been holding off the wolves so CeCe and Marc could save themselves, but it was wasted breath.

CeCe glowed with new power. Her magic was now on the outside for all to see. He watched her as she spoke to the werewolves, told them to be on their way—that they had no claim to anything inside this cavern. Even the alpha didn't question her. He simply motioned for his wolves to gather their clothes and leave.

Van Bom waited for Marc.

"We have the stake now."

"CeCe has the stake." She did too, shoved in her back pocket like a forgotten comb.

"Her vampire half came through."

"Her strength came through."

Van Bom tilted his head as if they were one and the same. "The human had no idea what he'd found."

"What do you know of Porter?"

"Nothing."

A quick response, too quick. "What did you do to him, Van Bom?"

"Nothing."

Marc's fingers crackled with power. He had kept his hand closed, hiding the new development from others and himself. He wasn't sure how he felt about the energy that had zipped through him and now, even without contact with the stake, seemed determined to stay.

However, despite his own unease, he spread his fingers wide so Van Bom could see the web of magic weaving around them.

"Tell me."

The show of power seemed to have the desired effect. The senior vampire's lips thinned. "I talked to him."

Marc flexed his fingers; power popped.

"When I heard you had been sent to find the treasure, I followed. I saw you leave that bar through a window. I went in after you."

"And found Porter."

"He was a mess."

Marc couldn't argue the statement. It is why he had been unable to get worthwhile information from the treasure hunter.

"I put him in thrall. He didn't come out."

"You killed him."

Van Bom waved his fingers in the air. "Not intentionally, and perhaps not at all. He was drunk and, from human reports, had a bad heart. There was no way for me to know that."

"And if you had?"

Van Bom's expression didn't waver.

"I'll have to tell the Fringe." Van Bom's actions with Porter were irresponsible, and his intentions—getting CeCe to man the stake for his benefit—unforgivable.

"Try."

"Andre is dead, isn't he?" It hadn't occurred to Marc before this that Van Bom would have gone that far, but of course, he would have, and based on his expression, had.

"I predict the current leader of the Fringe will be difficult to locate."

"Then a new leader will be found."

"You?"

Marc hadn't seen himself as the leader of the Fringe,

but it made sense. It would allow him to lead the vampires in a new direction, one where they worked against century-old prejudices. Vampires and werewolves had more alike than they had different. They should work together.

"Perhaps."

A look passed between the two, a look that perhaps told Van Bom too much about what Marc would do if he became leader of the Fringe.

Done with the werewolves, CeCe walked up.

Van Bom sprung toward her and jerked the stake from her pocket. He held it above his head, laughing. "Who has the power now?"

CeCe moved as if to take the stake back, but Marc wrapped his fingers around her arm. "Wait."

The stake, he'd decided, was more than just a cursed hunk of metal.

Van Bom listed side to side, his steps uneven and his attention locked onto the stake. With a laugh, he spun and careered toward the cavern's edge.

Marc vaulted forward, tried to grab the old vampire by the back of his shirt, but it was too late. Van Bom toppled over the edge.

As he fell, his laughter floated back up toward them.

"He's gone." Clinging to Marc's side, CeCe stared into the pit. "Will he survive?"

"Maybe, if the stake doesn't kill him."

Her nails scraped over his shirt. "Will it come back?"

Marc pulled her tight against his side. "Not if we don't give it a reason to."

"You think—"

He tipped her face up to his. "I think your mother

was smarter than anyone gave her credit, and your father was braver, and together they created the most magical creation of all time."

"The stake? But my father—"

"No. You." He pulled her flush against his body. Magic wound around them, warming his skin and his soul.

He would never be cold again, and CeCe would never be alone. They had each other, forever.

For once, the stake had done good.

* * * * *

YOU HAVE
JUST READ A
HARLEQUIN®
NOCTURNE™
BOOK

If you were **captivated** by this **dark** and **sensual paranormal romance story,** be sure to look for two new Harlequin® Nocturne™ books every month!

Available wherever books and ebooks are sold.

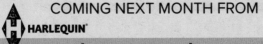

REQUEST YOUR FREE BOOKS!

2 FREE NOVELS FROM THE PARANORMAL ROMANCE COLLECTION PLUS 2 FREE GIFTS!

YES! Please send me 2 FREE novels from the Paranormal Romance Collection and my 2 FREE gifts (gifts are worth about $10). After receiving them, if I don't wish to receive any more books, I can return the shipping statement marked "cancel." If I don't cancel, I will receive 4 brand-new novels every month and be billed just $22.76 in the U.S. or $23.96 in Canada. That's a savings of at least 17% off the cover price of all 4 books. It's quite a bargain! Shipping and handling is just 50¢ per book in the U.S. and 75¢ per book in Canada.* I understand that accepting the 2 free books and gifts places me under no obligation to buy anything. I can always return a shipment and cancel at any time. Even if I never buy another book, the two free books and gifts are mine to keep forever.

237/337 HDN F4YC

Name _____ (PLEASE PRINT) _____

Address _____ Apt. # _____

City _____ State/Prov. _____ Zip/Postal Code _____

Signature (if under 18, a parent or guardian must sign)

Mail to the Harlequin® Reader Service:
IN U.S.A.: P.O. Box 1867, Buffalo, NY 14240-1867
IN CANADA: P.O. Box 609, Fort Erie, Ontario L2A 5X3

**Want to try two free books from another line?
Call 1-800-873-8635 or visit www.ReaderService.com.**

* Terms and prices subject to change without notice. Prices do not include applicable taxes. Sales tax applicable in N.Y. Canadian residents will be charged applicable taxes. Offer not valid in Quebec. This offer is limited to one order per household. Not valid for current subscribers to Paranormal Romance Collection or Harlequin® Nocturne™ books. All orders subject to credit approval. Credit or debit balances in a customer's account(s) may be offset by any other outstanding balance owed by or to the customer. Please allow 4 to 6 weeks for delivery. Offer available while quantities last.

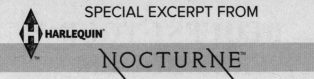
The fight had left him less staggered. Being *shot* had left him
less staggered.

Kai Faulkes, thirty years old and never been kissed.

Never like that.

He made himself step back, made his expression rueful and
his body still. Because he'd never known such *want,* and he'd
never taken such liberties, and he didn't begin to trust himself
not to take more.

Regan touched her mouth, her cheeks full of flush, her
brows drawn together in a faint frown. "I—" she started,
while he was still far from able to find words. *"You—"* she
started again, and then shook her head, impatient with her
own struggle. Then she shook herself off, pushing a wayward
strand of gold away from her face. "Later," she said. "I'll deal
with that kiss later. Right now, I've got too many questions."

For this, he met her gaze without flinching; he found words. "I might not answer them."

"We'll see about that. That needs care," she said, latching on to the most obvious need—looking at where the Core bullet had furrowed along the curve of his biceps.

But the arm would wait; it would heal faster than she could imagine. Other things wouldn't wait at all. For he needed to sweep through this area because the Core had finally infiltrated this remote and pristine place.

"Kai," Regan said, aiming a pale blue gaze his way with intent, regaining some of her composure—but not without the hint of remaining uncertainty.

Self-retribution slapped home. This woman wasn't Sentinel; she wasn't lynx. She wasn't born to be a protector. She'd been threatened and she'd fought back—but that didn't mean she wasn't still frightened.

She didn't need to walk back to the cabin alone.

She lifted one honey-gold brow, striking a note of asperity. "In case you haven't noticed, you're bleeding everywhere. If you faint from blood loss, I'm going to find my phone—" she glanced around, already looking "—and find a signal, and call for help. And somehow I get the feeling that's exactly what you're trying to avoid."

And Kai said nothing. Because Regan Adler saw—and heard—a lot more than she wanted to admit.

Even to herself.

Don't miss the dramatic conclusion to SENTINELS: LYNX DESTINY by Doranna Durgin. Available February 4, only from Harlequin® Nocturne™.

HNEXP0114

HARLEQUIN®

A *Romance* FOR EVERY MOOD™

Stay up-to-date on all your
romance-reading news with the
Harlequin Shopping Guide,
featuring bestselling authors, exciting new
miniseries, books to watch and more!

The newest issue will be delivered right to you
with our compliments! There are 4 each year.

Signing up is easy.

EMAIL

ShoppingGuide@Harlequin.ca

WRITE TO US

HARLEQUIN BOOKS
Attention: Customer Service Department
P.O. Box 9057, Buffalo, NY 14269-9057

OR PHONE

1-800-873-8635 in the United States
1-888-343-9777 in Canada

Please allow 4-6 weeks for delivery of the first issue by mail.